Dead for a Ducat

By the same author

THE NOSE ON MY FACE
TOO SMALL FOR HIS SHOES
DEEP AND CRISP AND EVEN
BIRDS IN THE BELFRY
SPY FOR SALE
EVEN MY FOOT'S ASLEEP
TAKE THE MONEY AND RUN
MALICE IN CAMERA
VIENNA BLOOD

Dead for a Ducat

Laurence Payne

HODDER AND STOUGHTON
LONDON SYDNEY AUCKLAND TORONTO

British Library Cataloguing in Publication Data
Payne, Laurence
  Dead for a ducat.
  I. Title
  823'.914[F]   PR6066.A93

ISBN 0 340 38541 3

Copyright © 1985 by Laurence Payne. First printed 1985. All rights reserved. No part of this publication may be reproduced or transmitted in any form or by any means, electronic or mechanical, including photocopy, recording, or any information storage and retrieval system, without permission in writing from the publisher. Printed in Great Britain for Hodder and Stoughton Limited, Mill Road, Dunton Green, Sevenoaks, Kent by Thetford Press Ltd, Thetford, Norfolk. Typeset by Hewer Text Composition Services, Edinburgh.

Hodder and Stoughton Editorial Office: 47 Bedford Square, London WC1B 3DP.

For
JOAN and PETER MOFFAT
two of the indispensable ones.
Thank you, both.

Thou find'st to be too busy is some danger
                                      Hamlet

Chapter One

Winter arrived overnight. High winds and rain stripped bare the trees and reduced the golden melancholy of autumn to a soggy morass of putrescent slime. Blocked drains and the bleak dripping of choked gutterings added to the general air of despondency.

To make matters worse the High Street was up again. Three large new holes at intervals of fifty paces had been opened up along the crown of it; three small groups of spent and silent workmen in caps and gumboots leaned gravely on their picks and shovels keeping an eye on them. Motionless city-bound traffic was piled up all the way down the hill, whilst a convoy of three 93 buses and a continental juggernaut pointing in the opposite direction put paid to anyone's hopes of getting to Croydon in a hurry.

The human race, for all its idle boasts of progress, had once again ground itself to a halt.

To relieve the monotony I ducked into the butcher's and for a few minutes bent an appreciative ear to Bill, the shopman cutter, as he explained the purpose of the three holes in the road to a confused and elderly customer in a flat pink hat.

"It's the go-slow on the Underground, see, madam? All the signals are up the spout, so they've had to dig down to the railway line, right? When a train goes through they pass the word to the bloke over there in the phone-box, right? and he rings up the station to say there's one on the way. They call it train-spotting in the trade and it's nice work if you can get it. 'Specially . . ." and he cast a laconic eye in my direction, "'Specially it being a Saturday when they get overtime . . ." Alongside him Buster Keaton was the laughing policeman. He called over my head to the butcher's wife enthroned in her cubby-hole in charge of the till. "One twenty-five for the lady in the pink hat, Vera, please."

Denis, the boss, tall and tired looking, leaned confidentially across the counter. "You don't have to believe everything you hear in this shop, you know, madam," he informed the customer in a kindly voice.

"Oh, I don't," she twittered, scrabbling gamely in an overstuffed purse. "I don't, believe me."

"So what can I do for you, Mr Savage, sir?" enquired Bill fixing me with a solemn eye. I told him a couple of chump chops and while he was sorting them out became aware of Vera waving at me with her chin. I edged over.

"What about the murder then?" Her voice was a hoarse whisper.

"Murder? What murder?" I thought she meant the one she'd seen on television the night before – Saturday's the morning we have a run-through of the films she's hated during the week. But no, this was a real one.

"Up on the Common. Last night. It was on the wireless this morning. Bloke got his head bashed in. Surprised you didn't hear it on the wireless."

I told her life was murky enough without listening to the wireless and asked if it was anyone we knew.

She made a disappointed face. "No, just a bloke. Hit over the head. From behind so they said. Marvellous, isn't it? Can't even walk on the Common o' nights now . . ."

"You'll be all right then," Bill chipped in, "seeing as how you live out in Sidcup. Two lovely chump chops, Mr Savage, sir," he added showing them to me with a flourish. "Two eighteen, Vera, for the gent in the sexy black mack."

Vera directed a disdainful snort in his direction. "Wish *you'd* go for a walk on the Common and get *your* head bashed in."

The lady in the pink hat who had somehow become attached to my elbow looked suitably startled. "You shouldn't say things like that, Vera dear. You never know who might be listening."

"Well . . ." Vera was unrepentant. "He gets on my wick, honest he does."

Further home truths were interrupted by the Pink Hat casting a handful of small change on the floor at my feet. "There!" she whispered with a hint of rising hysteria. "Now look what you've made me do."

8

I knelt in the sawdust recovering the scattered coins and a couple of wayward postage stamps.

"No need to grovel," uttered a deep and grainy baritone voice newly arrived in a smart pair of polished shoes streaked with fresh mud. "A kiss on the hand will do."

I looked up. Ex-Detective Inspector Sam Birkett CID bared pristine dentures at me. I regained my feet, returned the lady's spilled finances and dusted myself off. "Hi, Sam, how is it with you?"

He pulled down the corners of his mouth. "Mustn't grumble, I suppose."

The departing customer ducked her pink hat between us. "Thank you, young man, most kind . . ."

"There!" cried Vera, spirits reviving. "That's *your* good deed for the day done."

Sam frowned severely at her. "Which is more than may be said of you, madam. I hope you didn't mean what you said just now – about you-know-who getting his head bashed in."

Vera looked stricken. "You didn't hear that, did you?"

"The whole of Wimbledon High Street heard you."

"If I was you, Inspector . . ." began Bill.

"Which you're not . . ." finished Sam.

"I'd take it all down and use it in evidence against her . . . What can I do you for, Inspector, sir?"

Sam Birkett winked at Vera and turned away. She took my money with a toss of her head. "Can't say anything nowadays without someone on the listen."

I collected my change. "Used to be his job, didn't it?"

She leaned over her counter and lowered her voice. "I'll tell you one thing . . ." She jerked her head in Sam's direction. "They don't come like him any more. Some of the ones we've got over at Sidcup are still wearing their school caps. With him and his lot . . ." Sam again, ". . . well, you knew where you were, didn't you?"

I grinned at her. "Have a nice weekend, Vera."

"You and all. And don't do anything I wouldn't do."

I ranged up alongside Sam who was brooding over the ranks of deceased chickens hunched on the marble slab in the window. "How's Mildred?"

He gave me a preoccupied frown. "Who?"

Mildred was his wife.

"Mildred."

"Oh, ah yes, Mildred. She's all right, I think. Daft as ever." Denis hovered alongside him; Sam pointed a thickset finger at the bare chest of a mid-sized fowl. "That one." He sounded as if he were running an identity line-up. "And – er – " His eyes flickered coldly in the direction of Bill. "I'd like some stuffing."

"Wouldn't we all?" muttered the irrepressible William rising predictably to the bait.

Sam sighed. "There's always one, isn't there?" He glanced at me sideways "You on the wagon still?" The glint in the eye belied the casual delivery of the enquiry.

I shrugged. "Depends on how ugly it all gets."

He was thoughtfully silent for a second or two then turned away and wandered off to collect his packet of sage and onion from Vera and await the advent of his chicken now in process of being disembowelled.

I liked Sam Birkett, what little I knew of him, though I can't say I'd have been all that enamoured had I been tampering with the law and discovered him on my tail. Retired some years now, he was a formidable looking man, square and thickset with powerful shoulders, huge hands and the gentleness of mind and spirit so often intrinsic to one of such physique. The danger lay in the restless grey eyes and the subtle workings of the brain lurking carefully behind them. Retirement must have been anathema to him.

I hung about in the doorway getting into everybody's way and nodding at people I didn't know but recognised as locals. In a place like Wimbledon Village you got to know the residents by the shape of their hats, the size of their dogs and the way they dropped their eyes when they saw you coming.

I had come here to live shortly after my 'trouble' – when I had stopped being a so-called film star and gone off the rails, taking too readily to booze and pot for comfort. My not very loving wife, faced with the possibility of becoming consort to a living, breathing vegetable, had already removed herself. She'd gone before the booze and pot bit, otherwise I might well have been spared all that. I like to think so anyway, but I bear her no grudge.

Sam joined me with his parcels and we stood on the step shouting farewells over our shoulders before plunging out into the world again where the traffic was still stationary.

Sam said, "Did you know Denis was once a copper?"

"Denis the butcher?"

He nodded. "Got fed up with the red tape apparently, so he buggered off out of it. Quite right too in my opinion; can't say I blame him; it's pretty irksome when you meet it head-on for the first time. Pity though, he'd have made a damn good cop."

"And we'd have lost a damn good butcher."

He shrugged. "Can't win 'em all, can we?" He glanced up at the threatening sky. "Here comes the rain again. All of a sudden it's bloody winter. How about a gentle noggin at the Dog? Can I twist your arm?"

The wind nearly blew his hat off; he drew it down low over his eyes like a balaclava; an inch further and he would have blacked himself out altogether. With head bent against the wind I noticed again the fresh mud on his shoes.

"How was it on the Common this morning?"

"What?" I repeated the question. He glanced sideways at me, the brim of his hat flat against the wind – Napoleon hacking back from Moscow. "Who says I've been on the Common?"

"Mud on otherwise immaculate shoes."

He chuckled loudly. "Who says it's Common mud?"

"Your front garden is paved and it's pavement all the way from your house to here, so no mud. But after last night's rain there's an awful lot of it on the Common. Also on Common last night unknown gent gets his head bashed in. Conclusion: nosey ex-copper hears news on radio and rushes out with nostrils aquiver for clues overlooked by inexperienced whipper-snappers not yet out of their swaddling clouts. How's that?"

Sam stopped in his tracks. "My God, Holmes, you amaze me! How do you manage it?"

Chuckling together like a couple of schoolboys we went on. As we drew near the Dog and Fox he asked too casually, "Much on at the moment?"

I gave him a wary glance. "Workwise you mean? Not a lot.

Usual rubbish; you know the sort of thing. Forsaken wives with not enough to do, missing persons, tracking down aunties and uncles last heard of twenty years ago in some obscure part of the globe. I pass most of it on to poor old Mitch."

"Now I met Mitch once, didn't I? Tall, like a stick of celery? High heels? Blonde? Big blue eyes?"

"That's the one. Assistant, partner and silent sufferer, though slightly more vociferous lately and teetering I would say on the brink of rebellion. I think she's probably sickening for something."

As we pushed our way into the as yet scantily populated bar the inquisitive grey eyes roamed into every corner. It was probably no more than the usual reflex action of one who had spent the best part of his life beneath the brim of a deerstalker, but with Sam you never could tell. He may have hung up his policeman's boots but old habits die hard. He heaved his bulk on to a stool, removed his hat and swivelled himself into a position from which he could command an uninterrupted view of the door.

An unsolicited pint of draught Guinness appeared at his elbow and before I could say 'mine's a lager' he ordered an extra half pint and only then brought himself to raise an enquiring eyebrow at me. I told him a Carlsberg and gave up worrying about him. If he wanted to drink a pint and a half of Guinness out of two different glasses that was his affair, not mine.

"Written any good books lately?" I asked. It was a running gag. Sam had burst into print shortly after his retirement – accounts of some of the cases he'd been involved in, larded, I suspect, with a judicious amount of poetic licence. I'd read a couple of them and enjoyed them; a mite theatrical perhaps but none the worse for that. It confirmed my snide suspicion that there's an actor throbbing away beneath every good copper's helmet – how else could they deliver those boring old lines with such a stunning sense of spontaneous timing? 'I wonder if you'd mind just stepping out of the car, sir, please?' – 'P'raps you'd care to take a deep breath, sir, and breathe into this – er – bag, sir.'

He was telling me how he'd got bogged down in the third chapter of his latest epic – writers' block he called it – when the door behind me creaked open and I watched with growing amazement as his gnarled old face suddenly glowed and lit up as if someone had struck a match behind his eyeballs.

When I glanced over my shoulder I could see the reason why.

At a guess I would say she was in her middle twenties. Of medium height, slender and delectable, wide mouth, grey studious eyes bright beneath the brim of a jaunty rain hat, she possessed the sort of get-up-and-knock-'em-cold beauty which is apt to deprive all but the strongest of males of speech and hearing for some minutes. When she drew off her gloves I was rendered incapable and when she removed her hat and let fall a cascade of shoulder-length golden hair I grabbed blindly at my newly acquired Carlsberg and took a swig at it to keep my jaw from sagging.

"Down boy," breathed Sam in my ear, raising a hand to attract her attention. "She's mine."

I shambled off my stool as she came over and passed me by on the way to Sam who took both her hands and planted a vulgar great kiss on her cheek. He was the type who would have pinched Helen of Troy's bottom and started another war.

Then she turned back to me and with something of a shock I saw for the first time the clouding anxiety in her grey eyes and the dark shadows beneath them.

"Lindy," Sam was saying gruffly, "meet Mark Savage, known to one and all as Mark Sutherland, one time star of stage, screen and idiotic television plays, now, thankfully, retired. And this," he turned to me, "I would have you know, young Mark, is my daughter, Lindy."

Her hand was cold and needed warmth so I massaged it with diligence and since nothing was immediately forthcoming from my end, she made a gallant effort to shake off whatever was troubling her and with a show of perfect teeth informed me that I had been a childhood hero of hers.

I mumbled something about that making me feel elderly but she shook her head. "It shouldn't. You haven't changed a bit. I should have known you anywhere."

I followed her lead. "Didn't I read something about you in one of your father's books? Acting, if I remember rightly?"

She made a face. "In the school play, yes, for my sins. Lady

Macbeth at fifteen! It should never have been allowed. Now I'm an old married woman." Glancing almost furtively at her father, her eyes clouding again, she attempted a quiet laugh which didn't come off.

I gave her back her hand and comforted myself with the thought that wooing an ex-policeman's daughter wouldn't have been much fun anyway – like trying to go straight after ten years in the slammer with everybody on the look-out for the first sign of the flip-flops.

I took a stealthy peek at her left hand. The discreet gold marriage band was submerged and outclassed by a diamond the size of a carbuncle which didn't go with the rest of her and must have cost, as they say, a pretty penny. The shadowing of her eyes jolted my curiosity. Domestic problems maybe; married wisely perhaps but not too well . . . ?

The extra Guinness was for her of course. So he had been expecting her. A feeling of caution crept over me. She raised her glass solemnly. "Cheers." I grinned, lapped up some lager and nodded at the Guinness. "I see he's brought you up in the manner to which he has become accustomed."

Father then decided he wanted to sit somewhere else so we hefted our drinks and shopping-bags over to the corner table he had in mind, where he parked himself – again with a clear view of the door – and left the rest of us to fend for ourselves. I helped her out of her raincoat and spread it over a nearby chair. There was an inner restlessness about her which disturbed me intensely. My sense of caution now turned to unease. I encountered Sam's bland grey eye which told me nothing other than that he was up to something and had lured me here under false pretences. It was a set-up. It was also Saturday morning in Wimbledon Village for God's sake and he was behaving like Claude Rains in *Casablanca*. I took the chair opposite his daughter where I could stare at her without appearing rude and swept a keen private eye over the assembled clientele.

Some of them I knew by sight, none by name. Since my trouble I rarely frequented drinking establishments – self-preservation rather than choice – but I could still sort out the regulars from the casuals.

They were a job-lot, the regulars screwed immovably to

their chairs and stools hunched in silent ritual over their drinks and nothing short of a nuclear attack would be likely to unscrew them; the casuals looked as if they were actually enjoying themselves, one of them doing his best to interest the landlord in a bent silver candlestick he had just bought and didn't want. None of them looked suspicious.

A flurry of heavy rain gusted against the windows. A pallid flicker of lightning was followed by the dark murmur of distant thunder. I turned my head and found myself staring into the eyes of a man peering in at us through the window, his face distorted by the streaming glass, the rain beating on to his bare head and furrowing the dark, thinning hair; rivulets of water coursed down his cheeks and into his half open mouth; he seemed to be breathing heavily and I caught a fleeting glimpse of a broken front tooth and a dull glint of gold further back. Then he was gone.

I looked at the door half expecting him to erupt into the bar; I half rose to my feet.

"What?" asked Sam abruptly.

I stared back at the window for a second, frowning to myself. "Nothing. Thought I saw someone, or someone who thought he knew me . . ."

"Who doesn't know you? That old face of yours has been spread across the screens of the world often enough."

I shook my head. "It wasn't that. It was like . . ." I tried to remember what it was I thought I had seen in the eyes. ". . . as if he was – memorising me for another time. I don't know, it was just a passing thing, I expect. Poor bugger, he was probably just looking in to see if we were full up in here."

Sam's eyes strayed thoughtfully to the rainswept window.

I grinned awkwardly at Linda.

"Sam," I said.

"What?"

"What's all this about?"

After a second of silence he knocked back the remainder of his Guinness and reaching into a pocket placed a crisp fiver on the table. "Let's have the second half, shall we, Lindy?" I got to my feet. "No." Sam's voice was firm. "Be a dear, will you, Lindy? I want one quick word with Mark – out of your hearing. All right?"

Collecting his glass, she smiled at me. "For you too?" I shook my head. She touched my shoulder. "Don't let him bother you. He *is* my father, after all. He's been bossing me around all my life."

When she had gone Sam said almost without moving his lips. "She could be in danger." He paused as if to collect himself then added, "That's the quick word." He glanced almost surreptitiously at the window. "I think I could do with your help, Mark – professionally, I mean. If you've nothing else on. No favours: strictly business."

I stared at him with some incredulity. "What can I do that you can't? You've got the contacts. You're the professional."

"Ex-professional." The voice grated with sudden weariness. "I'm getting old. I'm not sure I could follow this through. Even if I knew what it was. It's too close to home."

I watched his finger tracing the circle of liquid left by his glass on the table. Overhead thunder muttered and rumbled restlessly. "Why me, Sam? Can't you shunt it along to some of your ex-mates on the Force?"

"No." He cut across me with a curt shake of his head. "It's nothing to do with them. Not yet. It might well be later on, but not now." He gave an irritable shrug. "Coppers always stand out like sore thumbs. Know what I mean? Big feet, funny hats, regulation rainwear."

His eyes were on Linda at the bar, the trouble in them deepening. I too looked across. She was engaged in conversation with the candlestick man.

"Her husband's gone," muttered Sam shortly, and after a pause added, "disappeared."

I waited for him to enlarge on the announcement and when nothing came asked, "How disappeared? Took off and left her, do you mean? Done a bunk? Another woman? What?"

His worried eyes met mine. "Nothing like that. They're devoted to each other." He hesitated. "He could have gone to ground somewhere." Another pause. "May even be dead." I waited patiently for the crunch line. He said quietly, "The man who had his head bashed in on the Common last night . . . Lindy's husband may have been the last person to see him alive."

"You mean . . ."

"I don't mean anything. Just telling you the facts." He took a deep breath. "At the moment they're treating it as a mugging which went wrong. The body had been stripped of valuables, money, wristwatch, cufflinks and, judging by certain marks on the wrist, a bracelet of some sort. His wallet had been rifled of banknotes, credit cards etcetera and then discarded, luckily with a letter inside it addressed to him, so at least they were able to put a name to him. Otherwise there was nothing. The night's rain washed away any hopes of prints and the like."

He looked at me intently, the lids of his eyes drooping deceptively. "Should you decide to come in on this and want to view the body for any reason I'm pretty certain I could arrange it, but at the moment it might be better if you were to keep your highly unforgettable face out of it. I wouldn't want to alert them to possibilities they haven't even thought of."

I wondered idly why he was so sure the killing *hadn't* been the result of a random mugging. I asked, "How long has he been missing?"

"Since last night." He raised a hand. "And before you make the obvious comment, bear with me, will you, while I put you in the picture?" He frowned down at the puddle of liquid on the table. "For some time now, he and some of his unemployed friends have been trying to get together some sort of business for themselves. First they tried a pop group – promoting, I hasten to add, not performing – and when that fell through they turned to the possibility of a theatre workshop project. Lindy is remarkably and, I may say, unusually vague about details. However, that's neither here nor there at the moment. The point is that last night he and his associates were holding a meeting at the house, so Lindy, who isn't really in on it – she's a desk-editor in publishing and is much too busy editing desks of course . . . ." He paused and gave me a glum stare. "That was a joke," he complained.

"Oh? Ah yes," I said. "Of course, sorry. Ha, ha."

"Lindy," he pressed on, "took Mildred to a concert at the Festival Hall. When she got back, the house was empty. At first she assumed that Anthony – that's her husband – had run some of his buddies home, but later she became a bit anxious and took a look in the garage; the car was there and the engine cold. She looked around for any note he might have left but there was nothing.

"Now, apart from one bloke – fellow called Geoffrey Earnshaw – she had no idea who was there last night, and that in itself is odd considering how close she and Anthony have always been – and still are, I hope. Whatever this workshop thing is all about he's apparently been playing it very close to the chest and obviously doesn't want her in on it – which, to a certain extent, she has accepted because she's that sort of girl, but it doesn't do a lot to help the domestic wheels run smoothly. Anyway, to get on . . . she tried to raise this Geoff Earnshaw on the phone but there was no reply. She then rings me to see if he's looked in on us by any chance. That was at two o'clock this morning.

"I told her to have another look around to see if anything had gone, like his toilet things, clothes and so on. But no, his razor was still there, his toothbrush and nothing seemed to be missing – no clothes gone, so far as she could see. So he obviously hadn't done a bunk – as you so elegantly put it. Also there was no sign of a struggle.

"Well, at three o'clock she woke me up again. He still hadn't come home. What should she do? I told her to leave it to me, I'd ring around the hospitals and the usual places – the old police routine, you know? I asked if she'd like to come over and doss down at our place for the rest of the night. No, she wouldn't do that in case he turned up. Funnily enough, she didn't sound all that anxious on the phone; if she had I might have gone over there, held her hand. She's pretty self-possessed, you know, one way and another – like her old man." He paused for comment. I made none.

He went on. "I said I'd telephone her if I came up with anything, otherwise I'd ring her first thing in the morning. Well, of course, nothing was to be gleaned from the hospitals and, quite honestly, I didn't expect anything. He could easily have gone off on a bender with this chap Earnshaw – the one she couldn't raise on the phone. It would have been out of character, but what the hell – we all surprise ourselves sometimes, don't we? If I'd really been worried I might have rung the police, but of course, they wouldn't even have listened to me. I'm damn glad now that I didn't. When I heard the early news this morning it all blew up in my face. The dead man on the Common was Geoff Earnshaw – they actually named him. The cops had already contacted his poor old mum."

He stared at me from beneath lowered brows. "Geoff was probably Anthony's only real friend – was in fact his best man at the wedding. Well, I was out on that Common with the speed of light, gossiped with the gendarmerie, shambled around and got nowhere. So then I called in on Lindy. She hadn't been to bed all night and looked like a dog's dinner." He glanced over my shoulder. "Still does, if it comes to that, poor old duck." His eyes dropped to mine. "I broke the news about Geoff – I had to, didn't I? But I said nothing to the cops because they'd have jumped to the very same conclusion that you've just jumped to – that Anthony killed Geoff, right?"

I wriggled a bit in my chair because, shall I say, it had crossed my mind?

He shook his head pedantically. "Whatever else Anthony may or may not be, Mark, he is no killer. Never, in a month of Sundays."

In the long pause that ensued Linda returned with her father's refill. "Sorry I've been so long. Someone's been trying to sell me a candlestick. I've only just been able to tear myself away."

As she seated herself, her eyes moved from me to her father and back again to me. "Dad's told you my problem, I imagine?" I nodded. "He said you might be willing to help."

I smiled. "I'd be willing to try." I brooded for a second or two. "May I ask you a few questions?"

"Of course."

"I gather there's no trouble between you and your husband?"

"None." The faintest flicker of a hesitation undermined the defensive asperity of the word.

I probed gently. "But something?"

She glanced obliquely at her father who raised a pair of lugubrious eyebrows and refused to come to her aid. A further moment of reluctance then she said with a slight shake of her head, "Nothing I could actually put my finger on – nothing specific. All I know is that for several weeks now there's been a sort of – remoteness about him. Did Dad tell you about this theatre thing he's been working on?" I nodded. "I'm sure that's at the bottom of it. He's been so secretive about it. We've never had secrets from each other before, never. There've been problems of course – every married couple have problems and disagreements – but we usually talk them out, get them into some sort of proportion. But not this time . . ."

She broke off, the shadows again in her eyes.

"And it's obviously disturbed you a great deal?"

She considered her answer gravely. "Frankly, yes. I just kept on hoping that things would sort themselves out and we'd be able to discuss them. But now, suddenly, he's gone . . ."

A burst of raucous laughter from a group at the bar interrupted her train of thought. She glanced at them abstractedly, her eyes brimming with hurt and desolation.

I met Sam's gaze. He was watching me intently, alert and knowledgeable, reading me like a book. He was an ugly bugger when he looked like that and one to be wary of.

I said tentatively, "You're pretty certain that this – er – preoccupation of his is the result of the work he's doing? The secrecy, I mean. Because if it's just some legitimate project, for example, I don't understand why he can't talk to you about it. Do you see what I'm getting at? Could it not be something else which is bothering him – something which might concern you more directly perhaps? Something he can't bring himself to tell you . . . I'm putting it badly, I know . . ."

"Not at all," she interrupted somewhat wryly, at the same time coming to my rescue. "You're putting it quite well. You mean another woman." I frowned at the table. "The answer is no. Another woman he would tell me about. That I know, absolutely and without any doubt whatsoever. If there were someone else I would know anyway – he wouldn't have to tell me." She smiled and touched my arm gently. "Does that answer your question?"

I shrugged and gave a sheepish grin. "Private detectives have to be grubby sometimes. I'm sure it won't surprise you to know how often these things are apt to boil down to some sort of – illicit liaison. The last thing I want to do is to embarrass you . . ."

Rabbiting away in my mind for some word of comfort I found myself searching Sam's hang-dog features in the hope that assistance might be forthcoming from that quarter, but he appeared to have taken himself off into a brown study all his own.

Linda said quietly, "He's gone, Mark . . . for whatever reason, Anthony's gone, and the least he could have done was to leave a note, telephone me, contact me in any way – not just walk out like that, without a word." Her eyes were bright with standing tears. "Something has happened to him, something bad. I know it, I just know it. And whatever it is, it's not an accident – not a street accident. If he'd been knocked over or – or killed or . . . you know what I mean . . . we'd have heard by this time. His pockets were full of identification – cards, papers, letters. Even Geoff had a letter on him . . ."

She pulled herself up with a stifled sob realising, as we all did, the bleak implication of her words. Her father stuffed a handkerchief into her hand, aware of the several pairs of eyes swivelling in our direction.

"Let's drink up and get out of here," he muttered sourly and lowering his voice still further added, "pull yourself together Lindy, there's a good girl. Tears aren't going to help."

She mopped at her eyes like a small girl. I could see the whiteness of her knuckles when she gripped his hand. If he had been talking to anyone but a daughter his words would have been hurtful and insensitive; as it was they were the right words and she quickly simmered down and gave him back his handkerchief. He winked at me solemnly over the rim of his glass.

"How about," he said almost jovially as he parked the empty glass on the table with a thud, "you coming to say hello to Mildred and having a quick bite with us? Cheese and biscuits and a snort of wine. How would that be? If you haven't got anything else lined up that is. Like some pulchritudinous maiden sprawled knickerless on your day-bed."

I was busy bundling Linda into her raincoat and couldn't see much of a way out of the invitation. There was nothing pulchritudinous waiting for me – more's the pity – but, I told him, I'd have to look in at the flat to put my chops in the fridge.

"Park 'em in our fridge." He screwed his hat on to his head, heaved himself to his feet and laid a fond arm about his daughter's shoulders. "All right, old lover?"

She gave a wan little nod and we set off for the door battling our way through a maddened hoard of drinkers on the swoop for the table we had just vacated.

Sam Birkett lived in an old dark house in Lauriston Road, three minutes from the Common at one end and a similar three minutes from the Swan at the other – an ideal position for one whose way of life embraced walking, bird-watching and drinking. If he wearied of the Swan, the King of Denmark was a mere dozen paces in a north-easterly direction. And with eleven hundred acres of wide and open country between him and Putney Crematorium he was unlikely to tire of the Common or of its avowed seventy varieties of resident and migrant bird-life.

Mildred Birkett was in the kitchen when we arrived, drinking gin and concocting something alarming in a large bowl. When she caught sight of me over her husband's shoulder she gave an owl-like hoot of pleasure, greeting me as if I were a long-lost son home from the wars, kissing me wetly on both cheeks and ordering me to take off my damp coat at once.

Somewhat unkindly portrayed in her husband's books as a gaunt and bony-elbowed 'strange looking woman in hair-curlers', Mildred was, in my eyes, none of these things, though I could, at a pinch, see what he meant about the incipient moustache. She had probably filled out a bit since he had complained about her elbows and I'd never had the privilege of judging her in hair-curlers. She was a thoroughly nice, if somewhat daunting lady in her early sixties or thereabouts, and to be married to Sam Birkett and stay sane you would have to be daunting.

Sam collected our wet rainwear and went off with it, telling her on the way about my chump chops and their need for refrigeration. She seized them and thrust them into her fridge without another word and placing a maternal arm about Linda's waist and a possessive one round mine ushered us into the comfortable sitting-room. "No news, I suppose?"

Linda shook her head. "Nothing," she muttered and

wandered over to the French windows where she stood, hunched and miserable, watching the weather. It had brightened a bit and the rain was slackening off.

"Nobody's rung," said Mildred forlornly. She shook her head at me. "It's too bad of him, you know, just going off like that. Dreadful thing to do."

Linda swung away violently from the window. I intervened hastily though with caution suggesting that we didn't really know whether it was dreadful or not, but that we ought perhaps to keep an open mind and hope for the best. When I lamely suggested he might have lost his memory and was wandering about wondering who he was and where he belonged, the idea went down like a lead balloon and a mighty gloom descended upon us.

The flushing of a loo somewhere close by came almost as a relief and heralded the return of Sam who also looked relieved. "Did you want to . . . er . . . ?" He jerked his head in the direction from which he had come. I shook my head. He turned to Mildred. "I want to borrow him for a couple of minutes if you don't mind. Man's talk. All right?"

She nodded comfortably. "I'll rustle up something to eat and give you a shout. Soup, cheese and biscuits, Mark, will that suit you?"

"And a bottle of wallop," said Sam. "I promised him a bottle of wallop."

Refusing a pre-prandial drink, I was practically frog-marched from the room, down a passage and through a back door into a sort of do-it-yourself lean-to conservatory – known *en famille* as The Jungle – full of sad-looking plants which didn't seem to be doing a lot.

"Sorry about all that," apologised Sam gruffly peering into a box of dead leaves, "but we'll get along better on our own. You really are a great lad, you know that? I do appreciate it." He pressed me down into the only chair, a creaking, paint-stained wooden affair which had seen far better days, and then stood over me like a threat. "Now then, I'm going to fill you in." He said it in much the same way as a Chicago hood might have said "I'm gonna rub you out."

Before he could get started an enormous black cat with startling pale yellow eyes landed with a thud on my lap. I leapt almost as high as he did. "Hello cat," I said when I had got over it. "Who are you then?"

"He walked in one day out of the rain and took us over," Sam explained. "Goes by the name of Magnificat and may not be staying. He's only been with us a few months."

Magnificat gave a cavernous yawn, took up a powerful purr, blinked contentedly, sharpened his claws on my knee and settled down to what was clearly a long overdue afternoon nap.

"I have a gut feeling about Anthony," announced Sam, prodding ineffectually among a further collection of withered leaves. "Just look at that, will you? Bloody white-fly . . . get in everywhere . . ."

"Sam . . ." I was growing impatient.

"What?"

"Get on with it will you?"

"I think he's been snatched." I stared at him wordlessly. "Kidnapped," he enlarged with the superiority which came only with rank.

"I know what snatched means. Why?"

"Ransom, what else?" He had unearthed a green aerosol and emphasised his words with a couple of sharp bursts of fly-killer which sent Magnificat into a frenzied paroxysm of sneezing.

"Oh Christ," I growled and snatched the green can from Sam's grasp. "Were you always like this? How in hell did Fred Saunders put up with you all those years?" Fred had been Sam's side-kick sergeant in the Force.

He sighed. "Ah, poor old Fred . . ."

"What, what? He hasn't died has he?"

"Worse, much worse. He's been promoted, poor old sod."

"Ransom," I pointed out with some asperity, "usually presupposes money, big money. How much big money has Linda got in her piggy bank?" I planted the aerosol in a box of earth out of his reach.

He looked smug. "Not Linda. It's father-in-law they'll be after." He allowed himself a dramatic pause. "George Raven." Another pause while he watched my reaction. "Sir George Raven?" and placed the slightest of question marks after the name.

I gaped at him. "Raven Industries?"

"The very same."

I pursed my lips in a silent whistle. "You've been very quiet about that I must say. That's money with knobs on. He must be one of the richest men in the country."

He gave a speculative nod. "Apart from the Arabs, I'd say one of two."

I shook my head in modest wonder. "That's a rarified atmosphere your Linda's been living in. When he shuffles off this mortal coil death duties alone will keep HMG going for at least a couple of weeks."

Sam shook a moody head. "Not much of it made its way into his son's pockets I can tell you. He was always kept on a very tight rein – and quite right too in my opinion. Bits of boys like you and him are far too apt to wax prodigal if you get half a chance. Mind you, if he hasn't done anything too drastic with the old man and blotted his copy book for good, he's still the son and heir and stands an almighty chance of also becoming the second richest man in the country, God help him."

I gave him a grave stare. "That's a weighty thought."

The smile didn't reach his eyes. "Yes, isn't it just?"

We listened for a second to the steady drip of water from an overflow pipe somewhere. Magnificat twitched in his sleep; the shudder of a feline dream rippled through the soft black fur like an electrical charge; a paw distended and stretched revealing the cruel crescent claws, then they were gone, hidden among the velvet pads.

"Raven knows about his son's disappearance of course?"

He nodded. "When Lindy became agitated yesterday morning the first thing I did was to ring his dad; thought perhaps Anthony might have called in on him on the way home. He lives over on Parkside, you know, one of those posh properties on the edge of the Common."

"This really is a local affair, isn't it?" I exchanged a second sober look at him. "I'm beginning to see what you mean about the Earnshaw killing. It's all too near home. Was – er – Raven worried at all about his missing son?"

He dismissed the suggestion with a short caustic laugh. "He hadn't seen him for months. I don't think they're even on speaking terms. A conflict of ethics I would guess. When

Anthony married Lindy a couple of years back he found a freedom he had never known before. Until then he had just about tolerated Dad the despot; the usual thing I imagine: do what I say or I'll cut you off without a penny piece. And Anthony, whom I have to admit – fond though I am of him – is hardly the most forthright and powerful character in the world, knuckled down and stayed where he was until Lindy turned up and whipped him away from it all."

"And how did that grab old man Raven?"

"Oddly and unbelievably quite well. He took a great liking to Lindy, thank God, and agreed whole-heartedly to the marriage; he was probably glad to get the boy off his hands. Set them up generously in a small property on the far side of the Common, small by his standards that is, only six bedrooms. So they too are Wimbledon worthies."

"The place is awash with us."

After a pause Sam said carefully, "I mentioned to him the possibility of kidnapping."

"And?"

"It was bound to hit him where he lives of course – all that loose change. The silence was the longest and barest I've listened to on the phone for a long time. But then he doesn't talk to me much at the best of times. We've only met once or twice and he's not exactly a confiding individual. There's no discernible Lady Raven. She certainly wasn't at the wedding. I think he's rather sad – and he probably thinks the same about me. I like him in a leery sort of way, though I'll never get on his dance-card. I can never understand blokes like that – blokes with money. There's no room for anything else, know what I mean? They don't get out and about, have fun like everyone else. They go into purdah, lock 'emselves away in their attics, go potty. Or maybe I've seen too many films. Perhaps they're not all like Howard Hughes. There must be happy rich people in the world somewhere surely? Though it's hard to imagine with all those government contracts of his; they're enough to sink the battle cruisers he helps to build."

"He's into armaments as well is he?"

"He's into everything, mate. Ships, arms, machines, electronics. Mad bloody lot! They invent something world-shaking, plan it, build it behind barricades – top secret all the way along the line – and when it's finished and the price is right, they sell it to everybody – potential enemies as well. What a lot of crap it is, isn't it? However . . ." He lifted his shoulders in a gargantuan shrug of amiable dismissal, and with head bowed and hands deep in his trouser pockets did a couple of turns up and down the narrow aisle between the home-made benches. Far away thunder still rumbled.

"You know something?" Sam again, a whimsical note in his voice. "These are the times when I wish I smoked. I'm sure it would do something for me. The waiting times . . ." He sighed loudly and hummed a couple of tuneless hums.

"Suppose you're wrong," I said abruptly.

He stopped in his tracks and stared at me gravely from beneath lowered lids. "Then we'll just have to sit back and wait, won't we? Nothing else we can do. If he's taken off on his own accord no one but he knows when he'll be back – if ever. As I see it, there are three possibilities. One, he's done a bolt because he's fed up with life as it is and pissed off to somewhere antiseptic like Canada or Australia; or he's frightened of someone or something and has gone into hiding. Two, he's been snatched and his kidnappers are being tardy about publishing their demands. And three, he's dead, killed by his own or someone else's hand. Frankly I think we can discard self-slaughter. He's no suicide." His eyes flickered uneasily. Picking up a pot of earth, Sam blinked at it, poked it with a despairing finger and then replaced it as gently as if it were Meissen porcelain. He stared up through the glass roof at the bare wet branches of a vast oak . . .

"So what do you want me for?" I enquired, gently running a soft finger along Magnificat's spine and watching the sensual ripple of fur.

"When and if the demand comes, it goes without saying that it will be with the usual codicil – no police. Any sign of fuzz and the deal's off, right? Well, for once I would agree with that sentiment and I'm sure Dad would too. We'll get him back if only for Lindy's peace of mind. But," I could swear I heard his heart beating, "whoever they are, I want them . . . personally. And I want you and me together to go out after them, and I don't want the bloody police buggering things up." I frowned up at him. He gave an impatient shake of his head. "Oh, I know, I know, I am a bloody policeman – was a bloody policeman – and an efficient one too in my own bumbling way. But somehow, Mark, somehow, when the thing comes as close as this . . ." He stopped, his eyes staring sightlessly at my chest. "I want them for myself. It's a personal issue. Family. You understand that?"

"Well enough." I nodded slowly. "It just disturbs me that you might be going out on a limb, your judgement impaired *because* it's personal. If you were still on the Force they wouldn't let you near it, you know that, don't you? I'd hate to see you blot your copy book for the sake of a few mercenary sods who are not worth the air they breathe."

"That's why I want you with me. I can't do it all – not the leg-work certainly, if there's to be any." He hadn't listened to a word I'd been saying. "What do you say, Mark? Will you come in? I'll pay your usual fees."

"I don't want any bloody fees – not from you," I quacked back at him with unintended violence.

"Then it's off."

"It's not off! We'll talk about it when and if it happens."

There was a protracted silence. He turned away again. I counted his footfalls. Six up, six down, five away . . . Silence again. He said quietly, "It'll happen. I know it will. It's not often I'm smitten with second sight, but when I am, by Christ it happens . . ."

The cat stirred, stretched, made a strange yowling sound and slept again.

Chapter Two

Sunday is a bad day to be alone. What God thought he was doing when he invented it only he knows. Me, I prowl about the flat like some demented Trappist monk, except that I talk a lot to myself and couldn't meditate even if I knew what it meant. I long for someone to help me burn the toast, hard-boil the eggs and back me up when I get incensed with the television and scream obscenities at the radio – someone nice and kind and gentle who thinks I'm the greatest thing since Steve McQueen. Unmarried if possible and looking not unlike Linda Raven née Birkett. I have a little woman of course who comes in twice a week to clean and dust and chase the Hoover around, but it's not the same.

On this particular Sunday morning I had already burnt the toast and snarled at some pompous, self-opinionated, know-all musicologist on Radio 3 who had smugly informed us that nothing of value had hit the fan in the musical world since the lamented and untimely demise of Mozart. "What about Beethoven then?" I bawled at the set. "What about Schubert and Wagner, Strauss, Shostakovitch . . . and bloody Albert Ketelby then? You stupid great ignorant twit!" But it was no bloody good, was it? He wasn't even listening and went on to prove how wrong he was by tinkling away at some puerile and prissy piece on his ill-tempered clavier; I was hurtling across the floor to the off-switch when the telephone rang.

Sam. On the bubble like a coffee percolator. "They've been on," he shouted. "We were right." The royal 'we' of course. I ignored it.

"What's the asking price?" Ever practical.

"Are you sitting down?"

"No."

He told me. I sat down. "Or else," I muttered.

"Or else." The phone breathed heavily for a second, then, "He wants to see you."

"Who wants to see me?"

"George Raven."

"How does he know about me?"

"I told him, didn't I? Said you might be willing to help."

I let that go. "When did they make contact?"

"This morning at the crack of dawn."

"How much time they giving him?"

"Unspecified at the moment."

"Did they say who they were?"

"They did, yes."

After a moment of listening silence I asked if he was going to tell me.

"You're not going to believe this." Another pause. "Swalk," he said and then went on to spell it in case I wasn't tuned in. "S-W-A-L-K."

I considered for a moment. "I knew a girl once who used to put that on the back of her envelopes," I told him. "What does it mean in present circumstances?"

"Your guess is as good as mine. They spelt it out for him and then hung up." He hissed between his teeth. "I'm never over-fond of these – what do you call 'em? – acronymous things. Is that the word? You know what I mean – IRA, EOKA and the like. They all spell the same thing in the long run: trouble with a capital T. And what's more they're usually political which is even more alarming."

"Listen, Sam . . ." Silence fell. I thought he'd hung up. "Sam? You there?"

"I'm listening, aren't I?"

"If it's political we're going to be well over our heads. God alone knows who we'd be taking on. Or what. I don't want to wake up one sunny day in Cuba or Libya."

He gave a jolly laugh. "I wouldn't worry about that if I were you. If you ever get to either of those places you probably won't be waking up at all."

"You have my point."

"Listen, Mark." He was being very patient. "If this lot is political the chances are they're not even off the ground yet. I've never heard of them and obviously you haven't either.

They could be on a funding spree, money-grubbing, you know? Out to attract the attention of the First Division as a bid to join in the Big League games at some future date. Everybody's got to start somewhere, even terrorists. Now, if I'm right and we play it cool – softly, softly sort of thing – we could have 'em on ice before they're out of the egg stage."

I smiled cynically down the phone. "Yes, well, if it's all the same to you, Sam old man, I think I'll stay with Mitch and her jealous husbands etcetera. Isn't there an anti-terrorist branch in your old outfit? Let them do it, that's what they're paid for."

The telephone said, "I'm not listening."

"What time's he want to see us?"

"Not us. You."

That alarmed me. "Why not you?"

"He only rang to give me the news-flash which was thoughtful of him, I suppose. But he did mention in passing that he wanted no advice and no interference from the police. 'And that,' he added, 'includes you, Mr Birkett.' He always calls me Mr Birkett. I told him once my name was Sam and he said he was sorry. Anyway I protested a bit, told him he oughtn't to try coping with this sort of thing on his own, pointed out the obvious dangers and dredged up your name as being the best in the business. Told him you hate the police like they were your nearest relations and got the impression that he would be quite happy with some outside help. So he said to fix it."

"What time?"

"Mid-day." He gave me the address on Parkside and told me not to be late.

I gave a loud sigh. "Does Linda know about this?"

A moment's hesitation. "Not yet, no. Nor Mildred. Sooner wait, I think, until there are more details – till I hear from you again perhaps. Right?"

"Well, you bloody wish me good luck, see?"

"*Merde.*"

"And the same to you."

I hung up.

The properties on Parkside are foursquare and considerable, each with a somewhat pretentious individuality and each set back from the road behind a modest crescent of driveway. Heavy traffic and the general rates would appear to be the residents' only drawbacks, the first countered by sturdy double-glazing, the second with the well-known, long-nosed resignation of the well-off. If such things depressed them there were always the wide open spaces of the Common to be viewed from their front windows and counted among their blessings.

Raven House overlooked the Bluegate Gravel Pit (disused and known locally as The Swamps) and was a disconcerting rectangle of dull red brick devoid of ornament and lacking in charm. Its staring, undressed Regency windows gave it the unwelcoming air of a barracks. A massive door of iron-studded black oak, recessed into a shallow porch above which, in a small niche, perched the gaunt and chipped effigy of a raven, was approached by a couple of stone steps, flanked on either side by monstrous iron footscrapers like poachers' traps. I noted the bell-push but settled for the heavy iron door-knocker. I gave it two hefty pounds and was gratified by the reverberating echoes set up within the house. The place thundered like a mausoleum.

As I awaited reaction to my summons a church clock struck twelve and as the last stroke died the door swung open with unnerving smoothness. No rusting bolts, no creaks or groans, not even a hunchbacked dwarf on the far side of it – just a manservant, pale as a troglodyte who had never seen the sun; pale hair, too, stuck close to his head like a plastic skullcap; washed-out flat blue eyes and a pair of raised eyebrows which said it all as he surveyed my person with frank disbelief. Dressed as I was in stormy black leathers and jack boots I must have been an alarming sight even to the most bomb-proof of gentlemen's gentlemen.

Since he appeared undisposed to open negotiations I told him who I was and that I was expected. He allowed me to slide crabwise into the hall, raised a pale silent hand to indicate that I should remain where I was and with the slightest whisper of alpaca mounted an impressive stairway and disappeared.

I wiped my feet on a doormat devoid of welcome and waited. He was back in no time at all, poised on the topmost stair, inviting me in a surprisingly rich bass voice to come this way.

The room into which he showed me was enormous and elegant with four windows overlooking the Common. It was furnished as an office-cum-sitting-room with a huge oak desk set midway between the two centre windows. I became aware of a presence and turned my head.

In the farthest corner, in a bulky wing-back armchair curiously like a throne, sat the man I had come to see, watching me over steepled fingers, a glint of sober appraisal in his eyes. The silent swing of a gilt pendulum on the vast mantelpiece was the only movement in the room.

Slowly I turned to face him and stood in silence for him to make the first move.

"Good day to you, Mr Savage," he said at last in a neutral voice. "You are punctual. I like that." He rose to his feet and moved noiselessly over the thick pile carpet to the window where he stood with his back to me and stared out over the Common. "We have a Canada goose in residence on the pond. Do you see him?" I moved in a little until I could see the bird with its graceful neck and tell-tale white patch behind the eye. "Know anything about birds, Mr Savage?"

"Not a lot, no. Sam knows about them though. Especially now he's retired and has more time for them."

"Sam?"

"Birkett."

"Ah yes . . . Mr Birkett." The name came to him from the middle distance. "Our Mr Birkett." He turned to face me. "An odd pastime for a policeman, bird-watching."

I shrugged. "It's a change from crime-watching, but I know what you mean. It's sometimes difficult to remember that policemen belong, as you and I do, Sir George, to the human race."

He took it like a man and allowed his eyes to wander languidly over my sartorial splendour. "You ride a motorbicycle, I imagine, Mr Savage?"

"Tied up in your drive at the moment."

We were of a height and stood for a second staring coolly into each other's eyes. His were hazel with a flicker of green in them, wary and suspicious, a lurking sense of humour in the lower depths. In build he was not unlike Sam, big and bulky; the two of them in a medium sized room would be enough. Thick-necked and broad-shouldered, he bore himself with the assurance of a one-time athlete – an ex-rugger blue perhaps – and although he must have been well into his sixties no hint of grey touched his temples, the dark mane of his hair and the heavy black eyebrows giving him instead an air of indestructability. The face was of the same mould, strong and muscular, wide-set eyes, a jutting nose and firm mouth whose thin ascetic upper lip was compensated by the projecting sensuality of the lower. I found myself prepared to like him.

"Please sit." He indicated the chair opposite the desk and I creaked down into it, the tight leather of my jeans squawking embarrassingly against the leather upholstery like the cry of a living thing.

He leant back carefully in his important, high-backed, swivel chair. "How much do you know of this wretched affair?" The question was abrupt and businesslike; no sentimentality about whose son was in jeopardy.

I told him exactly how much I knew in three sentences. When I'd done he sat on for a bit as if expecting more. Then, swivelling away from me, he turned his attention to the Common and the Parkside traffic moving on muffled wheels beyond his double-glazing. The silence was almost complete; I could just hear the whisper of the little ormolu clock on the mantelpiece behind me.

Suddenly he spoke. "Advice," he said. It was neither a question nor a statement of fact; whether he was about to offer it or required it was anybody's guess. I plumped for the latter and told him I wasn't there to give advice.

"What *are* you here for?"

"To keep an appointment."

"Your Mr Birkett said you were the best available."

"My Mr Birkett exaggerated. Until I know your intentions and the value set upon your son's well-being, it would, I'm sure, be a waste of time offering advice. That big desk suggests that you're quite capable of arriving at your own decisions." The speech was reasonable and without aggression.

He turned his head, the eyes dark and without expression. "How's that girl taking it?"

"Linda?" I shrugged. "As one might expect – upset."

"How much does she know?"

"That her husband has deserted her."

"Nothing about the kidnapping?"

"Not unless you've told her."

He frowned ponderously as he swung his chair back to face me. "I don't want her to get hurt. If I decide to pay the ransom it will be mainly on her account – not my son's." He waited for some sort of reaction and when none came added a trifle peevishly, "That doesn't surprise you?"

I gave him one of my thin smiles. "He's your son, Sir George. But I have to admit that I am no believer in the close-knit family syndrome. Families are sometimes more nuisance than they are worth. However . . . They're asking half a million, I understand?" He gave a curt nod. "That was in the early hours of this morning?"

"Six a.m. to be exact."

"And no further communication?"

"Not as yet."

I ground my teeth for a bit. "Half a million is a whole lot of money." He watched me in silence. "Is it available?" I tried again.

"Readily."

"What method of payment?"

"Diamonds."

"On tap?"

He gave me the superior eye, the way rich people look at the poor. "A phone call away."

I eyed the sleek Answercall machine beside the telephone on his desk. "You obviously didn't record the conversation?"

He shook his head. "Unfortunately no. I was taken unawares. I was still in bed. That machine isn't linked up to the bedroom."

"Can you remember their exact words?"

He paused, a heavy frown darkening his face. "They had trouble getting through initially. Marvell, my manservant, is touchy about putting on people he doesn't know – especially at that time in the morning. They told him it was a matter of life and death and concerned the family." The frown deepened. "I was half asleep. I can't vouch for the exact words, naturally. A voice said something like: 'Listen carefully . . . we have your son, Tony. If you want him back in one piece it will cost you five hundred thousand pounds. To be paid in diamonds.' Then . . . 'Think about it and stay close to the phone for further instructions.' He warned me about police interference of course – 'One word to the law and he's dead.' By that time I was beginning to think straight. I asked who he was and he said that ridiculous word, and the way he said it gave me the impression that he thought it was ridiculous too. When I asked what the hell it stood for and what it meant he simply spelt it out and hung up."

"The voice? Anything unusual about the voice? Accent, brogue, dialect – cleft palate? Anything?"

He shook his head. "Nothing that I can recall. Quite educated, light-weight, youngish I would say, fast speaking, a trifle breathless – probably nerves. And according to Marvell he was in a call-box."

"Was he now?" I squeaked sexily in my chair. "One thing . . . Has this come as a surprise to you?"

His eyebrows went up. "Well, I wasn't exactly expecting it if that's what you mean. Kidnapping in this country is hardly a daily occurrence."

"It happens nevertheless . . . And in Wimbledon if you care to cast your mind back a few years. What I'm getting at is, have you noticed anything unusual in your son's behaviour lately? Any sort of stress, as if he were under a threat perhaps? His wife sensed an edginess about him – a preoccupation. Were you aware of any such thing?"

He rose precipitately and moved away from the desk, his chair completing a violent revolution on its own and coming to rest with a gentle creak. His voice, muffled slightly, came to me from the direction of the fireplace.

"You must know that I have neither seen nor spoken to my son in over a year."

I turned and looked at him in surprise. "But I understand he lives not ten minutes away – on the other side of the Common."

He answered with sudden violence. "What the hell has that

to do with anything?" The words reverberated through the room and seemed to startle him; when he spoke again it was almost in a whisper. "We had a disagreement." He frowned, remembering. "One more disagreement . . ." The sudden bleakness in his tone suggested that he was on the brink of painful disclosures, about to peel away the dressing from an open wound, then he seemed to shake himself and glared at me with fierce belligerence. "Why am I telling you this? It has nothing to do with you. I have one question only for you: when the demand comes will you be available to deliver the ransom? No questions, no reports and no communication with the police. Is it a deal?"

"No, it isn't."

His eyes smouldered as they held on to mine in a lengthy challenging stare. Then abruptly turning his back on me, he spread his arms wide, grasping at the mantelpiece, fingers taut, as if clinging to a life-raft. "Then I have nothing more to say to you, Mr Savage. I wish you good day and will trouble you to keep this interview to yourself. I shall of course pay you for your time."

I got to my feet. "Right. If that's the way you want it." I loitered behind him for a second on the hearth-rug. "But for the record, I'm a private detective, not a messenger boy, and I am employed not by you, Sir George, but by our Mr Birkett. And for future reference, a good detective does his best work only when in full possession of the facts."

I had the door open and one foot over the threshold when he called me back. "Wait."

I waited.

"Come back here. Close the door."

I did so, stood with my back to it, waited again. The clock on the mantelpiece gave off a bright ping. He raised his head and glared at it, then with an effort pushed himself away from the fireplace, turned and studied me intently from beneath lowered black brows. He looked like a wrestler sizing up an opponent.

"Come and sit down." I made for the chair I had recently vacated. "No, not that one for God's sake. You sound like an outrigger in a storm with all that bloody leather. Have a go at this one – things'll be a lot quieter." He indicated the chair facing the one he'd been occupying when I arrived. "Drink?"

He gave me a sherry and helped himself to a half tumbler of raw Scotch. We imbibed in silence.

Lowering himself into the chair opposite he gave a low, self-deprecating growl. "I'm not a rude man usually; nothing can be gained by rudeness; I've learned that over the years. I apologise. You said nothing unreasonable." He lapped up some more whisky. "What are your theories about this business? You're obviously awash with them – views, opinions, ideas . . . tell me some of 'em."

So I told him about the talk I'd had with Sam on the phone and how we'd arrived at the somewhat shaky conclusion that SWALK, whoever they were, could be politically motivated. I pressed on as he was about to interrupt. "A newly formed group probably, wet behind the ears and short of the necessary funds to get 'emselves on the road – fed up with building their own bombs, perhaps, run out of fertiliser or something, want to spread their wings a bit. And these days they wouldn't have to look far for advice. There are always plenty of seamy characters ready and willing to pour poison into receptive ears."

"Terrorists, you mean?"

"Why not?" He looked sceptical. "Proof of professional advice could account for the ransom demand being in diamonds; it's a sophistication a fledgling group might not think of; it also means that they're not worried about quick conversion into hard cash, weapons, explosives, what-have-you. And since diamonds are the favoured currency for most international and nefarious practices, you could, in the long run, be dealing with almost anyone – Ireland, Libya, Syria, the Basques, Cuba, Lebanon . . . you name it, they're all in there somewhere. I'm sure I don't have to tell you that most of them run terrorist training camps open to all comers, and would never turn up a chance to nurture new growths – especially in this country where we all like to think such organisations are thin on the ground. The price would have to be right of course – they're nothing if not mercenary – and a half a million is a reasonable enough sum in all conscience for the initial membership fee or for the setting up of an arsenal. If all that is true, or even part of it, you could be on the verge of financing the birth of a terrorist organisation." I stopped and gave him a smirk. "It's your turn."

He took time pondering an answer. "Everything you've just said is, of course, pure speculation. We don't know that SWALK is politically motivated, and if it is we have no way of telling whether it's a fledgling organisation, as you suggest, or a splinter group of an established parent body, like the IRA or the PLF. I agree that the size of the ransom demand doesn't sound like the work of amateurs and the choice of Raven Industries as a target has unquestionable flair. To my mind the only juvenile leaning would seem to be encapsulated in their stupid choice of a name – SWALK . . . which I've always understood to mean Sealed With a Loving Kiss. Not quite what one would expect from a mob of terrorists."

He fell silent, thoughtfully swilling the remainder of his whisky around in his glass. "The fact remains," he said eventually, "if I want my son back in an undamaged condition I owe them half a million. Right?" I nodded. "Then there's nothing more to be said. The money's theirs."

"And you're not letting the police in on it?"

He shook his head emphatically. "They'd fill the place with bugs and telephones, tape recorders and technicians. Any fool of a kidnapper who watches television knows that if he stays too long gabbing on the phone he'll be traced, so he doesn't play along, does he? And a lot of time is wasted. Then, too, the press would get on to it, inevitably, and the whole of bloody Fleet Street would be down here. No, if it can be worked in any other way that's the way I want it." He drained his glass. "Get Anthony back for me, Mr Savage, and you can write your own cheque. I'll pay these bastards what they want and not a penny more. If he doesn't come back in one piece I personally will mount a private army and tear the living guts out of them – and to hell with the law. And if you think that's idle talk, try me!"

He got up, thudded over to the drinks and replenished his glass waving the sherry decanter at me: I shook my head.

There was a sour bitterness in the smile which twitched at one corner of his mouth. "My grandfather, Henry Raven, founded this company more than a hundred years ago. To be exact it opened its doors for business in 1871, the year Bismarck established the German Empire; it was then concerned purely with munitions. My father, and subsequently my elder brother and myself, followed in Henry Raven's footsteps. Son Anthony – my son – chooses, in his infinite wisdom and the intolerance of youth, to liken the four of us to the Four Horsemen of the Apocalypse: Conquest, Slaughter, Famine and Death. It has a certain ring to it, I suppose. The initial establishment of the firm made Henry Raven, Conquest; my father, in the saddle during the savagery of the First World War, was Slaughter; Famine was my brother, who, ironically enough, died of starvation and exposure somewhere up in the Himalayas in '37 – he was something of a mountaineer; he took care of things between the wars and sold arms to all and sundry – future enemies as well as allies. And yours truly was left to ride out the storm throughout World War Two . . . And has been here, wearily I may say, ever since. The lone pale horse – Death." He resumed his seat behind the desk.

"It never occurred to me that filial hatred could bite so deep." The voice was barely audible. "Anthony's I mean. Oh, I knew he disapproved of most of what I stood for – he was always a pacifist, even as a boy at school. I accepted it. I didn't attempt to change his views. On the contrary, I respected them and was under the impression that he respected and understood mine too. After all, the work I do, the business I run, is responsible for his home, his education, his wellbeing. But I never pressed him to join the firm – we talked about it, naturally, and he eventually busied himself in the electronics division for a few years, though, I understand, never very happily . . ." He was silent for a long time. When he spoke again it was almost as if he was unaware of me. "The last time we talked – in this room almost exactly a year ago – he informed me that my presence . . . polluted the air." I lowered my eyes and waited. "He stood at that door, looking very much as I must have done at his age. I remember thinking that his eyes were quite translucent, like the eyes of a seer. The last words he spoke to me – the last thing he ever said to me – were, 'Ride yourself into the bloody earth and see if I care. I, for one, shan't shed a tear for you and I doubt whether anyone else will either.' And he turned his back on me and walked out without closing the door." After another long silence he added softly, "I've not seen him since."

Hunched in his chair he sat staring stonily at the backs of his hands tightly clasped on the desk before him. A surge of sympathy welled up inside me but I knew better than to put it into words; he was not one, I thought, to seek commiseration from others.

He was watching me now, that same bitter, twitchy smile on his lips. He said quietly, "You may well be wondering why I am so anxious to have him back." He shrugged. "I can't answer that. Blood perhaps. Linda's need for him . . . The fact remains I want him back. Perhaps to assuage some feeling of guilt I may have. I obviously went wrong with him somewhere. Perhaps I'd like a second chance. On the other hand, he probably thinks he's had a rough deal. Maybe he has, I wouldn't know. I'm only his father. Linda could tell you more about that."

"Has she kept in touch with you since – all that?"

"She comes over occasionally, phones sometimes just to say hello. She's a caring girl – even cares a little for me I think. But I'm rarely here. I'm out of the country quite a bit and hardly ever in this house. I have an apartment I prefer over the works in Greenwich and spend most of my time down there."

Abruptly, as if the interview were over, he got to his feet. "Well, there's nothing more we can do now until we hear from them again." He turned and held me with his eyes. "If you're willing to help I'll be happy to place everything into your hands – yours and Mr Birkett's, if that's the way you want it." He ranged up foursquare in front of me. "But . . . if and when you make the drop, do me one favour please. Leave Mr Birkett behind. I don't want them getting the wrong idea. He may not be a policeman now but he was once, and a good one, I believe, with a reputation for tenacity. If they catch sight of him on the horizon they may take off again and anything could happen. That's why I didn't want him here this morning – they could well be watching this place."

"Suppose they want you to deliver personally?"

He shrugged. "The diamonds are more important to them

than Anthony. I'll tell 'em the truth. You're a private investigator paid to do the job and nothing else – no further interest. If they want the money that badly they'll play ball."

"Let's hope so." I held out a hand. "You've got yourself a deal." His grip was hard and firm. "You'll need my phone number." I unearthed a dog-eared card. "Incidentally, should you need to give me a name, I'd just as soon it not be my own. You never know, I might want to mingle with them later on. So call me – anything . . . what?" My eye caught a name on the spine of a book on the shelf behind him. "Eliot, how about that? Tom Eliot – he won't mind." I made for the door. "You'll hear from them before the day's out, I'm sure. They're not likely to let the grass grow too long. And you will remember, please, to record any conversation you may have on that thing, won't you?" I stopped. "Something else. I notice you call your son Anthony." He nodded. "Never Tony?"

"Never. We both dislike the diminutive – he more than I."

I frowned. "Curious, isn't it? From what you said . . ."

"That's right," he interrupted me. "The kidnapper called him Tony. So he did. Do you think it means something?"

"Probably not, unless perhaps a more intimate knowledge of him than one might have expected." I shook my head irritably. "I honestly don't know. These things add up sometimes; they're worth collecting and filing away." I hesitated. "Did you ever meet a chap called Earnshaw, Geoff Earnshaw? Friend of Anthony's?"

He shook his head. "Not that I can remember. He rarely brought his friends here. Why do you ask?"

"He was killed – over there on the Common. The night Anthony disappeared. There's a connection somewhere – there has to be."

His eyes bored into mine. "You're not inferring . . ."

"Not inferring anything. Anthony's kidnapped, his closest friend murdered. Make of it what you will. It's just another of those things to keep in mind."

For a second or two he stood staring at me then without further ado he leaned across me and opened the door. Marvell the troglodyte was hanging about outside within easy reach. "Show Mr Savage out, will you, Marvell?" Raven looked at me solemnly. "I'll phone you or Mr Birkett the moment I hear. If there's anything you need . . ."

I nodded. "I may well hold you to that. Getting Anthony back is only the beginning. That done, Sam and I will be off to the wars and could do with all the help we can get." I smiled. "And who knows, we may even be able to do the state some service while we're about it."

Chapter Three

When the Honda and I swung into Sam's front gate a few minutes later we churned up a small portion of his gravel drive and brought a peevish gargoyle of a face to the window – Sam's.

I heaved the machine on to its rest, hooked my crash-hat over the handlebars and made for the front door. The face was still there. I waggled cheery fingers at it but it was like making advances to a Hallowe'en mask. The door was open and I met him in the hall bulking largely beneath a portrait of someone who looked like the Duke of Wellington.

"Who's that?" I asked, not caring.

"The Duke of Wellington."

He led me into the room from which he had observed my coming. I stopped dead on the threshold. I thought for a moment he'd had burglars. I stared aghast at the jumble of junk and old newspapers on the floor, the shelves crammed with ill-assorted books and the untidy spread of litter on the desk in the window-bay. I gave a mental shrug and thought it best not to mention it; if he'd been burgled he'd soon tell me about it and, since he didn't, I could only assume that he liked it that way.

"Park yourself somewhere," he invited in a dispirited sort of way. "There." He pointed to a chair half hidden beneath several hats and an overcoat. "Bung those things on the floor. I was just tidying up. Mildred's been at me."

On the chair behind the desk sat an enormous hairy-looking pot-plant which seemed to intimidate even Sam, for after eyeing it for a second he left it where it was, cleared a portion of the desk and heaved himself on to it. "Now . . ." he said expectantly.

I lowered myself into the cavernous chair, three bowler hats clasped to my chest; my knees were on a level with my chin;

the chair wheezed ominously. "That was my father's chair," Sam explained. It didn't surprise me one bit.

The V-necked pullover he was wearing looked as if it might have belonged to his father too; it almost reached his knees: grey cable-stitch with non-matching leather elbow patches; he wore a shirt and trousers beneath it but you never really got past the pullie. He looked a heap.

I told him of my meeting with Raven. He sat with his back to the light, little more than a woolly silhouette, and made no comment during the recital; he nodded occasionally and hissed a bit between his teeth now and then but that was all. Eventually I droned off into silence.

I looked around for somewhere to put the hats. "Here, give me those." He rolled off the desk and gathered them up in his arms, peering into the lining of one of them. "This was my father's too. Used to fit me quite well when I was a young shaver." He put it on. It looked like a pimple on a haystack. "Doesn't now though, does it?" He took it off and threw it into a corner. The other two he placed carefully on the desk as if they were Oscars he had just won.

"Did you like him?" he asked suddenly.

"I didn't know him."

"Who?"

"Your father."

He gave me a narrow glance over his shoulder. "George Raven."

"Yes, I did as a matter of fact. He and I could get along quite well – especially with all that loot."

He crabbed his way into the window-bay and stood with his back to me eyeing the Honda perched saucily in his drive. "Odd they haven't contacted him again."

"Time enough," I said. "I've read all the books; the accepted thing seems to be forty-eight hours after initial contact; perhaps it's an unspoken law. Must be a complex business, kidnapping someone: accommodation, food, keeping him clean . . . working it all out."

"They'd have done all that. You don't just snatch someone and then wonder where the hell you're going to put him. It's all worked out beforehand – to the last sordid detail."

"How many kidnappings you been on?" I asked blandly.

"Discounting the Lesley Whittle affair – and her kidnapper was a nutter and not quite in the same class – there's only been one major kidnapping in this country, practically since mediaeval times I believe. And that was the McKay woman, poor thing – oddly enough just over the way on Arthur Road – and even that was a mistake on their part, stupid bastards. I wasn't on it, thank God, but it made one hell of a stir at the Yard – country-wide if it comes to that. They got 'em of course in the end but never the poor lady herself. Nobody knows what really happened to her – though a lot of ghoulish ideas have been aired. And here we are again – in our own backyard." He turned to face me. "Well, now we know for certain that the ransom's forthcoming, I think it's high time we put Lindy in the picture. I just hope she'll take it all right." He shrugged. "She'll just have to, won't she? To my mind, anything's better than not knowing, don't you think? Will you – er – stand by and lend a hand? I'd be grateful. I've broken worse news to all sorts of people in my time but . . . well, you know, it's my own flaming daughter this time, isn't it?" He rolled back the sleeve of his woolly and squinted at his watch. "Stay for a bite of lunch?"

I shook my head. "Thanks all the same. I thought I'd give old Mitch a ring, ask her over for the afternoon if she's free: put her in the picture. If it's all the same to you it might be good to have her in on this. She's got quite a head on her shoulders, in spite of what she looks like. We could do with an extra pair of hands and she could be holed up somewhere keeping an eye on things when I make the drop – check on the pick-up man perhaps."

"That's my job." He sounded a trifle tetchy.

"Raven doesn't want you there."

"I don't give a hoot in hell what Raven wants. If we don't get a line on the opposition we're back where we started, minus half a million quid."

"That's why I want Mitch standing by."

"Right, you've got her. But you've got me too. The more the merrier. I can fade into the woodwork a lot quicker than you can, young man, take my word for it."

I eyed his sturdy woollen bulk with slant-eyed disbelief but I took his word for it. Who was I to deny him? He had been on the job long before I was born and so long as he didn't turn up in a pointed helmet it would be a comfort to have him around. I shrugged my agreement. "We don't have to let Raven know, do we? I didn't exactly go bail for you. But you're the victim's father-in-law and the kidnappers will know you were once a cop and could well be on the look-out for them."

The telephone rang. He followed the cord and discovered the instrument sitting beneath an unsightly tweed fishing hat.

Someone called George. Grave news if Sam's face was anything to go by. He squatted on the arm of an overstuffed chair nodding and grunting, said 'Christ' once beneath his breath and when the metallic squawkings at the other end paused for a second put in quickly, "What's the general reaction down there?" More listening. "George, I'm grateful. You haven't told anyone about me being nosey I hope? . . . Good . . . Well done, that man. I owe you, George."

He hung up slowly, eyeing the instrument on his lap with increasing gloom. He appeared to have forgotten about me so I twanged a couple of strings in his father's chair to remind him of my continued presence. He frowned at me. "George Prewitt," he said.

"Ah," I nodded. "I thought it probably was. Who's George Prewitt?"

He stirred impatiently. "Forensics . . . police pathologist. Ancient buddy of mine, best in the business. Just performed a post mortem on Geoff Earnshaw."

"And?"

"Is of the opinion that the skull was crushed with the butt of a gun. Probably a Luger, he says, though how he can tell the difference between one butt and another in those particular circumstances God alone knows. The cavity in the cranium bone is consistent with such a blow, says George, and if that's the way he wants it, that's the way it is. It would explain the absence of a murder weapon; nobody's going to leave a gun lying about and they've been over every inch of that place and found not a thing." He frowned at me grimly. "Which means, Mark my lad, that we're in very deep waters." He lurched to his feet and parked the phone on his messy desk. "How I hate little pip-squeaks with guns." He was at the window again. "A deliberate killing made to look like a mugging – which is what I thought all along. The cops of course will now have to start digging deeper. A bore for us because they get so bloody possessive about everything – keep off the grass and all that. The good news is that George Prewitt, God bless him, has bent the rules a bit and leaked the information to me before submitting his official report. A couple of hours at most we'll have before the law gets itself into gear." He turned slowly towards me. "How about . . . ?" He pulled thoughtfully at his lower lip. "Geoff lived alone with his mother somewhere in Southfields. How about me going over there to offer condolences? Nothing wrong with that, is there? After all he was a buddy of my son-in-law, wasn't he? And I'll have a gentle sniff around while I'm about it. There could be something lying about which might give us a lead. His mum will give me the run of the place if I ask her nicely. And if the cops turn up while I'm still there – well, I'm a friend of the family, aren't I?"

"Want me to come with you?"

He gave me an oblique look. "What I'd sooner have you do . . ."

"Is break the news to Linda?"

"Would you?"

"Sure I will. Might be easier coming from me."

"She'll be at home, I expect. They live over on West Side, not far. Give her a ring if you like."

I shook my head. "I'll just drop in – make less drama of it."

The house on West Side, a hop, skip and jump north of Cannizaro Park, bore all the signs of having been there long before Lawn Tennis raised its nets at Wimbledon's All England Croquet Club back in the eighteen-seventies. Rambling gently and unsymmetrically behind a grove of lofty rhododendrons and spreading copper beeches it seemed to doze in the complacent pale sunlight of early afternoon, the sort of house I was apt to dream about during my less practical moments.

I parked the Honda just inside the slightly rusted wrought-iron gates and crunched my way importantly up the gravelled drive.

What looked like a home-made car – DIY kit perhaps – was there before me. Red and sleek with bull-nose and a pair of non-matching bucket seats, there was no doubt in my mind as to its potential. I eyed it with clinical appreciation as I reached for the door-knocker and wondered at the intrepidity of its creator.

The click of a lock and a direct descendant of the queens of ancient Egypt stood in the open doorway watching me, clearly of the opinion that I should have gone around to the tradesmen's entrance. I stared at her in silence, my vocal chords having seized up.

Huge almond-shaped eyes set wide beneath elegantly arched eyebrows returned stare for stare and offered no immediate assistance to my tied tongue. Glossy blue-black hair severely fringed above the brows framed the delicate olive oval of her face and it was this feature more than any other which lent her the ancient Egyptian air; the addition of a uraeus head-dress might well have thrown me on my face to kiss her feet except that she was wearing muddy black wellingtons with blue jeans tucked snugly inside them. The rest of her was done up in an unrewarding, sloppy purple jumper which had seen far better days.

I am bound to say in passing that she too appeared bereft of speech but whether as a result of my mesmeric personality or the abundance of black leather I was humping about with me I had no way of knowing.

"Er . . ." I said at last.

"Who is it?" A voice from the inner reaches of the house. Linda Birkett's. I shot a glance over Nefertiti's shoulder and there she was, Linda Birkett, homing in on the front door with an ugly looking knife in her hand and parcelled up in a blue plastic apron dedicated to Snoopy. "Oh, it's you, Mark. Hello. How nice. Do come in. This is Mark Savage, Cath, I was telling you about. Come in, Mark; do let him in, Cath, he's quite safe."

Cath stepped back a pace, grudgingly I thought, and I shimmied my way around her, registering as I did so a disturbing blast of perfume redolent of lotus-blossom, incense and the rest of the mysterious East. It was probably Ashes of Roses, but that wasn't my fault.

"Sorry if I've come at a bad time," I mumbled. "Just a word in your ear . . ."

"Stay to lunch, why don't you?" Linda interrupted in the sort of hectoring voice usually employed by her father and led the way through a wide hall into a classy and expensive kitchen. "I was just knocking up a salad. There's plenty – or have you eaten already? Do you like chopped carrot?"

"No, I won't stay," I told her, aware of the squeak of wellingtons on the polished wood floor behind me. "I just need a quiet word with you . . ." I managed to semaphore the fact that it would be nice to dispense with a third set of ears but she shot down the idea; Cath was family, she said, I could speak quite freely in front of her and was there any news?

Cath moved softly into my line of sight and stood disturbingly between me and the window. I shrugged away my unease at having a third party present but because of it broke the news with a bluntness which surprised even me.

"Anthony's been kidnapped." You can't get much blunter than that. I watched her go through the routine reactions to such tidings with the omniscient eye of one who had not only written the script but also directed the scene. Sam would have been proud of me.

When she sat down and deposited her knife among the chopped carrots she whispered only one word, "Why?"

I shrugged. "The usual reason. Money."

She frowned and looked blank as though the idea had never occurred to her. "How much money?"

"Half a million."

Her mouth fell open.

I took her gently through the remaining few facts, unembellished by comments of my own and waited in silence for further responses.

It was Cath who, predictably I suppose, was the first to utter and in doing so reminded me that it was also the first time she had spoken since my arrival. Her voice was of the deep blue variety, velvet nightfall over the pyramids with a touch of sphinx-like promise. "Who *are* these people? *What* is it they call themselves?"

"SWALK," I said and spelt it out feeling slightly foolish as if I had made up the whole thing.

"But surely that means . . . ?"

I nodded. "When I was at school girls used to put it on the backs of love-letters. But whoever they are they mean business." I glanced at Linda Birkett – Linda Raven – staring into the middle distance with a look of doom on her face. "Your father thinks there's some sort of politics behind it."

"Politics?" She came to life, her voice suddenly taut. "Anthony has no interest in politics. Why would he be involved in politics?"

"He doesn't have to be involved. He just happens to be the son of a rich father."

She looked at me steadily in silence for a second. "How long have you known about this?" A querulous note crept into her voice. "And Dad, how long has he known?"

"Only since this morning," I placated her. "That's the truth I promise you," I added hastily as she drew breath, "I volunteered to come over and tell you, rather than Sam."

A further silence. Her shoulders drooped as she smoothed the plastic of her apron against her knee. "So what happens now?" she asked at last. "My father-in-law's not likely to pay the ransom. He and Anthony haven't even spoken to each other for ages. And if he doesn't pay what happens then? Half a million? Dear God, he'll never agree to that . . ."

"He already has." I pulled up a chair and sat beside her, laying a hand on hers. "You mustn't have any worries on that score. I've just been with him. So there's nothing any of us can do now except wait for them to give us the time and place and then I, personally, will deliver the goods and your husband will be released."

"Do you believe that?"

"We have to believe something, so we may as well look on the bright side."

"And what about the police?" It was Cath who asked the question.

"They're not in it," I replied somewhat tartly. "Sam and I will be standing in for them and if there's anything we can do to bring the bastards to heel we'll do it."

She snorted. "I just can't believe it. It's a joke – the whole thing's a joke."

Linda swung on her. "Geoff Earnshaw's murder wasn't a joke."

Cath moved in. "What has that got to do with it? Geoff was mugged."

"Was he? Was he mugged? How do you know that? Dad

doesn't believe it." She turned back to me. "And neither do you, do you Mark?"

I hesitated then shook my head. "We believe it was made to look like a mugging." I didn't mention George Prewitt's theory about the gun-butt; it was classified information for one thing and I had quite enough on my plate for another.

I was staring idly at Cath's boots. She too had been prowling about on the Common; that same tell-tale mud clung to them. I raised my eyes. She was looking at me intently. "Did you know Geoff Earnshaw?" I asked.

She nodded. "Better than most, I suspect. We lived together for six months. He was going through a – er – difficult phase, I expect you would call it . . ." She frowned and ventured no more.

My hand, abandoned now on a small mound of chopped and forgotten carrot, felt cold. Linda handed me a tea-towel asking whether I thought there really could be any connection between Geoff's death and Anthony's disappearance.

I trod warily. There was no direct evidence of a connection, I told her, though of course the possibility couldn't be ruled out. I'd said the line before somewhere – on the stage or screen perhaps during my thespian days – it sounded mighty familiar. "Try not to worry too much," I finished lamely. "Don't think along those lines. Cath's quite right – er – Miss . . ." I smirked at Nefertiti. "I'm sorry, I don't know your other name, but you're right."

"Brenner," she supplied, "Catherine Brenner."

We shook hands. "Hello, Catherine Brenner." She had a grip of iron.

Linda said, "Sorry, I should have introduced you properly. Cath's my oldest friend. We went to the same school. We called her the Brenner Pass because she passed every exam she ever went in for."

"Since when," added Cath wryly, "I've failed in absolutely bloody everything. School blunted my wits."

Remembering my own dismal attack of the schooldays, I commiserated and got to my feet. "I must let you get on with your lunch." I gave Linda a grin. "We'll let you know the moment anything stirs, I promise. Okay?"

"Right." She led the way to the front door. "Thanks, Mark,

very much." On the doorstep she gave a small whinny of amusement. 'How do you like Cath's car?"

I grinned. "It's original, I'll give her that."

"Made it herself."

"Not without help," said Cath squeaking up behind. "I call her Mark One but maybe I should change that now I've met you."

Leaving Linda on the step we did a circuit of her handiwork, she pointing out various items of interest and demonstrating in passing the efficacy of the beautiful brass-bound, rubber-bulbed horn which gave off the hoarse wail of a tug in a storm. Becoming accustomed to the unconventional look of the machine I asked a couple of questions about licensing and road-worthiness, the latter almost destroying our relationship before it had begun, and came away with something rather more than a feeling of respect. "I don't know how you can say you've failed in everything since you left school," I told her. "I couldn't even begin to build a thing like that and I'm supposed to be a feller."

She gave me a sly smile. "Every feller to his own bent. I couldn't even begin to play Hamlet." Her eyes wandered over my shoulder to the Honda. "That's what I really want, I think – a motorbike."

I nodded. "Only way to travel. Perhaps . . ." Her eyes came back to mine. "Perhaps you'd like to come for a ton-up on the motorway sometime?"

She returned my look steadily holding it for a disturbing beat too long. "I'd like that."

The air steamed up again with that almost suffocating sense of eastern promise. A trickle of perspiration crept down between my shoulder-blades. I gulped a goodbye, crunched over to the Honda and fiddled needlessly with my crash-hat. Straddling the machine I looked back.

They were together now on the step, Linda with a hand raised in farewell, Cath, quite still, watching me.

Mitch and I were in the kitchen washing up when the doorbell rang. The clock said half past two.

"I don't answer the doorbell on Sunday afternoons," I told her comfortably.

"It could be important." She breathed on a glass and held it up to the light.

"Nothing important ever happens on a Sunday."

"Pearl Harbor happened."

"Not in England it didn't."

The bell rang again, longer this time with a sort of delayed action ping on the end for good measure.

"Whoever he is," Mitch pointed out, "he's not going away."

"Who says he's a he?"

"Only a he would perform like that on a doorbell."

She was right. The he was Sam Birkett, stacked up on the doorstep like a pile of old clothes, a stubby outstretched finger poised for a further onslaught on the bell-push.

He eyed my sensible rubber apron. "Did I interrupt something?"

"I'm in the middle of a gang-bang, if you must know," I told him tartly.

"Splendid. Knew you must be in. Hope I'm not inconvenient."

Mitch offered a neutral hand and peered at him closely through narrowed blue eyes. She looked like somebody's Aunt Augusta match-making for her favourite nephew.

"How were the chump chops?" Sam enquired with the nudge-nudge air of one entrusted with classified information.

"Over-refrigerated," I told him. "Coffee?"

"That'd be nice." He began unbuttoning his overcoat. "Sorry to barge in like this. I wasn't actually passing as a matter of fact, but Mildred's shacked up with Nelson Eddy on the telly and I was beginning to feel a bit *de trop* . . ."

"You're protesting too much, Sam," I said. "Take your coat off, come into the sitting-room and put your feet up. Mitch and I have gone off the boil; the gang-bang'll just have to wait, Mitch . . . sorry."

"I wasn't going to enjoy it anyway," she said.

He and Mitch reminded each other of how they had met briefly one wet morning on the stairs of my city office a year or so ago when Sam had paid a surprise visit to find out what made a private investigator's life so enthralling. He was so unimpressed that I took him to St Paul's over the road and showed him that instead, but even that didn't do a lot for him.

I gave him a cup of coffee and pointed him towards a chair but he wouldn't sit down, preferring instead to prowl about the room looking at this and nosing into that like a browser in a bookshop.

"Never been here before," he informed Mitch with a wink. "I like seeing how the other half live – what they've got and how they keep it. Possessions, like apparel, oft proclaim the man, you know." He prodded a finger at a shelf. "Ah, now there's a good book." I didn't have to look at it to know that it was one of his.

"How did you get on this morning?" he asked over his shoulder. "With Lindy, I mean. Was it all right?"

"She took it like a man."

"Thought she would. She's very sound, that girl, even if I do say so myself. She rang me after you'd gone to tell me she was okay. Just hope it wasn't too hairy for you, that's all."

"Not to worry. It was fine."

"Grateful to you. I owe you." He stood over the seated Mitch. "I trust Mark's told you what all this is about, Mitch – may I call you Mitch?"

"Please do – and yes, he has. He's even gone so far as to ask me to join the team."

"And will you?"

"With pleasure. It'll be a new experience. After pounding away in that office anything would be a new experience."

"How was Mrs What's-her-name?" I asked Sam.

"Mrs Earnshaw? Poor old duck, none too well, I'm afraid. She's got a lot older since Lindy's wedding." He shook a morose head and moved over to the bay window to stare out at the distant Surrey hills murky on the horizon. "Nice view you've got here," he mumbled. "Funny, isn't it, how some mothers seem to know so little about their own sons? I've often met that on my travels. If you want the truth about somebody, never ask his mother – because she just won't know. She even had difficulty remembering how old he was. He would have been twenty-four in October – she thinks."

There was silence for a second or two while he had a go at his coffee. Mitch and I exchanged glances.

Sam went on. "I managed to wangle my way into his room, made some excuse about Lindy having lent him a book and could I go and have a look for it? That room told its own story. Possessions again, you see. Che Guevara on the wall. Nothing in that, I suppose. Lindy had one of those on her wall too when she was at school – I gather most of the girls did. But they weren't all that interested in his revolutionary leanings; much more likely they were after his knickers . . . Sorry, Mitch."

"Don't worry," said Mitch. "I was too. He was beautiful."

"Mind you, judging by some of the literature lying about in his room, Geoff was probably after the same pair of knickers. On first showing I would say that sexually he was pretty ambidextrous. His other main interest would seem to have been anarchy, which in present circumstances is fascinating, wouldn't you say? Whether the interest was active or cerebral we shall probably never know, but there was a veritable gallimaufry of books on the subject, from Leila Khaled's autobiography to Claire Sterling's *Terror Network*; the Baader-Meinhof Gang, Carlos, Marighella - they were all there. Ah yes, and talking of Marighella . . ." He broke off, put down his cup and began searching through the pockets of his tweed jacket. Then he gave up with a quick shake of his head. "It's not here, must be in my other jacket. A book I stole which would interest you. Remind me to show it to you sometime.

"As a touch of light relief there was a picture of the wedding on his bedside table, with Geoff looking very proud and upright – he was a nice looking lad – newly washed and standing between Lindy and Anthony. I was there too looming in the background like a body-snatcher bent on business. And Mildred, God help us, with her hands clasped on her bosom, looking as if she was about to burst into a chorus of 'Oh What a Beautiful Morning'.

"I asked his mum about his friends. She couldn't remember them – she was in no fit state. Anthony, it seemed, was the only one she could be doing with. There was a coloured boy she didn't much care for – prejudice I would say rather than actual dislike. Then there was a girl he'd gone off to live with for a time. She hadn't met her and clearly didn't want to –

disapproved heartily of the whole set-up. That's another thing about motherhood. They spend a lifetime grooming themselves to become grandmothers and, come crunch time, won't let the boys out of their sight!"

"Cath," I said suddenly snapping my fingers.

"What?"

"I met a girl called Cath Brenner at Linda's this morning – you must know her, great buddy of Linda's."

"Cath Brenner . . . yes, I do vaguely. Old school friend . . ."

"That's the one. She said she lived with Geoff for six months and then it broke up. Her exact words were, I think, 'He was going through a difficult phase.' That would figure, wouldn't it, if he was ambidextrous, as you call it? And from the little I picked up of Cath's character she's hardly the type to hang about while sir makes up his mind who he is and what he wants. Sorry to interrupt. Anything else?"

A shadow passed over his face for a second then he slumped on to the sofa and looked suddenly weary. "I had a bit of a run-in with the local constabulary. A certain CID Inspector named Hodder, Tom Hodder – he of the pointed head and big black hat. They're right behind us, Mark. He and his side-kick, Sergeant Cohen, came pounding on Mrs Earnshaw's door like it was the end of the world and weren't at all welcoming when I opened it. As a matter of fact I toyed with the idea of leaping over the back garden wall because we'd already had a slight brush when I was nosing about on the Common early yesterday morning. Now here I was again opening somebody else's door to him. What the hell did I think I was up to and all that. 'Thought you'd retired.' You know the sort of thing. I pointed out that Geoff had been best man at my daughter's wedding and that I had every right to be there offering condolences. He wasn't convinced. Suspicion pours out of these people's ears, you know. He's really made up his mind that I intend to snatch this case right out from under his very nose."

"Fancy," I said.

"Can you imagine it?"

I shook my head sadly. "How can he think such a thing?" I turned to Mitch. "Now we have to contend with suspicious policemen yet! It's too much."

Sam wagged a warning finger at me. "But don't," he interjected, "let us underestimate Inspector Hodder. He's quite a fly one, believe me. Not perhaps the greatest cop in the country, but when he gets his head down we'll have to start looking over our shoulders, you take my word for it. We're only one step ahead of him, remember, only one. And he's got the law on his side, unlimited resources, stackloads of information at his finger-tips, men, vehicles, radio communication . . . And what have I got?"

"Us," I told him.

The look he gave us was one of infinite grief. "Exactly."

Chapter Four

The call came at precisely six o'clock the following morning. George Raven was in bed awake. When he rang me ten minutes later I was in bed too – asleep.

"They've been on," he said.

I groped around in the bleary limbo of my mind and muttered something inadequate like "Ho, ho . . ."

"Eleven o'clock tomorrow night." He waited. "Are you awake?"

"Does that give you time enough?" I asked him.

"For what?"

"To get the diamonds."

He said brusquely, "I could get them at eleven o'clock this morning if need be."

"What exactly was the message?"

"It's on the Answercall. I had Marvell switch it through to the office phone. If you need to know the exact text you'd better come over and listen to it yourself. The gist is that I'm to deliver the stones to Jubilee Market at eleven p.m. tomorrow."

"Where's Jubilee Market?"

"Covent Garden." He sounded a trifle terse. "The new shopping complex behind the Opera House."

I didn't know they called it Jubilee Market. To me it was just another old shopping precinct, expensive and touristy during the day, restless and sinister after dark when the sly and the sleazy came out of the woodwork and so-called musicians made night hideous with home-spun cacophony.

Raven continued. "I'm to put the stones into a Marks & Spencer carrier bag, take the Rolls, park it in King Street, walk across the square to Jubilee Hall and leave the bag at the base of one of the columns – then keep on walking and not return to the Rolls for at least half an hour."

"Yes, yes," I said, meaning 'no, no', "but it'll be me, won't it? Not you. That is if you're going to trust me with your Rolls." The thought of driving a Rolls was beginning to grow hairs on my chest. During the whole of my eminent film-career I had never got around to driving a Rolls – a 93 bus down Putney High Street, yes, but never a Rolls.

"No," he said, and he really meant 'no'. "It's got to be me, not you; they've insisted on that. When I suggested Tom Eliot they blasted off. They're not prepared to play our game, Mr Savage."

I thought about that for a second or two. "Well, we've got a day and a half to bat it around. I'd like to come and listen to that tape though."

"Any time."

"With Sam Birkett."

"No."

"It's the two of us or neither, Sir George, take it or leave it. Sam's a trained mind with years of experience. I need him and you need him. It's not just a question of getting Anthony back, you know that, it's a question of nailing these sons of bitches to the mast-head before they do any more damage. There's a rear entrance to your place, isn't there – Parkside Gardens? Secluded as I remember and could only be under surveillance by someone in a parked car. We'll check it thoroughly, I promise, and if you leave your back gate open we'll let ourselves in." I heard him draw breath and overrode him. "We'll be with you in a couple of hours. Did they say anything about Anthony, by the way?"

"I talked to him."

"What did he sound like?"

"Strained naturally and in some distress, I thought, but otherwise he seemed to be all right. They only allowed him to say a few words."

"You sure it was he?" He began to splutter. "The telephone can be deceptive. Stuff an old sock down the mouthpiece and you could be anybody."

"It was Anthony."

"Good. At least he's still alive. All right, we'll see you at – how about ten o'clock? That'll give Sam time to gather his old bones together."

"Mr Savage . . ." There was a lengthy pause; I could almost hear him wrestling with himself, then he said quietly, "All right, all right, I'll see you then . . . both of you," and hung up.

At seven o'clock, shaved and breakfasted, I rang Sam. Not only had he gathered up his old bones but he had taken them out for a walk on the Common. "He's always up at six," Mildred informed me, and when I repeated 'six' in a dismayed falsetto, added in a mildly reproving tone, "He's out by half past most mornings."

'And what time does he get back – most mornings?"

That would depend, she explained, on what sort of morning it was and whether he saw any interesting birds. Bad mornings he would just tramp around the windmill and back, nice mornings he would sometimes go as far as the pond. "He's usually back by seven-thirty."

"Well, I'll try and catch him in mid-peripatetics, I think. Thanks, Mildred." I hung up before she could ask any pertinent questions.

I ran him down on the far side of the windmill, stumping along at a sturdy pace, hands in his overcoat pockets, head thrust forward, chin on chest, his gaze, anchored firmly to the ground, paying no attention to Mother Nature and her undeniable attributes.

He was only mildly surprised to see me. "Couldn't you sleep?" he asked.

"Mildred made you sound like the Skylark trip around the lighthouse and back," I said, falling in step with him.

"News?"

I told him about the contact and what was expected of George Raven.

"No." He came to a sudden halt, shaking his head vigorously. "On no account must he make the drop himself."

I nodded. "My sentiments entirely, but you try to tell him that. There was no point arguing over the phone."

He squared up to me glaring ferociously from beneath his hat brim. "If they're asking half a million for his son how much more can they demand for *him* – Mr Moneybags himself? We can't risk that – no way – and neither can he. Lone millionaire prowling around on the loose in the middle of the night – it's sheer bloody lunacy. Some mad, greedy bugger, flushed and rich with the success of one crime, might well weigh up the chances of another and find it worth the gamble."

"I'm on your side, Sam," I said quietly.

"I know that!" He seemed to take my remark as a personal offence. "You don't mind me thinking aloud, do you? Old Fred Saunders had to put up with it for fifteen years, and if he could do it for that long then you can damn well do it for fifteen minutes."

"Sam."

"What?"

"I've got an idea."

His jowls trembled with disbelief. "I'm listening."

"How are you on disguises?" His eyes widened like hard-boiled eggs. "You said you were listening," I reminded him. "They're not going to let Tom Eliot do the job, right?"

"Right. Who's Tom Eliot?"

I told him who Tom Eliot was. "But . . ." I raised a dramatic finger. "Who among us has the magisterial build, shape and stature of our own Sir George Raven?"

He was sudden 'y very still. "I have no idea," he whispered hoarsely knowing very well who it was I had in mind.

"Put on one of his hats, climb into one of his overcoats, walk like a millionaire, and you, Sam, could do the drop yourself."

"And get kidnapped." He sounded very sour.

"You could get to drive his Rolls."

That did it. It was the casting vote. The eyes became almost beady as he began to consider the scheme seriously for the first time.

A distant man in a red pullover was shouting and making irate gestures at us with a golf club.

"We're in the middle of his green." I laid hold of Sam's lapel and drew him into comparative safety.

"God almighty," he growled peering with petulance at his watch. "What a time to start batting their little balls about." He threw off my restraining hand. "Will it work, do you think?" When the little red figure drove off into the blue Sam's baleful eye followed the parabola of the ball until it came to earth in a gorse bush some ten yards away. "Wonder why he wanted us to move?" he grunted and taking off his hat he waved it encouragingly at the man indicating with his other hand the beleagured ball. "Not surprising he gets up early if that's the best he can do."

I said, "Providing we all keep our heads and you get yourself under the skin of a millionaire I can see no reason why it shouldn't work. Is it on then?"

"Watch," he said. He tramped off along the path with the sort of loose slouch most people associate with Groucho Marx. "How's this?" he called over his shoulder.

"You'll have to do better than that if you want to get kidnapped," I called back drily.

At ten, having satisfied ourselves that no hidden watchers were shacked up in parked cars or disguised as milkmen and the like, we were easing ourselves surreptitiously into the rear entrance of George Raven's property. If anyone was peering through binoculars from an upper window, tough! Only Raven believed such caution advisable and we went through the motions to please him.

The colourless Marvell, awaiting us at the glass doors of a considerable conservatory built on to the rear of the house, ushered us speedily through the steamy tropics of the interior as if his job depended upon it – as indeed it might well have done, for the contents of the greenhouse consisted of orchids of every exotic shape and form.

Sam put on his horticultural look and dawdled ostentatiously, impervious to Marvell who clucked and twittered like an elderly marmoset. A man in a green baize apron and carrying an impressive brass syringe watched us warily from the sidelines. Sam gave him a companionable nod and lingered over a purple extravagance which, with its long chin and upstanding fair hair, put me in mind of Stan Laurel. The green baize man moved in. "Cypripedium Sanderianum," he muttered confidentially without moving his lips, as if he were giving a password.

"Ah yes, of course," nodded the blatant Sam loftily. "I thought so." And then went on to confound me by saying, "Sander's Lady's Slipper. Very nice, very nice indeed. You have an excellent show here – well done, well done . . ." He sounded like the Queen Mother at the Chelsea Flower Show.

And what's more, he took his grass roots into the presence of George Raven where, by enthusing over the orchid-house, he not only established a valuable bridgehead but laid down a durable invasion strip over which the pair of them passed into the euphoric sunset of botanical brotherhood. In five minutes flat Sam had Raven eating out of his hand.

Patiently I stood on the edge of the carpet just inside the door where Marvell had left me and waited for the mutual exchange of gardening news to expend itself. Eventually Raven noticed me and quietly pointed me out to Sam who smiled patronisingly and nodded a vague head in my direction as if I were some poor relation waiting for a hand-out.

I said rather grittily, "It would be nice if we could hear the tape, Sir George."

Without another word he moved to the desk giving the impression that I had ruined his day. He sat in his chair and touched a switch on the Answercall.

"Yes?" Raven's voice.

"Sir George Raven?" The second voice neutral and slightly muffled. (A sock in the mouthpiece perhaps.)

"Yes."

"I shall say this only once." He was obviously reading it. "The diamonds are to be placed in a Marks & Spencer carrier bag. At exactly eleven o'clock tomorrow night – Tuesday – you will take them to the Jubilee Market in Covent Garden. You will drive your Rolls Royce yourself – no chauffeur – and park it at the barrier in King Street. You will hear the church clock strike the hour. Then and only then you will begin to walk across the square towards Hammick's Bookshop. Place the bag at the base of the first column to the right of the bookshop. You will not pause but continue to walk through the arcade towards Russell Street. You will not look back. You will not return to your car for at least one half hour and then only by a circuitous route. Is that clear?"

Raven: "I would prefer not to make the drop myself."

"You will do it."

Raven: "I have already approached a private investigator

named Tom Eliot who will do it for me. He is to be paid for the job and knows nothing of its significance."

"No. If you do not obey these instructions to the letter you will not see your son again – alive."

Raven began to rant. "How do I know I will anyway? I have only your word for that. Let me speak to him. Prove to me that he is still alive."

"Your son will be returned to you."

"When?"

"In due course."

"That's not good enough. Let me talk to him, damn you. Either I talk to him or the whole deal is off and you can damn well do what you like."

There was a muffled moment of silence as if the caller had placed a hand over the mouthpiece, then another voice, lighter this one.

"Dad, is that you?"

"Anthony?" Raven's voice softened considerably. "Anthony? Is that you? Are you all right?"

"Sorry, Dad, dragging you into this mess . . ."

"Are you all right?"

"I'm okay, yes . . . all right. Not comfortable but . . ." The voice broke slightly. "Get me out of this, Dad, please . . ."

The other voice took over abruptly. "I hope you're satisfied. You've had your instructions. Carry them out and no one will get hurt."

The line went dead. Raven silenced the machine. "That's it."

There followed a long, uneasy pause. I stared stolidly at the now silent machine until Sam, leaning across the desk, rewound the tape; a whirring sound, silence, and then: "Yes?" . . . "Sir George Raven?" . . . "Yes." . . .

Rooted like trees we listened to the whole thing again.

Sam switched off the machine. "Was that your son's voice?"

Raven turned. "Of course."

"You have no doubts?"

"None. Have you? He's your son-in-law. Didn't you recognise him?"

Sam tugged doubtfully at his ear-lobe. "The identity of a

recorded telephone voice is not something I would care to swear to in court, even if such a thing were admissible as evidence, which it isn't." He looked at me. "Your thoughts, Mark."

"Did the call come from a public phone-box as before?"

Raven frowned. "I'm not sure. I imagine so. Marvell would be able to tell you. What's your point?"

"Only that if it came from a call-box then Anthony must have been there too, mustn't he? Standing cheek by jowl with the kidnapper ready and waiting to take the phone and talk to you. Not, as the book would have us believe, tied up and gagged in a damp cellar."

"Not all call-boxes are in public places," intervened Sam drily. "You can have a pay-box in a private house if that's the way you want it."

I nodded. "It was just a thought."

"Now wait . . . just one minute." Raven's voice was suddenly taut. "What are you getting at, Savage?"

"Well . . ." I eyed him with care. "If we bypass for a moment the possibility of his being trussed up on a truckle-bed with the telephone clamped to his ear by party or parties unknown, there would seem to be only two alternatives. First," I nodded at the Answercall, "what we hear on that thing could be someone impersonating your son's voice; he didn't after all commit himself in any way, did he? Nothing he said was particularly revealing, like what was his mother's maiden name, where did he go to school . . . Apart from your own assertion, which obviously we can't ignore, there's no positive proof that it was Anthony speaking."

"And the other alternative?" Brusqueness betrayed his deep anxiety.

"I've already mentioned that." I glanced at Sam but he was only a couple of raised eyebrows and a blank stare. "Anthony in the box with the kidnapper, egging him on."

It was a long time before anyone spoke then Raven said slowly, "That would mean . . ."

Sam nodded and came in on my side. "Exactly. A con job. Anthony having you on – to extort money from you."

He shook his head violently. "I won't have that. I won't believe that."

"It's been done before and will be done again." Sam was relentless. "Ransom paid, victim returns, haggard, overwrought, protesting a deal too much about how dreadful it all was, and then exits laughing – all the way to the bank. Who can disprove it?"

Raven bore down on his desk. "Marvell can." He lifted the telephone and touched a button. "Marvell, listen. The phone call at six this morning. Do you remember if it came from a public call-box?"

The answer was engraved on his face as he slowly returned the instrument to its rest. He raised his eyes and gave a brief nod.

Another long and oppressive silence. Raven seemed to have aged several years. Lowering himself into his chair he stared with distaste at the trim white rectangle of the Answercall. "So what do we do?"

Sam ambled towards the window. "The ball is still in your court. Nothing's changed." Pale sunlight encircled his head with a ghostly halo of radiance. "Pay the ransom or not – it's your decision. But before you decide there are various questions you should ask yourself. How well do you know your son? How prepared would he be, do you think, to practise such a deception on you? And how willing are you, George, to risk the truth – either way?"

Raven sat motionless, carved in stone. I sank into the nearest chair, Sam's eyes on me. He had turned back into the room and stood, bulky and formidable, etched against the window.

George Raven broke the silence. "We'll go ahead as instructed." The words were hard and decisive.

"No." Sam moved to the corner of the desk. "Not exactly as instructed." He raised a hand as Raven was about to interrupt. "George, please listen to me for a moment. We know nothing about this mob. Whoever they are and whoever they represent, they're greedy, ambitious and deadly serious. They're after money, big money, and there's every reason to believe that they will stop at nothing to lay their hands on it. And when I say nothing I mean up to and including murder." Raven's head jerked up. "Three nights ago Anthony's friend, Geoff Earnshaw, was killed on the Common – murdered. You may recall he was best man at Anthony and Lindy's wedding. Now my creaking bones tell me there's a connection between that death and this kidnapping. If I'm right then we're in trouble – up to our eyeballs, and being dutiful citizens we ought to call up the cops and leave them to sort it out because that's what they're paid for. On the other hand, should this snatch be genuine, a police presence could jeopardise your son's life. The one advantage the police have over us, as I see it, is numbers, and even that is a moot point. If we're going to get a line on this gang, our one obvious chance is to be on the spot when the ransom's picked up – not interfere with 'em but get 'em to lead us to wherever they hole up and keep them under some sort of surveillance until Anthony is released, safe and sound. Then we call in the law. Alternatively, of course, we could take that law into our own hands for a few glorious and rewarding moments and only then call the cops. We must see how we feel when the time comes."

He took off on a circuit of the room with the hunched and thoughtful gait I was beginning to know so well. George Raven stirred impatiently, watching Sam with a heavy frown and clearly coming to the end of his enforced span of silence. As he opened his mouth to speak Sam pipped him at the post.

"Our concern, George – Mark's and mine – is for your safety. Should you deliver the diamonds yourself you would, we think, be putting yourself into great personal danger. If I were in their shoes, having pulled off a successful felony to the tune of half a million, I think I might consider the possibility of upping it to a cool million, or even more, by snatching the goose who had just laid the first golden egg."

I watched Raven's eyes widen. "You think they'd actually try to kidnap me – in the middle of London?"

"The work of a minute. Why not? At that time of night the theatres are turning out, restaurants are booming, tourists on the loose, and just down the road the Mecca Dance Hall at the old Lyceum is pumping out its raving maniacs, all pepped up and nowhere to go . . . You could be picked up and stashed away on the other side of London in a couple of hours. And Raven Industries would be asked to foot the bill. There. It's melodramatic and far-fetched but can't be ignored. It could happen. And we, Mark and I, think you should consider a suggestion of ours before you shoot it down in flames."

Raven eyed us both now with cool detachment. "Go on," he said quietly.

A finger prodded at my shoulder from behind. "It's your turn, Mark," Sam prompted.

I opened bluntly enough. "Let Sam stand in for you. You are near enough the same build and height. If you have a distinctive hat or overcoat, a scarf or something, let him borrow them. Most of all, trust him with the Rolls. They mention the Rolls particularly, probably because it will stick out like a sore thumb – there'll be stoat eyes glued to it from the moment it trundles into King Street."

"And what if they decide to kidnap him – Sam I mean?"

I shrugged. "We're dealing with a whole load of imponderables but there will be three of us to deal with emergencies."

"Three?"

"Three." I didn't tell him that the third was a lanky female, short-sighted and blonde, called Mitch. He didn't press it.

"And who covers the actual drop?"

"The third of our number. If there is no ensuing excitement Sam and I will close with her and concentrate on the destination of the half million."

"Her?" He raised his eyebrows.

"Her," I repeated stonily.

Sam moved out from behind and took up a stance at the end of the desk. Raven followed him with eyes which glinted with wry amusement. "And what makes you think, Sam Birkett, that you are more capable of dealing with such a situation than I?"

"I don't. I just think you're a more valuable property than I am." He gave a tiny smirk. "Anyway, at your age you should be wary of the more boisterous games."

George Raven's mouth twitched. "All right, I get your point. I don't agree with it but I see it. And what am I supposed to do while you two – three – are playing your boisterous games?"

"Stay at home under cover. Your services and goodwill may yet be needed."

He took only a moment to make up his mind. He gave a

curt nod. "Expect you tomorrow evening – dinner if you wish. You'd be welcome."

Somewhat selfishly and without consulting me Sam turned down the invitation. "Dinner would be a bad idea in the circumstances – especially for my young friend here. Expect us about ten o'clock." He reached for his hat on the desk, nodded at Raven. "Grateful to you for seeing it our way. Only hope it works out, but . . ." He gave a silent shrug.

Raven said, "I'm prepared . . . either way. Anthony and I rarely saw eye to eye about anything, but I don't altogether blame him for that. I don't think badly of him – not that badly anyway. By the same token, I hope he would be incapable of . . ." He shook his head vaguely and left the sentence unfinished.

We moved in convoy to the door, Raven leading the way. "Oh, incidentally . . ." His hand was on the doorknob. "You wouldn't, by any chance, happen to have a Marks & Spencer carrier bag among your possessions, would you – either of you?"

Chapter Five

Tom Eliot stared back at me from the mirror. Unbelievably repellent he would have put an anthropophagite off his food.

The hair I had borrowed from a buddy of mine at Wig Creations and even he, who had seen most things in his time, was unable to repress a blench when I tried it on in his smart salon in Old Burlington Street. "Oh yuk!" he murmured good-naturedly, his deft and fastidious fingers working without hope on the lank black locks snaking greasily on to my shoulders. "You look 'orrible." The drooping black Mexican moustache reduced him to silence.

The secondhand jeans and orange T-shirt with *Stallion* scrawled in blood across the chest I discovered in a sort of clothing arcade in Long Acre. The young man who gift-wrapped them in a couple of pages of *Gay News* gave me a sly wink and eyed my crutch with interest. I felt wanted.

The jeans were bleached, patched, stained and deliberately frayed at the ankles. They were also two sizes too small; I had to bowl around on the floor to get the zip done up. They left little to the imagination and did much to change the character of my walk.

The wide-awake black felt hat with the floppy brim I purchased for 20p at a bookstall in Earlham Street, whilst the bomber jacket, ankle boots, studded black leather belt and wrist-strap came from my own personal collection of knick-knacks – as did the beads and the ear-ring.

A twenty-four-hour growth of bristle added a certain amount of sleaze but the final straw came with the umbramatic granny glasses which changed colour when faced with light. The camel's back wilted.

I glanced at my watch. Tuesday 21.00 hours.

Much as I would have liked to witness Sam Birkett behind the wheel of a Rolls I had opted out of the original idea of trailing along in his wake on the Honda and instead was going on ahead, early and solo, in the hope of catching someone with his trousers down.

Keep an eye open long enough on any particular centre of activity and a pattern of some sort will eventually emerge – however kaleidoscopic it may seem at first sight. An addition or subtraction, a subtle change of movement, even the shifting focus of a single pair of eyes could point the way to an odd man out . . . which was the one I would be looking for.

Mitch was also going in under her own steam. Having broached the subject over our Sunday meal I had filled her in with up-to-the-minute details at the office the following day; she had reacted to the invitation to join in the fun with the enthusiasm of a kettle on the boil. I told her what to look for and how to look for it, begged her not to wear either her stiletto heels or her best clothes and to make no recognition noises in my direction should she be clever enough to penetrate any disguise I might be wearing. I narrowed my eyes at Tom Eliot – he would be more than a match for Mitch.

Sliding my Swiss Army knife into a pocket of the bomber jacket, I hesitated over my bent bits of piano-wire and sturdy set of brass knuckle-dusters and decided against them. Lock-picking was unlikely to be high on the list of the night's excesses and the mere thought of being embroiled in a rough-house wearing those jeans turned my blood cold.

I took one last look at myself, shuddered, put out the lights and let myself quietly out of the flat.

At the front door I ran into the gent downstairs putting out his milk bottles. It was no good pretending I wasn't there; I was face to face with him looking like Guy Fawkes in dark glasses. He nodded, cleared his throat and said, "Evening, Mr Savage. Milk's going up again on Monday, did you know that?"

I gave a neutral growl, shoved past him and stamped morosely down the front steps feeling like an idiot. So much for bloody disguises!

A damp heaviness in the air predicted rain. There was no breath of wind and neither moon nor stars relieved the darkness.

Traffic was thin and I made good time. A little after nine-thirty I was parking the Honda in Henrietta Street near the hospital. I exchanged my crash-hat for Tom Eliot's floppy-brimmed number, shoved a slab of Wrigley's into my mouth and with thumbs hooked into the pockets of my jeans, hunched my way down Bedford Street and up into King. The self-consciousness I had anticipated soon began to wear off. No one giggled or passed derogatory remarks – or if they did they waited until I was out of earshot. Tom Eliot was the sort of latent nastiness which peace-loving citizens cross the road to avoid.

On the other hand of course he was a red rag to similar nasties, plenty of whom were already roaming the circuit. A plethora of approaching punks in full slouching order closed up into a ragged line as I drew near, challenging my use of the asphalt. I slowed to a halt and eyed them with care, legs straddled, head down, my hand beginning to crawl menacingly towards my empty hip-pocket – an ugly sight in anyone's book. After an age-long moment of tension their line wavered, buckled and broke up. I shouldered my way between them to live another day. When they were safely out of harm's way a barrage of catcalls and impolite biological suggestions hurtled through the night air.

Sweat slid like slime beneath my skimpy T-shirt. War-drums pounded in my ears. My trousers were far too tight. I was no Clint Eastwood – he could keep his fistful of dollars. Another small scene like that and I could end up in someone's emergency ward.

I sweated on.

The King Street approach to the market brought me face to face with Hammick's Bookshop. The column mentioned by the kidnappers was the first of four forming a portico above the entrance to the shop.

The sprawl of Jubilee Market – until 1974 the Covent Garden Fruit and Vegetable Market – is immense and solid looking, a monument to Victorian architecture, the renovators having cunningly preserved and rejuvenated the original iron-work, colonnades, porticoes and pediments. East and west of the complex lie spacious rectangular courtyards, paved and cobbled; the glass roofed arcade is flanked with smarty-crafty shops, restaurants, bars and offices, whilst between them, running the full length of the arcade, is a collection of open trading stands looking like vacant benches at a dog show; during business hours – and at a price – it would be here that you would pick up that quaint and modest gift for the friend who has everything.

Except for the bars and restaurants which were doing a rip-roaring trade, everything else was closed.

Too early for my purpose I slouched down to a lower level bar where the noise was awesome, bought myself a lager and slumped exhausted on to an uncomfortable metal chair tucked away behind a laurel bush. Lounging back with my legs spread dangerously wide, and tipping my hat down on to the bridge of my nose the way they do, I peered beneath its brim at my fellow imbibers.

No wonder no one was taking any notice of me: we were all look-alikes.

To be fair there was a sprinkling of other types, students and the like, one with a violin case upended on the chair beside him; another, a droopy and bespectacled blonde, feverish behind ballpoint and a pile of notepaper, appeared to be writing a book. Behind her again, back to the wall immediately opposite me and staring vacantly into space was another girl, dark and sullen, looking not unlike . . . I brought my knees together so violently that they cracked like walnuts. The table juddered. Jesus! I folded myself over the table, elbows clamped on either side of my untouched lager. I breathed heavily down my nose.

Cath. It was Cath Brenner. The Brenner Pass.

What in hell's name was she doing here?

Having coffee, that's what she was doing. Happened to be passing, felt like a coffee, dropped in . . . Chance, coincidence.

How far can you stretch coincidence?

I peered at her through my granny glasses. Her eyes were on me.

She's recognised you.

Balls. I look like the phantom of the opera.

Your downstairs neighbour recognised you.

I was coming out of my flat, wasn't I?

She was looking through me not at me. As far as she was

concerned I wasn't there. I peeked surreptitiously at my watch. Ten-five. Another hour to go. If she had any part to play in tonight's nefarious goings-on why should she arrive an hour early?

Why did you?

What?

Now she was looking at her watch. Reflex action. She had seen me looking at mine. Like when you see someone yawning and yawn yourself. That was it. She knew me, was watching me. Or maybe she just liked the look of Tom Eliot. Well, why not? *Chacun à son goût.* Maybe she was a horror movie fan.

I had to know. One way or another I had to know.

No point in sitting here wondering about it. Go and find out. But if she was here for a purpose – like picking up half a million quid's worth of diamonds or casing the joint for someone else to pick them up, a rash move on my part would raise the alarm and the whole thing would be called off and my friend Sam would drop his Marks & Spencer carrier bag outside Hammick's and some passing layabout would pick it up and go and live in the Bahamas for the rest of his life.

She was lapping up her coffee, looking at her watch again; clock watching, waiting for someone . . .

A well-set-up coloured boy, gangly in spite of his size, loped smoothly down the steps; handsome, late teens early twenties, he had the sort of lithe, hip-swinging, panther-like tread inherent to his race. With his tight, close-cropped hair, black pants, plain crimson boat-neck sweater and heavy silver chain about his neck, he outmoded and outshone everything in sight; his skin was purple ebony but the aristocratic features were those of the Moor – the Venetian one.

Cath had raised a hand high above her head. He caught sight of her and made a flat-handed salutation like a cop stopping traffic.

They didn't shake hands which suggested they knew each other quite well. He slid easily into the chair beside her, his right profile towards me, talking animatedly.

Except for its location which could have been fortuitous I could see nothing sinister about the meeting; a date pure and simple, that's what it looked like. Off to the Lyceum perhaps for a bit of the old stamp and wriggle or whatever they called it these days.

Both were keeping a close eye on the time. Synchronise your watches, gentlemen. Twenty-two hours, nineteen minutes and fifty-eight, fifty-nine . . . that's it. Good luck, everybody, and keep your heads down . . .

They were on the move.

Now what? They were moving up the steps, she in front, he following, his fingers hooked intimately into the back of her trenchcoat belt. I buried my nose in my lager until they reached the upper court and had moved out of sight, then, resisting the instinct to hurry – Tom Eliot went fast nowhere – clambered lazily to my feet. I climbed the stairs slowly, albeit two at a time, elbowed my way through a bunch of loud-mouths descending abreast, and paused at the top glaring about me.

Gone. Plenty of people milling around but not a fawn trenchcoat or blazing red sweater in sight.

Muttering obscenely beneath my breath, I took off down the arcade towards King Street and, beneath Hammick's portico, quartered the dimly lit square without success. I retraced my steps, prowled uneasily through the arcade, slid down each of the narrow alleyways dividing the shops to the Russell Street end and back again via the North Piazza. How the hell had they done it? They must have moved damn fast. Why? Had they known I was on their heels? I couldn't believe that, but beneath my big hat my brain throbbed with suspicions I didn't care to entertain.

Turning abruptly I walked slap into a man-mountain with a stomach the size of a beer-barrel. I staggered beneath the impact. His breath was like mustard gas.

"Watch it, punk," he growled, sweeping me from his path with an arm like a prize marrow. I fell backwards into one of the dog show benches, flattening my hat which had preceded me. He peered at me with pink, piggy eyes. "You wanna look where you're fuckin' goin', boy, or you'll get fuckin' hurt, right?"

He was a pantomime giant with none of the charm. With an approximation of jovial rumble he added, "Jeez man, but you're an ugly little sod . . ." If you were the size of the gasworks you could say things like that without fear of contradiction. As he lumbered off he broke generous wind leaving me gasping for breath and wondering what in hell he had been eating. I extricated myself from the dog show bench, resumed my hat and beat a hasty retreat in the opposite direction.

An untidy group of ethnics were in the process of putting down roots around the Hammick premises, one of them, a gawky youth with dandelion hair, hitching a guitar to his spare frame as if it were a safety-belt. My heart sank. All this and pop too. As if by some precognition the youth chose the 'drop' column as his centre of operations, curling his rambling body into a sinuously comfortable heap on the stone step with his back to the column.

I glanced up at the blue-dialled church clock of St Paul's – Inigo Jones' Actors' Church. Fifteen minutes to go. I eyed the intended concert with concern. In a quarter of an hour Sam would be tipping a fortune into that lad's lap.

Lounging up against a column cornering Culpeper's – the counterpart of Hammick's and twenty feet away – I studied the young musician with intent. He was one of a group of five, the others being two girls, a boy and an older man. Were they to be the fortunate recipients of half a million pounds' worth of diamonds? Terrorists – as Sam would have it?

The boy, in a threadbare jersey and big boots, was sullen, tired looking and barely in his teens. The girls, each with a scrawny hair-do braided with coloured beads, could have been sisters and probably were – their shapeless dresses had certainly come from the same bring-and-buy sale. The older man, dark-featured and balding with something of the gypsy about him, seemed at first glance to be no part of them, but when one of the girls offered him some sort of banter he replied with a tight grin and a playful flick of his hand which she laughingly ducked to avoid.

Kidnappers? I thought not. In the employ of kidnappers? Possibly. Positioned here to receive the loot, later to pass it on at some specified time and destination.

The music began softly enough, a smooth, rhythmical brushing of the strings resolving into a gently swaying motion, folk stuff probably. I watched the youth's long fingers moving adroitly over the metal frets. He was no slouch on the guitar. The innate brashness of the personality with the dandelion hair seemed to fall away as he folded himself about the instrument, head cocked, eyes closed. An overhead lamp etched deep dramatic shadows into the gaunt features. One of the girls began to vocalise quietly and wordlessly to an emerging melody, a haunting wisp of sound belonging to dark hills and sleep and the coming of night . . .

I gave myself an unwilling shake, turning back to the matter in hand – in particular to the whereabouts of Mitch who by this time should have positioned herself somewhere between Hammick's and the top of King Street. I could see no sign of her.

A sudden untidy influx of people was spreading across the square. I glanced at the clock; a theatre turning out perhaps. The Opera House. Some of them clutched the distinctive red programmes.

I slid down the pillar into a squatting position and listened to the clatter of their feet, feeling ever more desperate as time grew shorter and the square overflowed with homeward-bound opera lovers. Fortunately the weather was on the downgrade and no one seemed tempted to loiter. The warm moisture in the air had turned to fine rain; a thin, sinuous mist curled about the lamps.

Eleven minutes to go.

They had been to see *Aida*. A couple of them in not very good voice were giving us their version of the 'Triumphal March'. They appeared to be tone-deaf – like most music-lovers when tempted to vocalise.

A woman in an ankle-length white satin dress and sharply pointed shoes tripped over my feet. Her escort, a ruddy faced man in an incongruous tweed hat snarled at me rudely: "Damn silly place to sit!" I blew him a brisk raspberry and as he stopped and turned, grew slowly upright with my back against the column and stared down at the top of his country hat; he was all of five feet six. I thought he paled a little as he carefully digested my appearance.

"Come along, Wilkie," croaked the woman in white returning to collect him. "I'm perfectly all right."

"Good on yer, Sheila," I grinned.

She grabbed his arm and took him away. "Come along, Wilkie, they only spoil a lovely evening, people like that. They should be locked up – people like that."

And quite right too, I thought. I was beginning to hate Tom Eliot. I sank down on to my haunches again, my labouring jeans giving no quarter.

As the gilt hands of the clock crawled up towards the hour the crowd thinned and all at once the now gleaming square was empty again. Some roller-skaters appeared out of the darkness wheeling and weaving together over the wet cobble-stones, their vulcanised wheels making no sound other than a vibrant jarring against the uneven surfaces and the sudden swish of water as they swept through standing puddles.

Now that the crowd had gone the song filtered back. The second girl had joined the first, their voices blending in close and melancholy descant; Irish I would guess. The creeping mist and the soft rain, the stealthy swirling of the silent skaters all combined eerily with the lilt of the song, creating a dream-like sequence of ballet in blue and silver.

I caught sight of Mitch, tall and stooping, heron-like, between the parked cars, her flat sensible shoes making her somewhat less graceful than the average heron. She wore a diaphanous white waterproof with pointed hood tightly fastened beneath her chin which made her look like a ghost of some long-departed member of the Ku Klux Klan. Behind her, Poon's Chinese restaurant was disgorging a party of slightly merry diners. One of their number, about to step off the pavement, was hauled back by another with a garrulous cry of warning: they stood swaying on the kerb as the classic nose of a Rolls Royce stole silently past them. My heart leapt.

The clock again. Three minutes. Sam in borrowed glory . . .

The shafting headlights, silvered with rain, picked up the milky-white form of the waiting Mitch and threw her shadow long and black over the wet square. She turned abruptly, shading her eyes against the glare, then she too glanced up at the clock.

Only then did I realise that I had heard no sound from that clock and couldn't recollect having heard a peep out of it ever since I had arrived more than an hour ago. My feet began to feel cold. Were they having us on? 'You will hear the church clock strike the hour,' he had said.

Mitch had got herself out of the limelight and back into comparative shadow where she loitered, I thought, with intent and some ostentation.

The Rolls' lights were dowsed.

I eyed the guitarist narrowly. Neither he nor his companions seemed aware of anything other than their music. One of the skaters swept past me at speed splattering my overheated skin with the icy spray of his wake. I was sweating like a bull.

The skaters looked as if they were wearing some kind of uniform, neither male nor female, light blue jeans – dark now with rain – and the short unisex yellow and blue reversible anorak obtainable at most weatherwear stores; they wore them yellow side out, hoods up and clipped neatly beneath their chins thus rendering their features virtually invisible. The wet rubberised material glinted and slithered in the uncertain lamplight.

Whether by accident or design they had now drifted into a follow-my-leader ritual, swaying together rhythmically, step matching step, each flying body no more than a yard behind the one in front. Apart from the curious bone-rattle of the wheels on the cobblestones they made no sound.

I shifted in sudden uneasiness. Something sinister was beginning to stir beneath my sweat.

And then the music ceased and at the same moment, quite clearly, I heard the chiming of a clock. Not the one on the church. I looked at my watch.

It was time.

The musicians hadn't moved, the guitarist was tuning his instrument; the girls, their backs to the wall, murmured together intimately; beyond them and to the left, half submerged in background shadow, stood the glimmering sentinel form of Mitch.

There came the faintest slamming of a car door. The man who stepped away from the Rolls carrying the green Marks & Spencer bag ostentatiously in his right hand was thickset and moved with the deliberate step of George Raven. He wore a fur hat and a dark overcoat with an astrakhan collar.

As the distant clock slowly tolled the hour I rose carefully to my feet, every nerve on edge. Three stragglers moved silently across the square arm in arm; in the background the subdued clatter of the bars and restaurants; the wail of a distant police siren; the rattle of skate-wheels and the steady fall of approaching feet. The yellow-haired boy strummed idly on his guitar; the girls sat mute, one of them shrugging a raincoat over her shoulders.

The man with the bag was halfway across the square. The strollers passed beneath an overhead lamp and were gone. I hardly moved. The skaters surged by with a clatter, unconcernedly drenching me with spray. Preoccupied as I was I found myself counting them as they streaked between me and the figure in the fur hat . . . two, three, four, five . . . I blinked the water from my eyes.

It *was* Sam, but looking incredibly like Raven. He was close enough now for me to make out the sudden frown which darkened his brow as he pondered the group beneath the Hammick portico. His pace slowed a trifle. He flicked a glance in my direction; whether or not he recognised me I had no way of telling; he made no sign.

Three paces from the boy he changed the carrier bag containing half a million pounds' worth of diamonds to his left hand. The boy did not move. The clock ceased to chime and Sam reached his destination.

All at once from the far end of the square a single high scream rent the air; a woman in panic, brutal male voices shouting her down. As I half turned towards the sounds I saw with sudden alarm that the skaters were bearing down upon me, shoulder to shoulder in a close-packed line, black shadows where their faces should have been, their rain-wet anoraks glinting evilly.

I stood and froze for just a second too long. With militaristic precision they realigned themselves into single file, their leader coming at me like a bullet from a gun. I ducked too late from the reaching hands; he struck my shoulder hard thrusting me ferociously backwards against the column.

And now suddenly they gave tongue, maniacal, high-pitched animal sounds like a gang of drunken cowboys on the loose; now they broke ranks and ranted screaming through the arcade scattering pedestrians right and left. I saw Sam's startled face turning as the leader crashed into him and brought him down, the skater leaping high and free over his sprawling body.

Shoving myself away from the column I started towards him, a small part of my mind registering that he no longer carried the bag. A thudding blow in the small of my back threw me headlong as another skater flashed by me. I lunged at him wildly as I fell, grabbing at the flying skirt of his anorak; the wet material slid through my fingers but it was enough to unsettle him. Lurching drunkenly for a couple of seconds, arms flaying, hood slipping from his head, he spun into a clumsy pirouette and then, miraculously recovering his balance and sinking low on to his haunches, he thrust himself forward and upwards into safety. One of the flying skates came within inches of my head; I could hear the buzzing whir of its wheels. I grabbed at it, missed and received it full in the mouth. The singing wheels burned into my flesh. As I rolled over on to my back with a yelp of pain, hands clamped to my bloody and damaged mouth, I realised I had seen that face before somewhere recently, I had seen that face . . .

Sam's homely old features hung over me. In his borrowed fur hat he looked like someone high up in the Soviet Commissariat. "They got away," he said flatly. "Hook, line and sinker, they got away." He regarded me with a frown. "You all right?" The voice was, I thought, hurtfully lacking in concern.

I heaved myself into a more painful sitting position. "I got kicked in the teeth, didn't I?" With loving fingers I explored my swelling mouth; they came away wet with blood. Others, more curious than Sam, milled around muttering and staring as if we were doing it for their entertainment. I told one of them to piss off which he did with remarkable alacrity. My hat was lying in my lap like a dead thing. I picked it up and remodelled it for a couple of seconds, then asked Sam casually, "How did you know it was me?"

He squatted amiably enough beside me and with a pair of delicate fingers removed something which was stuck to my T-shirt; I crossed my eyes to get it into focus. Tom Eliot's moustache. "Also," he murmured gently, "your wig is on the skew and your flies are wide open."

"Oh Christ!" I slapped my hat over my crutch but not before I had caught a glimpse of my jolly multi-coloured Y-fronts glowing in the lamplight. Sam showed his dentures. "You're a rotten old sod, that's what you are," I mumbled. "Why don't we get out of here and I can go bleed all over your flaming Rolls. Are you all right?" The last time I had seen him he had been lying flat on his back.

"Bruised," he said shortly. He glanced over his shoulder. "I wonder what became of your lady friend, Mitch? Did she manage to get here? I don't think I'd recognise her even if I saw her."

My neck creaked painfully as I peered across to where she had been standing; she wasn't there now of course. He gave me a helping hand as I scrabbled untidily to my feet. "Put your wig straight," he muttered testily.

I threw a glance over my shoulder. The Hammick portico was deserted, the musicians gone. Several angry and dishevelled people were in the process of brushing themselves down and massaging bruised limbs; an elderly woman was being hoisted to her feet by a group of solicitous bystanders, one of them mutely tendering her smashed spectacles.

Of the skaters there was of course no sign. A surge of fury swept over me. I threw Sam off. "Let's go find Mitch."

Mitch was coiled around the base of a column in the North Piazza. Several people appeared to be trying to work her loose. We elbowed them aside. "Police," growled Sam waving a credit card. They looked at me. "I'm her father," I told them. They gave up and went away.

She was more or less unhurt but severely winded. She had, she told us later, received one of the flying skaters fully amidships. Having dogged Sam to the portico she had been close enough to register the drop one split second before the skaters had made their run-in; the third in line had snatched up the bag almost before it had touched the ground and continued his progress through the alleyway between Hammick's and Thornton's the confectioners next door. Unfortunately for Mitch she had timed her arrival at one end of the alley to synchronise with his entry into the other and he had simply put his head down and charged her full in the solar plexus. She had wound herself around the nearest column like a clockspring.

We were dislodging her with care when she became aware of my face; her china blue eyes widened with sudden alarm; when she caught sight of my Y-fronts alarm turned to hysteria. I couldn't immediately figure out why an uninterrupted view of a fellow's Y-fronts should render a female hysterical – even if the female were Mitch – but it did and Sam had to give her a smart slap on the cheek to bring her back to normal. She hung between us like post-Christmas paper-decorations, breathing heavily and in limp discomfort.

The heavy crunch of approaching feet heralded a policeman with a notebook at the ready who hove up through the alleyway and came to rest three paces away. We all stood and stared at each other.

"Anything wrong, miss?" enquired the policeman at last. "Are these gentlemen . . . ?" The unfinished sentence was far more telling than anything he could have found in his word book.

"I fell over," explained miss, still reaching for breath, ". . . and these two – er – gentlemen have just picked me up."

Not, I thought, a happy choice of phrase in the circumstances.

"You fell over?" Suspicion rocked his helmet.

"Well, I was knocked over actually – by a man on skates . . ."

"Ah, precisely." He grew in stature and confidence, took a couple of paces forward and flourished his pencil. "Several people back there have been injured in the same incident. Perhaps you could give me some details, miss . . . madam?"

"It happened so fast . . . He was large and on skates and wore a yellow mack thing."

He studied his book but didn't write anything. "And you gentlemen . . . ?"

"I'm her father," said Sam looking at me.

"And I'm her fiancé."

He eyed my T-shirt. "You've been hurt, too . . . sir."

"Right, mate. He come at me bull-headed like – like a ton of bricks, you know?"

"P'raps you'd care to make a statement?"

Sam said, "If it's all the same to you, officer, I think I ought to get my daughter home, don't you? . . . get a doctor to take a look at her – we're not far from here, just round the corner as a matter of fact." The officer looked doubtful. "Take the address if you like," offered Sam. "It's," he leaned over the man's notebook, "the name is Wingrave . . . Owen Wingrave . . . Captain retired . . . and the address . . . 33b, second floor, Floral Street."

"I know it, sir. And yours – er – sir?"

"33c – top floor. Budd . . . William Budd."

"Right, gentlemen . . . miss." He was easily satisfied and snapped his pocket book to attention with a rubber band. "Should we wish further information regarding the incident we'll contact you."

As he departed solemnly through the hole whence he had come Sam said tentatively, "Perhaps we ought to be on our way before he discovers we all live at the Opera House."

Having no wheels of her own Mitch had travelled up by Underground. I offered her the back of the Honda but was outbid by Sam who oilily suggested she might care for a ride in the Rolls (Rolls-Roycemanship they call it in the trade). She invited us to coffee and cakes at her pad in Fulham, adding with a cool smile in my direction that "you could follow on your bike, couldn't you, Mark?"

The Rolls went by the name of Silver Shadow Mark II and was one of the few remaining reasons for a possible upsurge of spirits in this waterlogged island of ours.

Mitch frowned up at my battered face as I helped her into the passenger seat, touching it with a gentle finger. "Do you know where to come?"

"If you wouldn't mind telling your driver to wait for me at the bottom of Henrietta Street, I'll be right up your exhaust-pipe." I shut her in carefully.

There came the soft whispering of engineering aristocracy and I stood with my eyes shut as he edged the large car without incident from the cramped parking space.

Back at the Honda I stripped off that hideous wig – to the surprise of a passing labrador who gave a little yelp of alarm – rustled into a pair of waterproof overtrousers to conceal my all-revealing jeans and straddled the wet saddle. The sheer exuberance of power which leapt from her exhaust as I switched on gladdened my heart and almost set the world to rights again. He could keep his Rolls.

Chapter Six

Mitch lived in Queens Club Gardens, her tiny apartment a lesson to us all. Sam had only to stand up in it to look untidy. Mitch, clearly aware of this, shoved him resolutely into the largest available armchair and, leaving me to fend for myself, disappeared off-stage to make coffee and toast, ignoring our scarcely audible offers of assistance.

Apart from the subdued clatter in the kitchen and some sporadic gunfire from somebody's television in the flat above all was quiet. Sam gnawed away at his lower lip for several morose moments, stirring himself finally with a chesty sigh. "I suppose we might safely say that the night's operation has been a resounding flop."

I nodded. "I think we might say that, all things considered. Though, in fairness, we could add that in the face of a superbly staged piece of theatrical diversion we didn't do at all badly. Mitch was winded, you were bruised and I was half killed . . ."

". . . While they helped themselves to half a million smackers in cut and polished diamonds."

"Which," I pointed out, "was the object of the exercise."

A pause.

"The object of *my* exercise," muttered Sam a trifle huffily, "was to find out who they were and where they went."

A second pause.

I nodded glumly. "A resounding flop."

He picked up a book from the table beside his chair and stared marble-eyed at its title. "She doesn't really read this sort of thing, does she?"

"What's it called?"

"*Everyman's Companion to the Brontës.*"

I nodded. "It's food and drink to her."

He crossed his eyes and returned the book reverently to its place.

Upstairs John Wayne was busy winning the Second World War. I said, "The one who knocked me down . . . I've seen him before somewhere."

"You already said that."

"But I don't know where."

"Fat lot of good that is."

I shot him a grieved look. "Don't ride me, Sam. Or yourself for that matter. Without a pair of bloody skates there was no way we could have got after them – no way – and even if we had we'd have been risking Tony Raven's life . . ."

"If he's still alive." Sam wagged an unhappy head. He began probing around in an inside pocket and abruptly changed the subject. "I told you I stole a book from Earnshaw's place, didn't I? I remembered to bring it for you to see. Tucked away in his bedside drawer it was. Just have a peer through it – it'll make your hair stand on end."

He threw over a torn and grubby, much fingered, paper-covered copy of something called *The Anarchists' Cookbook*. "God alone knows where he picked that up. I've heard of it, read about it, but never actually handled a copy. Originally published in Havana, I believe, and then smuggled into the States. No acknowledgement of origin of course, as you'll see."

I could feel his keen eyes upon me as I leafed swiftly through it, alarm and despondency increasing with every turning page. It contained everything you wanted to know about how to be a successful anarchist – a do-it-yourself manual of how to wage urban warfare in ten easy lessons; weapons, explosives, strategy . . . Lenin had once said, "The purpose of terror is to terrorise." And that's what this tatty little book was all about.

When Mitch returned with coffee and toasted wholemeal and set about clearing tables and so forth I remained oblivious to her until, as I flicked over the last pages, I discovered her looming over me with a bowl of steaming water in one hand, a sponge in the other and a bottle of TCP within easy reach on a nearby table.

"That," I said, pushing the book over to Sam, "reads like a horror comic. It's terrifying."

"Which is the name of the game: terror. That's why I think he's dead."

Whilst Mitch, keeping her own counsel, mopped and bathed and soothed my wounded face Sam embarked on a monologue which had the hall-marks of an all-stations political broadcast.

"To get their grubby hands on half a million these people have killed once and maybe twice. With that sort of money they can go shopping anywhere they damn well please. If they lacked weapons and explosives before, they need lack them no longer. They have only to raise a finger and the dissidents will come crawling out of the woodwork in their hundreds, ready and eager to jump on the arms wagon with our dear friends the IRA leading the way. They're a whole lot thicker on the ground here in England than we like to admit. Being British of course, we shrug 'em off, as always, pretend they don't exist – until they park bombs in the Underground during the rush hour and slaughter men and horses in Hyde Park; Airey Neave was killed on the doorstep of the House of Commons, Mountbatten was blown up in a boat, the entire bloody cabinet was within an ace of annihilation in a Brighton hotel. So either they're pretty bloody good at it, or our security is pretty bloody bad – or maybe ineffectual is a better word."

He was flipping idly through the pages of *The Anarchists' Cookbook*. "There's another nasty little book like this, you know, probably even more dangerous. This one tells you how to make it, the other how to do it. *The Mini Manual for Urban Guerillas* it's called and it's by some Brazilian gangster called Carlos Marighella – dead now, thank God, hoist with his own petard, killed in a police ambush. The *Mini Manual* is standard text for all terrorists – their Stanislavsky, their Bible – and has been translated into a dozen or more languages. It tells them how to set up shop, keep a low profile, insinuate themselves with the common people; how to shoot first at point-blank range, how to blow up bridges, and railway lines, how to liquidate policemen and high-ranking army officers; hijacking, bank heists, kidnappings – 'Have victim, need money, will ransom.' It's all there. 'Operate in absolute secrecy,' he says, 'and in cold blood . . . Shooting and maiming are to the guerilla what air and water are to human beings . . . Always be sure to identify with popular causes . . .' Notice the nice distinction between terrorists and human beings.

"Well, you have only to cast a cursory eye over present conditions in this country to see and understand how it works. Stir up enough trouble in the streets and the police have to step in, if only to be seen preserving a semblance of law and order – house-to-house searches, scuffles, arrests . . . and who turns out to be the Big Bad Wolf in the end? Why, the bloody copper. Remember the miners' strike of '84?

"And how much easier it is to be a terrorist in a so-called free society like ours with no secret police breathing down your neck – and how much more satisfying! The de-stabilisation of western democracy is the target for tonight, chaps, and no holds barred. Dear God, I've never been one to see snow on the boots of everyone who feels himself moved to stand up and cry havoc, but it's bloody criminal to shut one's eyes to the possibility."

By the time he had reached this stage of his peroration Mitch had long finished whatever it was she was doing to my face and was squatting beside me on the arm of my chair staring with open-mouthed admiration at Sam as if he had grown an extra head.

He stopped abruptly, his eyes moving from mine to hers and back again to mine. "Or am I being a bore?"

I grinned. "Protesting too much perhaps, but never a bore. So tonight we blew it. Where now?"

The answer was immediate and to the point. "We wait for the reappearance of Anthony, dead or alive. Until that happens there's nowhere to go, is there?" He paused and repeated thoughtfully, "Or is there?"

He bit into a piece of toast and crunched his way through most of it before he spoke again. "You thought you recognised one of them. And Mitch here said . . . What did you tell that copper, Mitch? The man who knocked you down was a big man, you said. Did you mean that, or was it just that he looked and felt big?"

She thought for a second. "He was big, I'm sure of it. Bulky and broad. I couldn't see his face because of his hood – he could have been black for all I could see of his face."

"Coloured, you mean?" I was suddenly alert.

"I didn't say that."

"But he could have been?"

She shrugged. "I suppose so, there's no reason why not, but you're putting words into my mouth."

I downed a cup of tepid coffee and told them about Cath and her coloured fellow in the bar. "I can't believe they were there by accident. It's too much of a coincidence." I frowned and muttered half to myself, "She might even have been one of those skaters."

Mitch said slowly, "It occurred to me that a couple of them might have been female." Sam looked at her sharply. She forestalled him. "It crossed my mind, that's all, a couple of them could have been girls. But I would never swear to it."

"Two girls, three blokes – one of 'em big." Sam eyed his coffee-cup crossly. "What else do we know of this Cath girl? I've only met her as an appendage of Lindy's and then not very often. Lindy's always kept her friends to herself – even as a small girl. She seemed to prefer going to their houses rather than bring them home to us." He added as if it had only just occurred to him, "Maybe she was scared of Mildred."

Replenishing his cup Mitch said delicately, "Maybe she was scared of you."

"Mildred?"

"Linda."

"Rubbish. Who'd be scared of me?" He appealed to us with a face as bland as a York ham.

"The prisons," I told him drily, "are groaning with people who were scared of you, Sam."

He thought of something else and pointed a recollecting finger at me. "Cath, now I remember, was in that school production of *Macbeth* we were talking about the other day; in fact, she was not just in it, she was the man himself – Macbeth – with a big bass voice and a red wig I seem to remember. She was a ferocious child."

"She's still fairly ferocious," I told him. "She builds her own motor-cars now."

He nodded. "That figures. Which makes her also no mean mechanic."

"Well," the male chauvinist pig in me stirred a little, "let's say she knows something about cars, not necessarily about mechanics. She admitted that she had help with it. The coloured boy perhaps. They seemed to be on fairly intimate terms."

"Such a one, you may remember," put in Sam, "was also to be found in Geoff Earnshaw's latter days, according to his mum. Up to something, she thought they were, but didn't know what."

"The best way to find out, I would have thought," Mitch said mildly but with the slightest hint of peevishness at the stolidity of men's deliberation, "would be to ask your daughter, wouldn't it? Cath seems to be her best friend; Cath knows the black boy; the black boy – if he's one and the same – knew Geoff Earnshaw and Geoff Earnshaw was Anthony's best friend. And Anthony is married to Linda. Could it be, perhaps, that Linda knows all the answers?"

During the silence which then ensued Mitch cleared her throat and buried her nose in her coffee-cup. Sam and I exchanged glances. I looked up at Mitch. "Just because you live here there's no need to hog the entire bloody screen."

"She's right though." Sam gave her a congratulatory nod. "You're quite right, missus. Well done."

I groaned. "She'll be impossible in the office tomorrow."

Sam said, "I'll have words with Lindy. Maybe she'll come up with something interesting."

Mitch rose suddenly and began loping about the place like a disturbed stick-insect. "They're all young, aren't they?"

"Who're all young?"

"Everyone concerned with this business. Linda, Geoff, Cath, the coloured boy . . . the skaters . . . all young . . ."

"The one I saw wasn't all that young," I reminded her. "Not what you mean by young. I'd put him in the middle thirties, though he might have looked older because his hair was going. He was quite gaunt looking . . ." I stopped and snapped my fingers. "I've got him. I remember where I saw him. He was the one at the window of the Dog and Fox on Saturday. Remember my saying I thought I'd seen someone who knew me? Dark, sort of lantern-jawed with a broken front tooth. He was tailing Linda, that's what he was doing. And what's more he was the bastard who clobbered me tonight."

They were silent for a moment mulling over the information, then Sam said, pouring cold water, "Doesn't help much though, does it? With Anthony in their hands what could be more natural than to keep an eye on his nearest and dearest – if only to find out who she was contacting . . . police, private dicks and so on. More to the point is whether he recognised you tonight under all that bumph you had on. If he saw that daft moustache of yours drop off . . ."

I shook my head. "When he kicked me in the teeth he was already on the turn. He wouldn't have seen it. And even if he did, so what? They must have known there'd be someone there keeping an eye on things. Otherwise why all the diversion tactics?"

"All that screaming you mean?"

I nodded. "Classic example of pure theatre – the sort of thing Guthrie would have thought up. All that sudden screaming off-stage-left at exactly the moment the audience should have been concentrating on stage-right. It's the surprise tactics that matter; everyone present turns to look if only for a second, but it's enough – that second is all that's needed. The timing was perfect – just as you dropped the diamonds. And then all those flaming skaters letting rip, throwing everyone else off balance, physically as well as mentally. It was well conceived and well executed, I'll give 'em that . . . Brilliant, that's what it was." I stopped. "My tooth's aching," I told them. "I got hit in the mouth, remember?"

"More coffee anyone?" asked Mitch suddenly as if not wanting to get involved. Sam and I looked glumly at our empty cups, then at each other. She was not the world's greatest expert on the coffee-bean. Sam glanced at his watch. "I must get that old heap downstairs back to her stable at Wimbledon."

"Will he be waiting up, do you think?" asked Mitch.

"Raven?" He nodded slowly. "I reckon so. I would also reckon that he'll be expecting us to bring Anthony back with us, alive and well. What are we going to tell him, I wonder?"

"That we made the drop," I said somewhat tersely. "That's what we've done and that's what he'd have done in the same circumstances. What else was there? Now all we've got to do is just to sit and wait until something happens."

There was a long silence then Sam creaked out of his chair.

He looked very untidy. He nodded again, slower this time, frowning at each of us in turn. "That's right. All we've got to do now is sit and wait – see what happens."

Upstairs the war was over. They were playing the 'Stars and Stripes'.

Chapter Seven

Three days we waited. Three long and miserable days yawing in the doldrums of George Raven's displeasure. Our credibility slid down the barometer of his expectations, sinking rapidly through changeable, cool and cold, to finish up well below freezing point; the telephone crackled with permafrost – if you listened you could hear his breath steaming.

Every morning and evening the same question: "News?" And always the same answer: "None." There was little we could do about it other than counsel patience, and nothing at all to offer in the way of hope or comfort. In two attempts to break through his self-imposed barrier even Linda was met with the same icy aloofness. "He never gave a damn about Anthony when he was around," she complained, "now he's behaving like a bereft and inconsolable father."

It would change of course. The ice would melt into fury and fury into action and though it was difficult to see quite what could be achieved if the present impasse continued. I, for one, did not particularly want to be on hand when he saddled up that pale horse of his and went galloping off on his own private war.

Mitch and I did our best to get our heads down at the office and concentrate on other things but unfortunately there didn't seem to be a lot of other things to concentrate on. A solicitor buddy of mine in Redhill had hired us to run to earth the missing deeds of a large Elizabethan property in South Godstone about to come on to the market for possible conversion. Mitch went down there on the Thursday and miraculously discovered the ancient papers lurking between the pages of an enormous family Bible in the loft of a falling-down farmhouse near Lingfield. Flushed with success she spent the rest of the afternoon on the racecourse where she lost twenty-two pounds fifty on the Tote.

The same day, Thursday, Sam telephoned to tell me about Geoff Earnshaw's inquest which had taken place the day before. Murder by person or persons unknown. When George Prewitt, Sam's pathologist crony, gave his evidence about the possibility of the murder weapon being the butt end of a Luger pistol the coroner was singularly unimpressed. He had stared at Prewitt over his half-glasses with mild disbelief and a touch of the official condescension. "Did you have, Mr – ah – Prewitt, a particular – ah – model in mind perhaps? The Luger, as you are doubtless aware, has been in service for almost a hundred years – since, I believe, 1898 . . ."

"A P08!" George Prewitt had snapped back, irked by the man's nit-picking attitude. He had later confessed to Sam that he had no idea what the bloody model was and had been quite put out that the coroner should have known what a Luger was in the first place, let alone its bloody birthday.

Over the phone Sam gave a loud and succinct snort. "Expert witnesses, by their very nature and calling, never fail to get up coroners' noses. So what it all boils down to is that the CID is now in the process of launching a full-scale murder investigation – which is what we all expected. Did you see the local rag this morning? Full of uneducated speculation, pictures of Geoff and his mum, the house he lived in – with the headline: *When did you last see Geoff?* So far, thank God, no one's got on to his friendship with Anthony but it's only a question of time. And I'll tell you one thing – if Anthony now turns up dead we're going to find ourselves in a whole lot of hot water. At least, I am. I'll make it my business to keep you out of it as long as I can and see to it that George Raven does the same. So even if our hands are tied at least you'll be free to snoop around on your own. Mitch too, if that's how you want it. And incidentally, I took her advice and had a word with Lindy. The coloured boy's name is Roberts – Skip Roberts. You were right about him and Cath Brenner putting that car together; wrong about Cath being unmechanical. According to Lindy she knows more about engines than I do about crime or you do about acting. Otherwise, I'm afraid Lindy's not been all that much of a help. Apparently they have some sort of centre of operations, a one-time drama school – at least that's what Lindy thinks. She doesn't seem to know much about anything, but that's his doing, not hers. He just hasn't taken her into his confidence and that's what's really upset her."

"He obviously doesn't want her involved in whatever it is."

"Obviously. But why?"

"That's what we've got to find out, isn't it? We don't know where this place is, this school thing?"

"No we don't. He let slip one day that they were doing some work there – 'at the school' were his words. When she asked what school he looked bothered and said it had to do with this theatre scheme of theirs."

I broke in. "Look, Sam, why don't I get on with this? Give me the okay and I'll find that bloody place even if I have to put Cath and her black boy-friend on the rack and scream the truth out of them. But for God's sake, let's do something constructive instead of sitting about studying our navels and getting nowhere."

My impassioned plea fell on a lengthy interval of heavy breathing. "Sam," I urged, "speak to me. I know you're there, I can hear you breathing . . ."

He said stolidly, "Until Anthony turns up one way or the other I think we should lie low."

"You think he's dead!"

"If he isn't and we start nosing around there's a good chance he will be."

"Look, Sam, today's Thursday. The ransom was paid on Tuesday. How long do we wait, for Christ's sake? If he's alive why hasn't he turned up? Why would they still want to hang on to him?"

"Maybe they're having trouble shifting the diamonds. I don't know . . . I just don't know." I listened to the dull clicking of his tired old brain – or maybe he was just tapping out a distress signal on the telephone wire. At last he said, "Mark, one more day, right? One more, then we'll get together. Tomorrow. Maybe launch a pincer attack on George Raven and get some motivation from him. I'm so – personally tied up in all this that maybe I'm being too leery; but bear with me, will you, old son . . ."

"Okay, Sam, tomorrow."

On the Third Day, the Pentateuch informs us, the waters under the heaven were gathered together and the dry land appeared. On this particular third day the heavens were split asunder, the land submerged beneath an inch and a half of rain, and to round things off the calendar had decided to call it Friday the thirteenth.

A perfect day for a funeral. Geoff Earnshaw's funeral.

I spent the early morning grouching about the flat glaring dyspeptically through the condensation on the windows. Putting in an appearance at the cemetery hadn't been my idea but Sam's who had pointed out that funerals (*clambakes* had been his word) were rewarding affairs to attend if you wanted to see people showing their slips: "No more revealing place for the conscience-stricken than the brink of an open grave," he had informed me with the sort of heartlessness one might expect of a copper – retired or otherwise. "Of course, I've *got* to go," he had added with not a little ire, "because of Lindy and Thing – what's-her-name? – Cath, being on good terms with Earnshaw. And for his old Mum's sake, of course; she'd appreciate me being there. But you, Mark, if *you* could bring yourself thither it might well be worth your while. If you do manage it please don't stand about in all that black leather of yours and make an exhibition of yourself; stay in the background somewhere and keep a low profile if you've got one, and whatever you do don't be seen hobnobbing with me."

The first thing I saw on arrival at the cemetery gates was Cath's home-made vehicle staring rudely through the rear window of an elderly Allegro which could well be Mildred's.

I parked the Honda alongside and plunged in among the tombstones still wearing my crash-hat as a token sop to Sam's mutterings about keeping a low profile.

Though the cemetery was large and densely populated it took no time at all to locate the freshly dug grave with its attendant crowd of sober-suited mourners most of whom huddled beneath a shining canopy of dripping umbrellas. I was faintly surprised at their numbers until, wandering quietly on the outskirts, I realised that the majority seemed to be local sightseers, drawn by curiosity to witness the laying to rest of one of their number who had met death by violence in his own backyard. A narrow strip of no-man's-land separated them from the close-knit, black-clad huddle about the grave itself. The priest, hunched protectively over his book of words, cowered beneath an outsize umbrella held over him by a grubby looking individual in mud-stained black oilskins – the gravedigger perhaps.

Sam was there, without an umbrella, the rain dripping from the brim of his tired old hat; occasionally he wiped the end of his nose with a gloved hand. Beside him Linda, pale and drawn, stared bleakly at the plain coffin and looked as if she had forgotten where she was. The tiny bundle in black beside the priest with a handkerchief pressed to her mouth could only have been the dead boy's mother, whilst alongside her, resplendent in a bright yellow sou'wester – apart from the flowers the only splash of colour in sight – stood Cath Brenner, one comforting arm about the mother's shoulders, the other supporting an umbrella over the older woman's head.

Opposite her, facing me and staring blankly over the heads of the other mourners, was the gangly coloured boy I had seen with Cath at Covent Garden – Skip somebody – Skip Roberts. He was clearly ill at ease and certainly not into funerals, jigging gently from foot to foot, as if longing to take off; his shoulders jigged too, keeping time to some restless secret rhythm in his head.

The coffin was lowered into the grave as a great jumbo jet lumbered thunderously overhead, and the rain redoubled its force, beating down upon the surrounding umbrellas like a battery of side-drums.

Skip Roberts was right. Funerals weren't for me either. Sam could keep his theories; if there were any slips showing they weren't immediately visible to me.

I was about to move on when a voice said at my elbow, "You Mr Savage?"

A small boy of ten or thereabouts in a tattered school cap and a blue raincoat stood in a large puddle alongside, his eyes screwed up gargoyle-like against the teeming rain. I gave him a nod which he exchanged for a folded paper slid into my hand with the dexterity of one inured to the ways of secret agents the world over. "Bloke said to give you this," he muttered in a gravelly voice. "No answer," he added glancing furtively over his shoulder, and melted forthwith into the crowd as if he had never been.

I felt suddenly guilty, like a wartime spy being passed the latest sabotage reports whilst chatting up Adolf Hitler. I sensed watchful eyes. Cath had turned her head and was looking directly at me. She could not have missed the sabotage reports changing hands. Our eyes locked for what seemed like the best part of a quarter of an hour then I stuffed the paper nonchalantly into my anorak pocket and waggled some fingers in her direction.

Beneath the brim of her back-to-front sou'wester the cool watchfulness faded and was replaced by the faintest glimmer of a smile. A heavy clod of earth thumping on to the coffin in the grave drew her attention back to the matter in hand.

Like the boy before me I stepped back and faded into the crowd.

Beneath the wing of a crouching stone angel I peered at the paper.

Meet tonight 11.30 Windmill. Come alone. No Sam.

It was signed *AR*.

I turned the paper over. On the back of it was printed SWALK in thick black letters. Not hand-written but in heavy printer's type.

I heard myself give a deep prolonged groan.

Dear God, not another nocturnal appointment! What the hell was the matter with him? Why didn't he just look me up in the phone book and give me a ring like any other normal human being? The prospect of poncing around that flaming windmill not only in the middle of the night but also in the teeth of a screaming monsoon made me want to throw up. I glared belligerently at the paper before stuffing it away in the pocket of my anorak.

So he *was* part of SWALK. The entire operation had been nothing more than a con job to lighten his father's bank balance by half a million. But for what? And why so much?

I was aware of a growing distaste for Master Anthony Raven and the thought of meeting him face to face gave me no feeling of satisfaction other than being in a position to kick him in the crutch – hard.

From the shelter of a yew tree the boy who had delivered the note was watching me shrewdly. I strolled over to him slowly not wanting to scare him; he didn't budge.

"What did he look like, this bloke who gave you the note?"

He shrugged. "He was just a bloke – you know . . ."

"Tall, short, old, young . . . what?"

"Old. Nearly thirty I'd say. Tall."

I stared down at him. Anyone would be old in his eyes. And tall. "What did he say exactly?"

"Don't remember. He just pointed at you. 'That bloke in the crash-helmet' he said. 'Give him this, will you?' And he give me a quid too."

I made a face at him. "Big money. *Then* where did he go?"

"How do I know?"

"Was he fair or dark?"

"He had his hood up. He had a yellow mack with a hood."

I gave a heavy sigh and parted with a fifty pence piece. The information wasn't worth it but it might help him to buy a new cap.

Turning away with a mumbled thanks I caught a sudden glimpse of movement fifty yards away behind some tombstones – yellow movement; someone ducking away swiftly, darting between the graves towards the shelter of a clump of bushes.

Without looking where I was going I hared off after him, tripped and finished up sprawling over a muddy grave occupied by a J. Rex Hartington who, his stone informed me, had gone early to his rest in 1934.

I pretended not to hear the giggles of the boy behind me, brushed myself down and decided against further pursuit. To hell with it! It was the windmill at eleven thirty or nothing. I raised a thumb in the direction of the yellow rainwear. "Be there!" I bawled into the air.

The funeral was over. I elbowed my way through the throng of departing mourners cluttering up the narrow paths, pausing for a second or two to watch the man in muddy oilskins languidly take up a shovel and commence grave-filling operations. Morbidly I listened to the hollow thumpings of earth on wood and turned away.

Sam's Allegro had gone. Cath was straddling the Honda waiting for me, rain dripping from the brim of her sou'wester.

We stared at each other in silence for a couple of seconds then she nodded and said, "Hi".

"And 'hi' to you too."

She smiled. "When are we going on that ton-up you promised me?"

I stared up at the sky. "Not today, that's for certain – not in this weather."

She raised her face to the rain until it was a mask of wetness. "I love the rain."

"So do I," I told her, "but in its place and when I'm dressed for it."

"I love it to soak me – right through to the skin."

I eyed her rain-dark denim jacket and jeans and the purple jumper beaded with water. "What's the sou'wester for then?"

She removed it, flung it into the back of her car and ran her hands through her hair. "Come back for a drink," she said suddenly her eyes wide with challenge.

"Where's back?"

"Home." She swung herself off the Honda. "I'll lead the way. I'll give you a drink and a bath in that order."

My throat seemed to have closed up. I opened my mouth to say "no" but nothing came of it.

"Is it a deal?" Her lips curled in amusement at my obvious dilemma.

"Where's home?" I croaked.

"Not far, you'll see." She climbed into her car. "Follow me." She thumped hard at a starter button and the engine racketed into life, blue smoke pouring from the exhaust. "Come on," she called above the din. "Don't be a spoil sport."

The little car shot backwards from the cemetery gates, swung around almost within its own length and paused, trembling like a living entity. She ducked her head and peered at me from beneath the leaking hood. "Okay?" she mouthed.

I needed no further invitation. I felt suddenly light-headed and reckless. I buckled the strap of my helmet and straddled the Honda. She was away before I had rammed home the key.

Trapped in the perennial traffic-jam on Putney Hill I bubbled up alongside and eyed her impatient fingers drumming on the steering wheel; square efficient hands devoid of rings.

I leaned in at her open window. "Where's home?" I asked again, bawling to be heard above the din.

She gave me a sideways look, the only sort of look she could manage, and said nothing.

She lived on the river, on a boat which was no longer a boat but bobbed up and down and did all the unnecessary things boats do when left to themselves. I might have guessed she wouldn't have lived in an ordinary house built for normal human beings. The address, she said, was Cheyne Walk but it was a boat for all that, moored within hailing distance of Battersea Bridge.

Everything was on the move, wet and treacherous, including the look she gave me when she caught me dexterously in a grip of iron as I set foot on the first of a series of slippery pontoons and all but disappeared into the slurping drink below. I followed her with care, clutching at heaving wet rails and doing my best to keep upright. We arrived at last and she delved for keys.

"And mind your head," she warned, too late, as she safely ducked her own and led me down a set of steps into a surprisingly warm and comfortable cabin whose *Gemütlichkeit*, however, was somehow offset by the wall hangings: elegant prints of deadly weapons and destructive machines as devised by Leonardo da Vinci.

She caught me frowning at them. "You not like Leonardo?" she enquired in pidgin English.

"The world's most boring painting," I told her, "is the Mona Lisa."

I watched a raindrop roll fatly from her fringe on to the tip of her nose where she fielded it with the back of her hand. She grinned suddenly. "I hate it too. Take off your clothes and have a drink. What would you like?"

A smart little bar was tucked away in a corner; she edged herself behind it and began rattling bottles and glasses. "Whisky, gin, sherry, vodka . . . milk?"

"I'll have something unbruising," I said. "A tiny whisky-mac if you have such a thing. And I mean tiny," I added as she laid hands on a bottle of Teachers with considerable intent. "I'm not good at it any more – certainly not in the middle of the day, like now."

There was a warmth in her smile I had not seen before. "I read about your problems, didn't I?"

"Didn't everybody?"

She measured out a careful tot of spirits, added an equal amount of green ginger wine. "You were headlines for a whole week." She handed me the drink. "In danger of becoming the bore of the year, in fact. Was that the reason you never went back to acting?"

I shook my head. "I just . . . My nerve gave, that's all."

"Because of the accident?"

"That too, I suppose. But I'd probably have gone the same way without it. Acting's a mug's game if you're not a fanatic – all that dressing up and spouting other people's lines. It's no different from any other job in the end. It just *has* to pall – like going into an office every day."

She built herself a gigantic whisky-soda and disappeared through a door into another room.

"Do you like bubbles?"

"What?"

"In your bath."

I heard the running of water, went over and leaned in at the door of an unexpected and minute bathroom.

"Look," I said, "forget the bath. I'm only here for the beer."

"You're having a bath if I have to strip you off myself."

"That could be difficult," I growled, my throat dry and contracting steadily for the second time that morning.

She was squirting Badedas into the bijou bath with the prodigality of a car-wash machine. "Oh, I don't think it would be all that difficult," she murmured silkily, turning to look up at me, "do you?"

She drew down the zip of my anorak and when I took her hand in mine, slid voluptuously into my embrace. I felt the dampness of her hair against my cheek and the warmth of her body through my wet clothes. We steamed together for several sultry seconds. Over her shoulder I gave the pint-sized bath a critical eye. "There's not going to be room for the two of us in that thing," I said.

But we managed.

Half unconscious and listening with only half an ear to the incessant drumming of the rain on the deck above our heads, I lay beside her in the narrow, bunk-like bed, spent and utterly replete. It had been a remarkable afternoon. I had been well and truly, willingly and superbly laid.

If Nefertiti had anything like the physical guile, drive and attendant attributes as those wielded by Cath that afternoon, then Akhenaton must have been a very happy and contented – if exhausted – pharaoh. No wonder he died young.

Unaccustomed as I was to the quaintly acrobatic nature of moored river-craft I twice fell out of bed, striking my head on both occasions on the telephone which was tied up alongside and gave off a hollow clang like the end of a round in a boxing-ring; on both occasions I ignored the wild cackle of laughter and the quasi-tender concern from my companion and clambering breathlessly back on to the bed took up where I had left off. The second time it happened she packed me up like a parcel and wedged me rewardingly between herself and the wall – or bulkhead or whatever they call it.

I opened my eyes and stared blearily at the ceiling – or was that another bloody bulkhead? I turned my head and studied her sleeping profile.

The nose wasn't as nifty as Nefertiti's but it was still pretty splendid – good enough to breathe with anyway, which is all noses are about in the long run. A slight smile was playing about her lips.

I couldn't help but admire her. At the same time I didn't have to be told that any natural and physical charms I might possess had little to do with her flat-out endeavours to get me into her bed. I had been drawn into her riverside web as part of some as yet obscure plan of hers and she would have to be pretty thick not to realise that a smoothly smooth operator like me would be lying awake beside her at this very moment wondering what the hell she was up to and hoping that her next move would be as transparent as her first.

A stealthy glance at my watch told me it was coming up to four o'clock. To my right a tiny window was draped with a discreet and chintzy-type curtain. With a cautious finger I drew it back an inch or two and set my eyes to the crack of fading light.

A pair of black gumboots stood a yard away looking abandoned; when I raised my sights a couple of inches I discovered they were occupied by a sturdy pair of legs in wet jeans. I slid gently down into the bed; the steadily dripping skirt of yellow rainwear came into view. My ears began to thud. I let the curtain fall.

"What is it?" whispered Cath. She was watching me, a slightly amused frown on her face.

"Thought you were asleep," I grunted.

"Is something up?"

"Not a thing. Just a pair of wellies lounging about outside, that's all. You expecting anyone?"

She sat up, leaned across me and twitched the curtain aside and stared out into the rain. "Well, there's no one there now."

I laid my face alongside hers.

The boots were gone.

"Perhaps I imagined them."

She gave a secretive sort of smile. "Nothing like a pair of wellies to stimulate the imagination."

I made a show of studying my watch. "Time I was up and away."

"Where you off to?"

"I have work to do. I can't loll about here for the rest of the day."

She gave an uncharacteristic pout. "Just when we were getting on so well."

"So we were, so we were. You're a dear girl and full of hidden talents and I'd like nothing better than to shack up with you for the rest of the afternoon, but I have an office to run, things to do, papers to sign . . . and so on . . . Know what I mean?"

The telephone rang. She reached down for it with one hand, the other remaining flat against my bare chest, thus effectively pinning me to the wall. "Yes?"

The instrument babbled frenetically into her ear, and she jerked suddenly into an upright position. "What?" She turned a pair of startled eyes upon me, as if whatever it was she'd been told was my fault. "I don't believe it!"

"But why? Why would anyone do such a thing?" she cried. "It's so senseless . . ." She was listening again in some distress, staring at me intently as if I was aware of what was going on. She interrupted suddenly. "There's nothing anyone can do, is there?" I heard the word 'police' clearly. "Yes," she nodded impatiently. "I'm sure they are – like flies. God, what an obscene thing to do . . . Yes, yes, okay, Skip. Thanks for ringing . . . Yes . . . yes . . . Bye now."

There came a click as the caller hung up and I heard the dialling tone take over. She lay back on the pillow, frowning to herself, her eyes tight shut, the instrument cradled and forgotten on her shoulder.

"Something bad?" I asked tentatively.

Two tears seeped from between the closed lids and forged slowly down her cheeks.

"That bad?" I took the telephone from her grasp and lowered it over the side by the cord.

Her eyes brimming with tears were open now and she was staring at me in dogged disbelief.

"Someone's blown up Geoff's grave," she whispered.

Chapter Eight

The loitering gumboots were nowhere to be seen. A boy in football shorts and a woolly hat sheltered beneath a nearby tree, one industrious finger halfway up his nose; across the road, implacable on his plinth, sat Sir Thomas More resplendent in black and gold; both stared at me without interest as I started up the Honda and took off.

Though the rain had slackened a little and the sky seemed a touch brighter more wet threatened from the west.

I had phoned Sam from the boat. He was decently appalled and said to meet him at the cemetery. Where was I? Chelsea? Twenty minutes.

Cath showed no desire to accompany me. Rigid and silent she had sat staring blankly into space, naked until I had draped a bathrobe over her shoulders.

"Will you be all right?" I asked.

She looked at me as if she had never seen me before so I gave her a wave and departed.

Picking a serpentine path through the steady build-up of traffic along the Embankment and into the Fulham Road, I pondered the phenomenon of the exploding grave. What was the point of wiring up a coffin? To warn? To frighten? Threaten? Kill . . . ?

Cath's reaction to the incident had been excessive, I thought, but not noticeably tempered either with fright or an awareness of possible danger. As I saw it, the shock she had sustained had been caused by something other than the desecration of a grave containing the earthly remains of a one-time lover. If my first meeting with her, little more than twenty-four hours after Earnshaw's death, was anything to go by, she cared not a hoot in hell about him or his remains. No sign of loss or bereavement had betrayed those immaculate features.

I arrived at the cemetery ten minutes later than Sam had

stipulated. The usual crowd of sightseers had collected around the half-closed gates, many of them, I guessed, reporters and press photographers avid for the odd shot of scattered limbs. I elbowed my way through them and was doing quite well until I came face to face with an evil-looking policeman the size of a house and wearing a pointed helmet which made him look like a block of flats. He was wedged in the narrow opening between the gates and stared down his considerable nose at me with intense dislike. "You got business here, sir?"

"It's all right, constable," said a sour and familiar voice behind him. "He's the deceased boy's uncle." Sam's old tweed hat appeared around the law's massive shoulders.

The constable's face opened up like an empty suitcase then half closed again as an expression of sympathetic concern took over. He stepped back smartly on to Sam's foot and waved me through.

"Where the hell have you been?" growled Sam, limping a little as he stumped away down the main path. "And how did you get on to this? Don't tramp all over the graves, there's a good lad."

"Somebody rang up."

"Who somebody?"

"Skip Roberts."

"You don't know Skip Roberts."

"So?" I was beginning to feel and look a bit sheepish. "He rang Cath." He waited. "Brenner? You know Cath Brenner? Lindy's buddy?" I put question marks behind everything.

"I know who Cath Brenner is." He sounded cross.

"What are you so cross about?" I asked mildly. "I just happened to be with her at the time, that's all. Any questions?"

"Oh ho . . ." He sounded like Father Christmas. "Hobnobbing with the Brenner, are we?"

"Hobnobbing," I told him primly, "is a disgusting word the way you use it. Everything I did was in the line of duty."

"I'll bet." He moved on speaking over his shoulder. "How did she take the news?"

"She went into a decline."

"Did she say it was Skip ringing?"

"She called him by name on the phone; I was there and heard her."

"How'd he get to know about it, I wonder?"

"Heard the bang p'raps. Was it a big one?"

"Pretty big by all accounts and by the look of things over here. Bomb in the coffin apparently. Good title for a book that, *Bomb in the Coffin*." He stopped again. "Listen. You're Geoff Earnshaw's uncle if anyone wants to know. We've got Tom Hodder on the job here at the moment – my favourite inspector. He's a nosey blighter. Don't want him to rumble you. Don't let him get you into a corner whatever you do – he's a pretty sharp operator."

"You're a great help, I must say."

An awestruck silence came between us as we reached our destination.

What was left of the grave, and several others adjoining, was heavily screened and cordoned off by the police. Our arrival seemed to trigger off half a dozen arc-lamps which, powered by a rumbling generator parked nearby, splatted into life lending to the scene an air of utter and grotesque unreality – a horror film on night location. Though it was yet by no means dark the sudden illumination brought down the night like an iron curtain. Hunched black figures with pale hands and white faces prowled among the gaunt and toppled tombstones like grave-robbers caught in the act, stooping and squatting every now and again to snatch up some obscene piece of rubbish and stow it away with exaggerated care in glossy black plastic bags; one of them, silhouetted behind a green linen screen, knelt, hump-backed and misshapen, scrabbling with both hands in the mud and slime like some huge black dog digging up a bone.

A short figure in a massive overcoat and a large black hat detached itself from a tight group of others and moved with slow intent in our direction.

"Here he comes," muttered Sam out of the corner of his mouth. "Hodder, Inspector of that ilk. Mind how you go and keep that lip of yours buttoned up. And don't expect a welcome."

"Thought you'd left," said Hodder unsociably as he

came to a halt foursquare in front of us; he was talking to Sam but his beady black eyes never left mine. "Who's this?"

"The boy's uncle," said Sam.

"What boy's uncle?"

"That boy's uncle." Sam's eyes shifted to the scene of devastation. "Thought he had a right to be here – with your approval of course, Tom."

Hodder's moustache twitched irritably. "I hope you're suitably appalled," he said.

A sudden scurry of ice-cold wind whipping around us brought a shower of raindrops on to our shoulders from the branches of overhanging trees. Hodder glowered up at them. "Flaming weather doesn't help either. More rain, that's *all* we need." He stamped his feet and shivered inside his huge overcoat.

The same scurry of wind swept up a footloose piece of paper and stuck it firmly on to my chest. I snatched at it, glancing at it idly as I was about to dispose of it. In the bright spill of light I read the black letters: SWALK. In spite of the cold I felt my pulses jerk into some sort of life. I glanced sideways at Sam but he had noticed nothing. I turned the page over and narrowed my eyes at the reverse side. Nothing. It was blank.

My other hand crept stealthily into the pocket of my anorak. The note given me that morning was still there. So where the hell had this one come from?

I nudged Sam behind Hodder's back and offered him the paper. He took it slowly and stared at it for a full minute in silence. Our eyes met. He expelled his breath in a long drawn-out sigh. Hodder heard it, turned and sourly eyed the paper in Sam's fist. "And that's another thing," he grumbled. "What's all that about? They were everywhere, all over the place. We've collected dozens of them – all the same."

"SWALK," read Sam ponderously. "What's it mean?"

"Don't ask me. Like I said they were scattered all over the place. Stuffed away in the coffin I reckon, that's the simplest explanation. The bomb was probably wrapped up in them. How do I know?" He eyed me narrowly. "What about you? Do you know what it means?"

"Me? Why should I know?"

"You're his uncle, aren't you?" He was so unreasonable, this man.

I gave a heavy sigh. "All I know is that when I was at school it meant sealed with a loving kiss."

"Doesn't make sense anyway, does it?" he said huffily and stalked away.

"Tom," Sam called after him. He stopped and turned. "Would you mind very much if we went a little closer?"

The Inspector gave us each a searching glare then shrugged his shoulders mightily, as if relinquishing all responsibility. "But don't touch anything," he growled ungraciously and rejoined his group of stand-arounds.

Sam removed the paper from my grasp with a pair of delicate fingers and studied it moodily. "What the hell *does* it mean, Mark?"

"It means," I said bleakly after a pause, "it means that it has begun. They got their money and now they've got their bombs. And to prove it . . ." I gestured to the ghoulish proceedings before us.

Sam folded the paper meticulously. "The coffin of a dead man," he said slowly, "is an odd sort of choice for a first target, don't you think?"

I watched him reach for his wallet and stow away the paper carefully inside it. "But think of the publicity," I muttered unhappily. "Sealed with a loving kiss . . . A coffin for God's sake."

He frowned at me uncertainly as he tucked the wallet away again. "Publicity stunts are for actors," he said gruffly.

We moved slowly forward into the light, fastidiously careful of where we set our feet. Hodder's eyes were upon us. Sam's hand on my elbow steered me away from him.

"So . . ." he rumbled half to himself. "We have a bomb in the coffin and a handy set of pamphlets to tell us who put it there." He turned his head to look at me. "Right?"

"I'll buy that," I nodded. "That's easy. *How* they put it there's another matter."

"By busting into the undertakers presumably, or wherever the body was last night." He brooded in unhappy silence for a moment. "We haven't a hope in hell of getting there before

Hodder and his mob." His breath clouding about him isolated his head gargoyle-like from the rest of him.

I stared speculatively at the small static group huddled about Hodder, and came to a thoughtful halt. "Or have we?" I eyed Sam with a quizzical leer.

A whiff of something unmentionable from a gaping grave nearby made my nose wrinkle; a policeman with a mask over the lower half of his face was ferreting around in it with a certain amount of unwilling industry. "I'm not all that mad about this place anyway, are you?" I asked.

I couldn't see Sam's face but his mouth was on the twitch. "Then why don't we find a better 'ole to go to?" he murmured with a quick flash of dentures. "But . . ." He caught my arm as I strained forward like a greyhound in the slips. "Let's not make it too obvious, eh? Just ease ourselves out gently."

A couple of SWALK's calling cards fluttered at our feet; he stooped to pick them up; they were charred at the edges. "Bomb damage," he muttered. He thrust them casually into his pocket as he strolled out of the limelight with the sort of bumpy nonchalance which would have brought him a hoot from the gallery had he been on a stage. As an actor he was a ham – lovable, but a ham nevertheless.

The sudden upsurge of darkness as we left the lights sent us stumbling among the tombstones like a couple of drunks but we managed to make the gates without mishap. Giant Despair was still in charge. "Is there a telephone near here?" Sam asked. A great gloved hand pointed to a kiosk over the road only a few yards away.

"You're a good lad," Sam told him and made his day.

"Who're you ringing?" I asked as we sprinted heavily across the road.

"George Prewitt to start with. It's possible he'll know the undertaker who collected."

I let him get on with it. He emerged eventually in a cloud of steam and with a satisfied smirk on his shoulders.

"Merton High Street. Dickens and Jordan, Funeral Directors. Let's go."

"Leave it," I said as we approached Mildred's Allegro and he began scrabbling in his pocket for his keys. I released the Honda from her rest. "Jump on."

"Never!" He was being a ham again.

"Speed," I told him ramming my head into my crash-hat, "is the name of the game. Otherwise we'll have You-know-who breathing down our necks." He was a game old bird and climbed aboard without another word.

We lurched to a standstill outside Dickens and Jordan in three minutes flat. *Twenty-Four Hour Service* proclaimed a black and gold frame on a small brass easel in the window. "That's encouraging," muttered Sam as he unwound himself.

Mr Jordan turned out to be a small round jolly man, pink-cheeked and fastidiously elegant in black jacket and pin-stripes. He bowed from the waist as we entered.

"I was on the phone to you a moment ago," said Sam crushing the man's hand in his. "Inspector Chumley . . . And this is my sergeant – Sergeant York."

"Ah yes, Inspector . . . Sergeant," whispered Jordan sibilantly. "You have means of identification?"

Sam plunged a hand in his pocket and whilst Jordan was still scrabbling in a spectacle case for his glasses, flourished his wallet containing credit cards. By the time the glasses were on the undertaker's nose Sam's wallet was back in his pocket. I sweated. He was taking one hell of a chance but fortunately for both of us the little man took our identity as read.

"Perhaps you'd care to come this way, gentlemen?"

We followed him through a black-padded door into a narrow passage lit by a dim blue lamp. Except for the occasional creaking of Sam as he breathed the silence was intense. Mr Jordan paused at a door which sported a brass cross on its centre panel. "This particular Chapel of Rest is, at the moment, occupied but the bereaved relatives would, I'm sure, be the first to understand your – intrusion, if I may so put it?"

Noiselessly the door swung open. The sweet stench of countless wreaths made me want to reel.

At the head and foot of a half-draped open coffin resting on a plinth covered with purple silk burned huge candles in massive brass candlesticks; wreaths and other floral tributes banked on and round the plinth made the place look like a village flower show. I found myself cowering from it. Similarly

I avoided looking too often at the pink, shiny faced lady who lay snugly in the coffin her dead head resting on a whiter-than-white satin pillow. Mr Jordan noticed my reluctance. "She's only sleeping," he murmured softly in a slightly reproving tone. She looked dead to me.

Sam had ignored the entire set-up and was studying a hideous stained-glass window which glowed avidly in the gloom behind the coffin. "Is there any way in or out of this chapel other than that door?"

"None," Jordan assured him. "There's a window behind the stained glass but that hasn't been opened in years."

"May I?" asked Sam and without waiting for the go-ahead disappeared with a flourish behind the black velvet drapes backing the stained-glass monstrosity which I could now see was free-standing and lit from behind by a forty-watt electric bulb. Mr Jordan stirred uneasily in a pair of slightly squeaky shoes.

The lady in the coffin was very quiet. Sam had gone very quiet too. The minutes ticked by. I was about to explore the black depths of the wall-hangings when he reappeared alarmingly behind us, clearing his throat in the doorway and looking a trifle more dishevelled than usual.

If I was startled poor little Mr Jordan leapt a couple of inches in his shoes and gave a small hoot of dismay.

"I'm sorry to have to disillusion you, Mr Jordan, but far from that window not having been used in years, I would guess it was opened as recently as last night."

"But surely it is fastened from the inside?"

"Not just now it wasn't," Sam told him. "I climbed out of it and into your side passage and to prove it – here I am."

Mr Jordan, his mouth working silently for a moment, turned and sped through the curtains, to reappear a moment later hanging on to them like an elderly actor taking a curtain call.

"Do you keep a record of visitors to this – er – chapel?" Sam asked him.

"Record?" Jordan frowned through his confusion. "No, no, we don't. I fear not."

"Do you remember who came to view Mr Earnshaw's remains?" Sam persisted.

Jordan closed his eyes and screwed up his face.

"Owing to the unfortunate nature of the poor fellow's demise we only took delivery of the body yesterday." He glanced apprehensively at the still figure in the coffin. "I think perhaps, gentlemen, it might be more fitting if we were to – er – move elsewhere . . ."

Sam smiled wanly as we moved out into the shop.

"Last evening," Sam pressed him. "Did anyone visit him last evening?"

After a moment Jordan nodded. "A woman. Yes, a youngish woman, and later there was a man. The boy's brother he said he was."

I fielded a glance from Sam. "Do you remember what he looked like?"

Jordan shook his head in desperation. "We have three chapels here, you know – all were occupied – and there was a stream of visitors all evening. The woman was youngish as I said . . . in her thirties perhaps. I just don't seem to be able to remember anything. I'm really very sorry." He was wringing his hands.

"The man then," I interjected sensing Sam's growing exasperation.

Jordan thought for a moment. "An elder brother I would say. An accent of some sort, I think, but I couldn't place it. Northern . . . I don't know. Soft spoken, very polite. Wore a leather cap. I remember that particularly because he removed it almost at once as he came in. Overcoat . . . black, I think . . . that's all."

"Was he carrying anything? A parcel, suitcase . . . ?"

"No, I'm sure not."

"Fair or dark?"

"Mousey. Receding hair. Oh, and a green turtle-neck pullover . . . or polo-neck perhaps."

"Any gold teeth?" I asked. Sam glanced at me sharply. "Did you notice his teeth?"

A slow shake of Jordan's head depressed us all.

Sam looked pointedly at his watch. "Well, Mr Jordan, we may as well call it a day, I think. You've been very patient with us, and if you do remember anything else, the slightest thing, perhaps you'll be good enough to give me a ring." He scribbled a number on a pamphlet he found on the counter. "And I would ask you not to pass that on to anyone. It's a private line. And while we're about it, I think it might be best if you didn't mention this visit to anyone. Forget we've even been here. This is by the way of being an undercover investigation, you understand? Anti-Terrorist Squad. The local police are inclined to get twitchy if they know we're poking about in their manor and we're liable to tread on each other's heels quite badly if we're not careful – which can put up the prey before we're ready." He drew on his gloves. "The local inspector's name is Hodder, by the way, and he'll be with you very shortly I imagine. Please give him all the help you can – but you haven't seen us, remember? All right, Mr Jordan? Sorry about all this cloak and dagger stuff but it's sometimes essential. It's the upstairs administration which is at fault, not us, so it's out of our hands."

We shook hands all round, the distressed little undertaker standing forlornly at his door waving us off and wondering, no doubt, at the Anti-Terrorist Squad's unique form of transport.

We had got halfway to South Wimbledon Underground with Sam laughing merrily in my ear about the success of our mission when he suddenly remembered that we had left Mildred's Allegro standing outside the cemetery gates.

I did a smart U-bend and was turning into Haydon's Road when a police car steamed by going in the opposite direction. Sam gave a loud snort. "We cut that pretty fine, didn't we, old lad?"

"I'll tell you one thing," I bawled over my shoulder. "If old Hodder finds out about your goings-on this evening you'll end up behind bars."

"I won't be alone," he promised me loudly. "Impersonation of a police officer, remember?"

Chapter Nine

The BBC ran the story on the Nine o'Clock News.

Hugging a meagre splash of vodka in a large glass of apple juice I caught a gargantuan glimpse of Giant Despair regulating the traffic at the cemetery gates and watched with fascination as Inspector Hodder, looking like Napoleon in a moustache, tip-toed his way through a minefield of pertinent questions put by an astute and out-of-shot reporter. He had taken his hat off for the interview and spoke with that strangulated articulation which is apt to beset those unaccustomed to public speaking in front of a camera.

So it was out. SWALK had gone public. Tomorrow the papers would be full of it. *The Kiss of Death* was the banner headline Sam most favoured. We'd had a fifty pence bet on it.

I'd followed him back to Lauriston Road and we'd dawdled over tea and cream slices in his chronically untidy front room, trying to make some sort of sense of the latest development – or what *he* thought was the latest development.

What he *didn't* know about, and what I'd fought my better-self hard to keep from him, was the piece of paper with Anthony Raven's scrawled invitation on one side and SWALK on the other.

My decision to keep it to myself had nothing to do with its insistence on my keeping the appointment alone. I just felt that any exchanges to be made between AR and myself would be made a whole lot easier in the absence of an interested father-in-law.

He had employed me because I was younger and prettier and more capable of coping with the leg-work. So, toiling up to the windmill on a dark and stormy night was leg-work with a vengeance and if he'd still been a Chief Inspector he'd have sent his poor bloody sergeant to do it. Sergeant York, for God's sake!

I was in the kitchen clearing up the usual havoc created by my culinary efforts when the phone rang.

It was Sam. "You watching the news?" he demanded without preamble.

"I've just seen it, yes."

"Get back on to it. There's something else."

I flung the instrument on to its rest and doubled back to the set punching up the sound on the controls as I went.

Flames engulfed the screen; in the foreground the milling silhouettes of firemen fighting the blaze. The commentator was saying, ". . . . less than a hour ago. The windows of private dwellings and warehouses were blown out by the blast which was heard several miles away. It was thought initially that the explosion was caused by a leaking gas-main but firemen, forcing an entry into the rear of the building, have discovered what they believe to be a considerable *cache* of arms and ammunition. One fireman recovering after having been overcome by smoke warned of a pile of what looked like steel ammunition boxes stacked against an inside wall; he was unable to get closer to ascertain either their contents or the markings on the boxes."

The commentator appeared against a background of swirling black smoke bawling into a hand microphone to make himself heard above the din. "This extra hazard – the possible presence of live ammunition on the premises – has placed the firefighters in extreme danger and the police have spread a wide cordon around the stricken building and sealed off the area to all civilian traffic."

As the camera tracked back from his face he flourished a handful of familiar looking leaflets. "The presence of these papers has led the police to believe that this apparently disused house was the headquarters of a terrorist organisation calling themselves by the initials S-W-A-L-K which you can see on each of these. These leaflets are similar to ones discovered earlier in the day in the desecrated grave of Geoffrey Earnshaw who was found dead of head wounds on Wimbledon Common last week. So far no organisation has admitted responsibility for either of these incidents." The picture dissolved and the studio newscaster appeared.

"Because of the extreme danger of further explosions the police are advising all road traffic and pedestrians to keep clear of the area. Road blocks have been set up and alternative routes designated. And now sport . . ."

I cut the sound and sat staring soberly at the silent scoreboards.

The phone again. Sam. "Did you catch it?"

"Sounds like they blew themselves up," I said. "I missed the location of the fire – where was it? And *what* was it? Residential, warehouse or what?"

"An ordinary dwelling house, dilapidated and falling to pieces, officially unoccupied but with a local rumour that squatters had moved in. No bodies so far, but it looked pretty hairy in there – they could be buried in the rubble." He paused. "This is getting out of hand."

I said, "It's getting out of *our* hands, that's for sure. We're not going to be able to cope with that scale of things."

Another pause. "So what do we do?" Uncertainty thickened the words. "Give up?"

I passed the buck. "You're the boss."

"Perhaps we should go over there – have a bit of a recce."

"Where's there?"

"Wapping."

"Dear God! I've always wanted to go to Wapping on a night like this. Nothing doing, Sam." I inserted a hacking cough. "I'm sickening for something, I think. As a matter of fact I was just about to go to bed with a hot lemon." He cleared his throat. I raced on. "What could we do anyway? The place is crawling with cops and firemen. We wouldn't be able to get near."

"Wanna bet?"

"Sam, no. You'll get the chop if you're caught loitering around these trouble spots. Better me than you – at least I'd have an excuse – but I'm sick. Why don't we go over there tomorrow when things have died down a bit – and I feel better . . . perhaps?"

"Fred might get in there," he mused quietly.

"Fred? Who's Fred?"

"Saunders, my old sergeant, now inspector. He could inveigle himself in there."

"For God's sake, Sam, he's still a cop. He's not going to throw up the Force and start working for you."

"He owes me."

"Come off it, Sam. How sympathetic were you to the old boy network when you were active? Eh? What?" Silence. "That's better." It was like talking to a child. "Tomorrow will be soon enough. I'll go down there first thing in the morning – if I'm better – and mingle with the press. Right, Sam?"

"We've *got* to get in there, Mark," he growled stubbornly.

"You can't until they put the fucking fire out!" I yelled at him, suddenly incensed.

"Don't swear at me, there's a good lad."

"You make me mad."

"That's your problem, not mine."

"Tomorrow, Sam," I pleaded. "We'll talk about it tomorrow morning early. I promise." I slipped in another bout of coughing.

"You sound as if you might be dead tomorrow," he complained mildly.

"In my present mood that would suit me fine."

"Goodnight then, old man, and sleep well . . . And Mark . . . ?"

"What?"

"What's the hot lemon's name?"

"Go to hell."

The grunt he made as he hung up sounded mighty like a chuckle. I dialled his number. It rang once.

"What?"

"Sorry, Sam."

"You're welcome," he growled. "Go to bed."

The weatherman, backed by an impressive set of closely woven isobars, was clucking and gesturing over his charts like a stand-up comic. Even without sound the doom-laden message came over loud and clear.

I switched off the set and went back to finish up in the kitchen feeling guilty about Sam and wondering whether he would in fact haul himself off to Wapping.

The phone rang again. I snatched up the instrument. "I've gone to bed, Sam."

"It's not Sam," said a cool, taut voice. "It's me . . . Cath." There was a slight pause. "Have you really gone to bed?"

"Why?"

"I need to talk to you."

"Talk away."

"Not on the phone. Can you . . . could you come over?"

"What now?" I scarcely suppressed a groan. It was nice to be wanted, I suppose – nice but inconvenient. "Not tonight I can't, I was just on my way out."

A pause. "I have things to tell you, Mark. Important things."

"Tomorrow . . . won't that be soon enough?"

"I don't think they can wait that long." She sounded pretty fed up, I thought. She wasn't the only one. She added hesitantly, lowering her voice a little almost as if she were looking over her shoulder, "Did you happen to see the news tonight – on the box?"

"I just did, yes." Everyone had been watching the news.

Her voice dropped another notch. "That's what I want to talk to you about – Geoff and me – and – er – other things . . ."

For an indecisive second or two I listened to her breathing. It was an invitation I couldn't afford to turn down. "Cath, listen, I've got a date later on tonight but if you really and truly want me to come over . . ."

"Please, Mark . . ."

I frowned. There was an urgency in her voice which worried me. "You all right?" She didn't answer. "Look, it's just after nine thirty. Give me twenty minutes, okay, and I'll be with you. But I can only stay for an hour at the outside, right?"

"That'll be fine. I'm so sorry, Mark, it's a hell of a night to turn out in . . . thanks."

"Think nothing of it . . ." I hung up abruptly.

Now what was she on about? Damn and blast! I needed a trip to Chelsea and back like I needed a hole in the head. I had intended to get to the windmill early so as to sniff around a bit before my date arrived; now I'd be lucky even to get there on time.

I peered out into the darkness. It was the night of the deluge. Noah was building his ark; I could hear him hammering. "Oh shit!" I said aloud. Why didn't I ring Sam and make *him* come too? I would serve him right, poor old sod!

I drew a pair of waterproof trousers over my jeans, thick

socks and Hunter boots, climbed into a sturdy rubber trenchcoat, and rammed a flashlight into its pocket.

A couple of minutes later I was hurtling through the maze of red lights guarding the holes in the High Street, and all but drowned a lone pedestrian who was minding his own business on a traffic island.

The river was black oil and except for the spanning lights of the bridges hardly discernible from the rest of the murky sludge. I had no idea what the bloody boat was called and couldn't even remember where it was berthed.

I did, however, remember Sir Thomas More, so I went to look him up, knowing that he'd give my sense of direction a jolt and put me right. He looked as fed up as I was, sitting there on his plinth without an umbrella. He said to leave the Honda with him and walk the rest of the way, which I did. Heavy with rain and misgivings.

The slap and swill of high water together with the creaking and bumping of moored craft made the whole thing sound like a scene out of *Moby Dick* and increased my chronic feeling of depression and uneasiness. I had a creepy feeling that I was walking into a trap.

Stumbling along the pontoons and wishing everything wasn't so desperately on the move, I managed with the aid of the flashlight to single out the vessel I was looking for – blue and white with a crooked chimney.

Painted on a theatrical looking life-belt to which I wouldn't have trusted my worst enemy was the word *Chessene* which must have meant something to somebody but did nothing for me. A light was burning in the cabin. I pushed open the door and leaned in. "Ahoy there . . ." I called quietly. "Chessene . . . ?"

My scalp began to crawl. The stairs creaked loudly beneath my weight. I steadied myself with a hand against the wall as I descended.

The cabin was empty.

"Cath . . . ?"

The faint odour of tobacco smoke twitched at my nostrils. Did Cath smoke? I couldn't remember seeing her with a cigarette.

The vessel strained and creaked in the heavy swell; rain

thudded monotonously overhead and the overture to *The Flying Dutchman* was working its way to a climax on a neighbouring hi-fi. I could heard another sound, a faint familiar humming I couldn't immediately place.

The bed was disturbed but no more than when I left it a few hours before. The telephone, upended on the deck beside it, was off its rest. The humming was the dialling tone. I replaced the handpiece. No need for panic stations; had the instrument been on the bed a sudden roll of the boat might easily have dislodged it.

Quietly I shoved open the bathroom door. You couldn't have hidden a cat in there. Half a glass of something was balanced precariously on the edge of the bath. I sniffed at it. Whisky. Probably the one Cath had been drinking when our mutual yearnings had got the better of us. I replaced the glass; it teetered perilously; I put out a hand to save it but it didn't fall. I stared at it soberly. Any undue motion of the boat which could have dislodged the telephone would also have toppled the glass.

Turning my back on the bathroom I surveyed the cabin with care. Various small discrepancies began to assert themselves. One of the Leonardo prints on the wall was off true; a crack in the glass, a corner of it splintered. On the carpet beneath it lay an open book, a page torn, its spine slightly damaged. I picked it up. Beneath it was revealed a large muddied footprint, the tell-tale crossbars of a rubber boot – a man's boot. Beside it and a little behind was another. He had stood facing her and she had heaved the book at him; he had ducked, the book had struck the picture frame . . .

I riffled through the book. *Kidnapped* by Robert Louis Stevenson. That was apt too. On the fly leaf, in fair round childish hand, the name *Katherine Brenner*.

I put it down on a low bookshelf alongside an ashtray in which lay the residue of three filter-tipped Dunhills. Another, half smoked, had been ground with determination into the carpet just inside the door.

I stood havering for a second or two reviewing both the situation and the compact little cabin. She wasn't here, that was for sure, so I'd have to search the bloody boat. Muttering gloomily to myself I climbed the steps to the door. When I turned the handle the bloody thing flew open and all but impacted me into the wall. The wind and the rain howled past like a couple of rowdies intent on vandalising the cabin. Shouldering my way out into the filthy night I dragged the door shut with all my strength and stood panting for a second to get my breath back.

It was then that I realised I was not alone. Something moved on the periphery of my vision, something bulking blacker against the darkness, something which ducked and disappeared from the skyline.

I dutifully froze and groped around blindly in the hope of finding a weapon of some kind. To hear better I quietly removed my crash-hat. The murk was only slightly relieved by a filtering of pinkish illumination from the street lighting on the Embankment; I could also make out some overhead lamps presumably intended to serve the little community of boat-dwellers, but for some reason they weren't burning.

The shadow I had registered had been to my right. Flattening myself against the upperworks of the cabin I moved cautiously, step by step, in the opposite direction. The wind, which had increased considerably since I had first set foot on this miserable barge only a few minutes before, now tugged at the skirts of my heavy mack and flapped and beat them against the walls of the cabin like a tattoo of drums. All I needed to announce my whereabouts, I thought venomously, was a fanfare of frigging trumpets.

My foot came upon the weapon I had been looking for: a sturdy wooden off-cut, two inches by two, and a couple of feet long. Enclosed in my fist it made me feel a whole lot better.

Crabbing cautiously around a corner, I found myself with relief in the lee of the wind and breathed more easily, my back to the wall, a narrow decking of about eighteen inches between me and the outside rail. I latched hold of this frantically as the vessel gave a sudden lurch. Beyond the rail the neighbouring boat, separated only by a couple of old motor-tyres hanging over its side, heaved and groaned alongside.

I arrived at another door, let myself in to whatever it was and closed the door quietly behind me. The heat after the outside cold was intense. It had to be the galley.

Not wanting to risk the flashlight I groped my way in utter

darkness until my foot encountered a downward step. Eight down . . . four more than those into the cabin.

I was right about the galley. The dull glow of what looked like an Aga stove was the source of heat.

I stiffened. Somewhere I thought I heard the sound of a stealthy footfall. Galleys being notorious for suspended kitchen utensils – I could hear them clanking in the swaying darkness – I stood quite still for a full half-minute allowing my eyes to accustom themselves to the gloom.

The glow of the lamps on the Embankment filtered through the two small windows which came complete with curtains. I closed the curtains and risked a guarded beam of torchlight. Apart from the usual accoutrements the galley was empty.

A mat of some sort fouled my foot. As I stopped to rid myself of it a metal ring sunk into the deck beneath it glinted in the light. A trap-door.

Dowsing the torch I knelt and heaved on the ring. Hinges creaked appallingly. Stale, tobacco-polluted air surged up from below like a plague.

Sticking my head into the aperture – the best way I know of getting it shot off by anyone who had half a mind to have a go – I swept the beam of the torch around the confined space revealed below.

A small bunk-bed, a littered table and a plain kitchen chair appeared to be its only assets. No steps or ladder by which to descend.

Curiosity got the better of me and shoving my two by two into one pocket and the flashlight into the other I swung myself down and closed the trap behind me.

I could barely stand upright. The darkness was absolute. I groped for the torch.

The place was claustrophobic and windowless, the only way in or out by the trap . . . trap being the operative word.

The narrow bunk bearing rumpled sheets and blankets had clearly been occupied quite recently. Across the foot of it lay a white raincoat. I went through the pockets. A grubby handkerchief, a pencil without a point and a key to somebody's castle door; it was enormous and looked so interesting that I shoved it into my pocket and turned my attention to the table. It was all pretty sordid: a hurricane lamp and the remains of a do-it-yourself meal – fish fingers and chips at a guess – a half-empty Thermos flask, a dirty glass smelling strongly of gin, a crumpled packet of Player's Specials and a noisome ashtray overflowing with fag-ends. On a corner of the table, a small pile of notepaper; at least that's what it looked like until I turned over the top sheet and found the letters SWALK staring me in the face.

I riffled through the rest of them.

Well, well, Cath Brenner . . . who and what have we here, lying low in the bilges of your floating homestead?

I felt sick and disillusioned. God knows why. It was not as if I had ever really trusted her. But even a one-night stand can have its complications. Cath was my sort of female – intelligent, capable, forthright with nothing of the helpless little woman about her, and being so, the very fact that she had called me and was not now on hand to greet me was beginning to fill me with the sort of forebodings I was not anxious to contemplate – especially when faced with the small but irrefutable evidence of a scuffle in the cabin.

I wanted to wash my hands of the whole thing and probably would have done had I not been incarcerated in the bilges of a houseboat with an unknown adversary prowling the decks above me and probably lusting for my blood – and had I not also, at that very moment, taken a belated look under the bed and discovered, alongside a pair of muddy shoes, an ordinary black canvas airline bag.

Squatting beside it I drew open the zip. I sighed. Just what I needed: somebody's dirty laundry. Yet the bag was heavier than somebody's dirty laundry – heavier by a good couple of pounds of something swathed in a striped pyjama top.

I knew exactly what it was before the torchlight picked up the sinister, elegant lines of a Luger pistol. A P08.

I laid it carefully aside and scrabbled on through the bag like a customs officer on the rummage. A smaller bundle folded neatly into a yellow duster. I placed its contents one by one alongside the gun: a Seiko Quartz wristwatch, a gold signet ring and a man's silver bracelet. I didn't even attempt to unravel the entwined monogram on the ring for the single word engraved on the name plate of the bracelet made it unnecessary: GEOFF.

With sober disbelief I regarded the incriminating evidence of a brutal murder.

A sudden heavy creaking overhead plunged me into darkness. I put the torch on one side and by touch alone collected up the various items, silently rewrapping them and placing them inside the canvas bag.

He was in the galley above, his careful steps audible above the straining and shifting of the boat. I withdrew to the corner furthest from the trap and waited. Only then did I remember the Luger.

Snatching up the bag again, I freed the gun from its shrouding and checked the magazine. My fingers told me it was fully loaded. I slid the magazine back into position and, since I had no intention of firing the thing, thumbed down the safety-catch.

As I pressed my back against the wall I peered at the glowing green digits of my watch. Twenty-two twenty. If I was to make it to the windmill by eleven thirty, time was already running out. Why couldn't the silly bugger have jumped me the moment I set foot on board – we might have got all this over by now.

I heard him stumble and stopped breathing. I knew exactly what he had done – he'd tripped over the mat as I had done. Then there came the faintest clink of metal against metal as he touched the brass ring sunk into the deck. My throat went dry. If he guessed I was down here he would only have to lob in a fireball and I'd go up in a cloud of smoke. I shoved my head into my crash-hat.

The hinges of the trap-door grating together sounded like the crack of doom. A narrow sliver of diffused light appeared on the wall opposite and grew less narrow as the trap was raised slowly and with extreme caution. I knew exactly how he felt but when I had arrived the place had been unoccupied; now it was packed to the gunwales with flesh and blood, bone and muscle – 168 pounds of it – not to mention a fully loaded Luger P08 and a two-foot length of two by two as a sturdy standby.

Frankly I didn't go a lot for his chances.

Now I could make out the shape of his head and the shadow of his arm supporting the trap.

A voice whispered hoarsely, "Tone . . . ?"

A narrow shaft of light played for a second over the table and steadied on the bunk. I stared at it mesmerised, wondering whether I'd left anything around to arouse his suspicions. The white raincoat was sprawled obscenely across the bed like a legless body . . .

"You there, Tony?"

The creaking ceased, the trap fully open.

Then he did what I had done, but with less good fortune. He stuck his head into the aperture and with it the torch, the beam of which caught me full in the eyes as I reached up, locked my left arm about his neck, hung on to it like a giant squid and dragged him down with every ounce of strength I could muster.

He gave a strangled cry and came rocketing through the trap like a cat out of a tree, landed on his head at my feet, uttered a deep-felt groan, rolled himself into a ball and passed out.

The sound his head had given off as it made contact with the deck turned my stomach.

I caught up his fallen torch and directed its beam on to his face. There appeared to be no blood and he was still breathing – stertorously, but breathing. He had probably concussed himself.

Lighting the hurricane lamp, I trimmed it and placed it by his head, listening anxiously for a moment for any extraneous noises up top indicating that he might not have been alone.

I moved the chair out from the table, parked it beside the lamp and straddled it, holding the gun loosely in my hand. When and if he revived, and I hoped he wouldn't take too long about it, he'd have a nasty shock. Sitting there with the light shining up into my face I would look like the Phantom of the Opera.

I leaned over the back of the chair and peered down at him.

Late twenties or thereabouts and looking not unlike the late Tom Eliot: narrow-faced, long, lank black hair straggling now across an unshaven jaw. The skin was pallid and slightly blotchy. I am bound to say that he didn't look at all well.

He was wearing indecently tight blue jeans tucked into gumboots mighty like those I had glimpsed through the window after my exertions with Cath – though gumboots being gumboots there is little to distinguish one pair from another – and, almost unsurprisingly, a wet yellow anorak similar to those worn by the skaters at Covent Garden.

From the exposed hip-pocket of his jeans I extracted a wallet and took a quick gander at its contents. He was not doing very well – two pounds and a thirteen pence postage stamp. His name according to an Access Card was Leonard O'Toole. A coloured, passport-size photograph showed him cheek by jowl with a vapid-looking blonde piece who looked like Monroe without the Mouth. They both looked drunk and probably had been at the time.

I stuck the wallet back and went through the rest of him. The pockets of his anorak were like a schoolboy's crammed with bits of junk, and a small diary, containing it seemed little else than assignations with one Wanda – she of the photograph I guessed. Today's date bore the words *G's Funeral*.

As I flicked through the rest of it I came across a piece of stamp-paper stuck across the inside back cover. WEST, it said, and a telephone number, the last four digits, curiously enough, being the year of my birth. With a modicum of effort I might remember that. The exchange number, 265, meant nothing to me.

A low groan came from the prone figure at my feet. I shoved the rubbish back into his pockets, reached for the Thermos flask and poured cold black coffee over his head. He spluttered a bit, and made a couple of hand gestures like someone swatting a fly, then slowly opened his eyes to find himself staring up the muzzle of a Luger pistol.

"Hi Len," I greeted him cordially. "You've been fighting again."

With considerable effort the eyes focused on my face, then closed again in disbelief.

I gave him a friendly kick in the ribs.

"Fuck off . . ." he mumbled querulously, and then, stirring himself, wiped his coffee-stained face with the palm of his hand. "You lousy sod. You've split my head open."

"I didn't do anything of the kind – you fell on the bloody thing."

With an ungainly effort he struggled to his knees, peering up at me through black narrowed eyes. Kneeling at my feet with his hands still on his head he looked like a prisoner waiting for the *coup de grâce*. Something stirred in me uneasily. I jerked the gun at him. "Get over there by the bed." He made a sudden lurching movement in my direction. I jabbed the gun in his stomach. "Don't even try it, mate."

"Fuck you!" he snarled again.

"And please don't swear at me, there's a good lad," I added gently, taking a leaf out of Sam's book, "or I'll put a bullet through your foot."

His teeth closed over his lower lip forming the initial "f". I pushed up the safety-catch and pointed the gun at his foot. For some reason he took me seriously and after a tense moment half crawled to the bunk where he squatted on the floor and watched me with sullen distaste.

"What do you want?" Suddenly he was whining. "What have *I* done? And how do you know my name?"

"One, I want some answers. Two, you're you, that's what *you've* done; and three, I know a lot more about you than just your name – believe me. And four . . ." I glanced significantly at my watch, "I have just ten minutes to waste on you – after that . . ." I gave him a theatrical shrug which didn't mean anything but seemed to put the fear of God into him.

"What do you want to know?"

"Where's Cath?"

"I don't know." I sighed loudly. His voice went up a notch. "I don't, I tell you, honest I don't. I was just told to come and – look after you . . ."

"Look – after – me?" I repeated slowly. He lowered his eyes. "*How* look after me?"

"I was supposed to – keep you here."

"How? Kill me?"

"Don't be bloody daft. Why would I want to kill you?" He spread his hands in a sudden reasonable gesture which made his head ache and brought a grimace of pain to his face. "Look . . . I just work here, right? 'Knock him out if you have to,' he says, 'but don't let him off that boat.'"

"Who says?"

"Get stuffed! *You're* so f . . ." he pulled himself up hastily as the gun muzzle dipped a little, "so frigging clever *you* tell *me*!"

I didn't have a notion who he was talking about. But for

some completely irrelevant reason I remembered that scrappy bit of stamp-paper stuck so importantly to the back cover of his diary.

"West," I heard myself say. Not a question but a statement and it hit the jackpot. It was a chance in a million – like backing an outsider with everything you've got and watching it take to its heels and run like the clappers – but it came off. And he didn't even evince any surprise.

"If you know it all, why bother to ask?" He sounded fed up.

I did my best not to show my satisfaction. "And Cath's with him?"

He shrugged. "How the hell should I know? I don't know what they do in their spare time, do I?"

"If she *is* with him she wouldn't have gone of her own accord, would she?"

"Why wouldn't she? Nobody tells her what to do – not even him." His eyes narrowed suddenly and he squinnied up at me with a sort of knowing leer. "You've got something on him, haven't you?" He shook his head slowly and made a hissing sound between his teeth. "You watch your step, mate. He's like a cartload o' monkeys, he'll have you before you know what day it is . . . . What you got on him?"

"You mind your own bloody business."

"Okay, okay . . ." He raised his hands. "Keep your hair on."

"What's happened to Tony?" I asked. "Where's he got to?"

"Search me, I don't know. I thought he was here. He's hopped it, I 'spect. No good asking me. Nobody tells me nothing. If you really want to know what *I* think . . ." He stopped.

"What do you think?"

"I think somebody's grassed on us, that's what I think."

I nodded slowly. "West thinks it was you."

He stared at me wordlessly for a couple of seconds his eyes widening with growing fear. "Me?"

I wobbled my head. "That's what he said. 'Old Len's been spilling the beans.' That's just what the man said . . . his very words. 'Can't trust old Len, can we?' he said."

Slowly he climbed to his feet, his eyes mesmerised by the gun directed at his midriff. He licked his lips. "I haven't said a word to anyone," he whispered hoarsely. "I don't know anything or anybody. How the hell could I talk if I don't know anybody? You're all fucking mad . . . No don't!" Panic stricken he raised his hands in front of him as if to push the gun away. "Sorry . . . I'm sorry . . . I didn't meant it, it just come out natural like . . ." He broke off when he saw I wasn't about to shoot his foot off. There was silence for a bit while he ran his fingers gingerly over his bruised head. Then he frowned suddenly. "What about Cath?" he asked, a cunning look in his eye. "Cath would have known someone, wouldn't she? She knows everybody. She could have let something slip . . ." He caught sight of my face. "Not knowingly of course – she'd never do it knowingly . . . not Cath . . ."

I nodded at the littered table. "How about him?"

He looked surprised. "Tone?" He shook his head. "Nah . . . He's been holed up here all the time. He's been stuck here for days."

"He's not here now though, is he?"

He stared at me blankly. "That's right, he's not, is he? I wonder . . . ?" Another heavier frown darkened his pale features. "No, it wouldn't be him. Why would *he* bugger it all up? Him of all people. He started it all. It was his money."

"His dad's money," I corrected mildly.

"Same thing, isn't it? But if it hadn't been for him and poor old Geoff . . ." He broke off.

"Exactly," I said succinctly. "Poor old Geoff . . ."

He eyed me steadily, lapping again at his lips. "What are you getting at?"

I waggled the gun at him. "This was the thing that killed poor old Geoff."

He stared at it as if it had grown a head. "That?"

I nodded. "This. Found under Tone's bed. That bed. There . . ." I pointed.

"Never."

"True."

He just stood and stared. He had nothing more to say to that. Then he shook his head abruptly. "He wouldn't hurt a fly, Tone wouldn't."

He was so emphatic that I almost breathed a sigh of relief. It was something *I* wanted to believe too.

"Is he scared of West?" I asked suddenly.

He brooded for a bit, staring at the remains of the meal on the table as if for inspiration. Finally he said, "He doesn't scare easy, but he doesn't go a bundle on him. None of us do. But he gets things done. He's got the contacts, hasn't he?"

"Who are we talking about?"

"West, who else?"

"What contacts has he got?"

I sounded too eager. I could have bitten my tongue out. I cursed my big unthinking mouth.

He regarded me nastily, his lip on the curl. "You're a bloody nark, aren't you?" The eyes had become alert and watchful.

"I'm nobody's nark," I told him as calmly as I could. "But I think you're in a lot more trouble than you realise. Were you at Geoff's funeral this morning?" He didn't answer but a flicker of his eyelids told me he had been there. "And *you* put the bomb in the coffin, didn't you?"

That got him. Rearing awkwardly to his feet he stood glowering at me, his useful hands clenching and unclenching themselves spasmodically, only the gun levelled at his chest preventing him from putting his head down and charging me. "Don't be so f . . ."

"If *you* didn't, who did?" I interrupted. "Tell me that, Len. Was *West* at the funeral? Well, was he? Did *you* see him? Because *I* didn't. I was there and didn't see him. I saw Skip, I saw Cath, I saw you, but there was no sign of West, was there? Do you know something?" I paused only for a second before grasping the nettle. "That bomb was scheduled to go off when all of you lot were gathered round that grave. You didn't know that, did you? Fortunately for you and Skip and Cath – to say nothing of a lot of innocent people – the mechanism got stuck and the thing didn't explode until later when, thank God and your lucky stars, no one was around to get hurt. Otherwise you'd all be up on a murder charge. And you'd better believe me."

He was glaring at me with his mouth half open. "I don't know what the hell you're talking about," he snarled eventually.

I lurched precipitately to my feet, reached for a handful of the papers on the table and threw them at his feet. "That's what I'm talking about. Those things were wrapped round the bloody bomb and only you and the rest of your mob had access to them, right? And you can deny that until the cows come home and nobody, nobody at all, is going to believe you."

"I never had nothing to do with it," he shouted. "None of us did. None of us knew anything about how those things got to be there."

"*I* do," I yelled back at him and after a pause added more quietly, "West."

"Why? Why would he do a thing like that?"

"Who's got the money, Len?" I asked gently. I was making up the script as I went along but suddenly, instinctively, I knew I was on the right track.

"Money?" His brows contracted slowly as an ugly suspicion began to curdle his already stricken features.

"One half million pounds' worth of diamonds, Len. Who has the custody of that? Who was responsible for converting the stones into ready cash? Who is it who – *knows* the sort of people who have five hundred thousand pounds stashed away at the ready in their piggy-banks? Not Cath, nor Skip either, not by a long chalk, and not Tony who's just a means to an end. And certainly not you, Len, not you . . . So who?"

The seconds ticked by remorselessly as he digested this diatribe of claptrap. But claptrap or not I was on to it – I knew I was on to it. I was almost trembling with excitement.

He was staring at me without seeing me, rehearsing and recollecting actions and conversations of which I knew nothing and had only guessed at. "West," he whispered at last, his lips barely moving. "West had the contact, a man named . . ." He paused endlessly then shook his head in vague despair. "I can't remember the name. Some – American I think he said. I can't remember. Cath will know . . ." He looked at me with a pathetic sort of hope in his eyes. "I'm sure she'll remember."

"But we don't know where she is, do we?" He shook his head gingerly, clearly distressed by his ignorance, and slumped slowly on to the edge of the bunk. "Or West?" I pressed him roughly. "Do you know where West is? The sooner we find him the sooner you'll be off the hook. For God's sake, try to remember. What did he say to you?"

He was a long time making up his mind then he shrugged in sudden helplessness. "Wimbledon. He said he had to go over to Wimbledon."

I stared at him in growing horror. I glanced quickly at my watch. Twenty-two forty-five. "Oh my God!" I stepped over to him and jerked him to his feet by the front of his anorak. "Listen, is Tony really a buddy of yours? Do you care anything at all about what happens to him?"

He tried to throw me off, startled by my sudden violence. "Course I care."

"Right, then you bloody well come with me. I may need your help."

"Where? Why should I?" He stopped struggling and eyed me with hatred. "You're a cop, aren't you?"

"No, I'm not a cop! Haven't you got that into your great thick head yet? I'm on *your* side, for Christ's sake – yours and Tony's. And if we don't get a move on Tony's going to get the chop. Geoff bought it, didn't he? Now it's Tony's turn and then it'll be yours. Now come on!"

I turned my back on him abruptly and, pocketing the Luger, reached up and swung myself out of the trap hoping and praying that he would be right behind me. As I stumbled up the steps and on to the heaving deck I could hear him lumbering in my wake. I stamped across the pontoons hardly pausing to get my bearings and more by luck than judgement made it to the Embankment without mishap.

It was still raining but the wind had dropped a bit and even the rain had slackened. I broke into a jog in the direction of Sir Thomas and the Honda. Len gamely ranged up alongside. I had him, I thought with a fleeting sense of relief and satisfaction, I had him for the moment. I just hoped I would be able to hold him.

"Where we going?" he panted struggling, as he ran, into the hood of his anorak.

"Wimbledon," I grunted. "Where else?"

Chapter Ten

What should have been a headlong dash to the rescue in Wimbledon disintegrated into a nightmare of delays and frustrations.

An articulated truck had jack-knifed and overturned bang in the middle of Putney Bridge and the south-bound, after-theatre traffic was stacked up, bumper to bumper, all the way from World's End to the bridge.

Biking in such circumstances can sometimes turn out to be an unmitigated delight, saucily nipping in and out among the stationary vehicles, overtaking on the wrong side, mounting pavements and all the rest of it. But tonight, aided and abetted by the stinking weather, it was a pain in the arse, with Len O'Toole breathing heavily down my neck, clutching at me like a drowning man at a straw and moaning and groaning with terror as I weaved a mystical path between buses and cabs and the occasional Rolls Royce full of lounging money. Twice I told him to belt up, the third time I banged his right knee against a sturdy Land Rover telling him I'd do the same to the left one if he didn't withhold his criticism of my roadmanship. It shut him up but not for long.

Apart from the physical problems there were other, more disturbing anxieties which scratched away at my mind.

The revelations extracted from my peevish companion required more attentive and judicious consideration than could be achieved astraddle a great throbbing CB900 Supersport. I felt the need to bring everything into focus, then mull it over in some quiet spot with Sam.

My concern for Cath's well-being now outweighed the resentment I felt at her double-dealing. That she had run up against West at his ugliest was my uneasiest concern. My actor's instinct had cast him for the villain of the piece.

Instinct also told me that I knew West. He was the one I

had seen through the window of the Dog and Fox and had later tangled with at Covent Garden – and got my face cut open in the process. If I was right, then I owed him.

The chaos on Putney Bridge looked more like a train crash than a road accident. Blazing arcs and a couple of mobile cranes had been set up around the monstrous truck which sprawled on its side and spanned the road like a dead dragon. Under police supervision alternate one-way traffic mounted the shining pavement and edged gingerly between the truck and the parapet of the bridge.

Once through, we steamed up the High Street and Putney Hill in record time, the Honda shaking off the traffic like a dog ridding itself of fleas.

As we swung around Tibbet's Corner and into Wimbledon Parkside my chronic apprehension for the safety of Anthony Raven increased with every yard we covered. A clock in the High Street had given the time as eleven thirty-five, so we were five minutes late already.

Then we were there. To our right loomed the shadowy bulk of Clock House on the corner of Windmill Road which led across the Common directly to the mill itself, a narrow road ostensibly closed to traffic after sunset but with a barrier rarely secured. I toyed with the idea of parking the Honda and approaching the mill on foot, thus obviating the sound of the engine proclaiming our arrival. But speed was of the essence.

I swung the bike across the road, told Len to hop off and open the gate and leave it open, exits being sometimes more urgent than entrances. I dowsed the headlight and when Len was up again cruised softly up the road towards the mill.

Though the night had quietened and most of the rain had gone the wind in the trees might still mask the sound of our approach.

The road was no wider than a driveway, with a shallow ditch between us and open ground on one side, and a narrow grass verge on the other, beyond which creaked a Stygian forest of trees. At a fork branching to left and right I turned the machine to face the direction from which we'd come and stilled the engine.

Now there was only the restless fidgeting of trees, a final

spattering of rain and the wind, a thin wail of it, high above our heads.

Heaving the machine on to its rest I removed my crash-hat to give my head an airing and leaned in to Len. "Listen . . . I'm supposed to be meeting Tony on my own. If he sees someone else it might scare him off, so keep your distance, will you? I'll yell if I need help and for Christ's sake come quick if I do. West's probably here gunning for Tony," I improvised meaningfully. And in case the message hadn't gone home, I added, "*You'd* better keep your head down too or you'll find yourself on his list."

The darkness was intense. It was some time before my eyes became accustomed to it, and though I had a torch I felt it was wise not to proclaim my presence too soon.

The grass underfoot soon gave way to a strip of tarmac leading to the car-park behind the small complex of buildings surrounding the windmill itself – a cafe, the club-house of the London and Scottish Golf Club and the Ranger's house and stables.

The dark bulk of the windmill reared up before me, sails lost in darkness creaking dismally to themselves as if longing to be active once more.

Peering anxiously into the rustling gloom hoping for a glimpse of a waiting figure I moved in closer and stood quite still for a second or two, listening.

There was a plaque somewhere, I remembered, commemorating the fact that Baden-Powell had written some of *Scouting for Boys* in the mill. Be Prepared. I reached into the pocket of my anorak and felt for the cold comfort of the Luger.

"Anthony . . . ?" I called in a voice which didn't sound a lot like mine.

With the mill on my left I moved slowly up towards the car-park, past the cafe and public conveniences, on up to the club-house. A light glowed in one of its windows.

Softly I called again. Nothing.

Retracing my steps I strained my eyes for any sign of movement. Past the mill and on to the Ranger's gate. Lights there too in the house.

All at once everything became deathly quiet as if a giant hand had stifled the wind and stilled the trees. The hairs stirred on the back of my neck. I stood rooted drawing the gun slowly from my pocket as there came what sounded like a deep groan. At that same moment the wind gusted in again, spattering my sweating face with stinging drops of rain whipped from the branches of an overhanging tree and I wondered whether I had imagined the sound.

I raised my voice. "Len!"

No answer. A sudden sense of imminent danger began to close me in. I felt exposed and vulnerable. The sweat on my face was ice-cold and congealing like drying blood. Slowly I began moving back towards where I had left the Honda, reaching for the torch as I went.

Around me now everything seemed to be stirring and whispering, poised, waiting for something to happen.

Then, unmistakably this time and somewhere to my right, I heard it again, a long drawn out moaning sound, almost inhuman, like an animal in deep pain . . .

Turning towards it, the Luger in one hand, torch in the other, I flicked on the light and stared in silent horror at the glistening, yellow-hooded figure suspended in the darkness, crumpled and folded like an unstringed puppet, a vanquished character in a Punch and Judy show sprawled head first and forgotten over the lip of the stage.

A second or two passed before I could bring myself to get any closer to it. When I did, I discovered why it appeared to hang in mid-air with no apparent support. It had been flung over an enormous iron wheel six or seven feet in diameter – at a guess, a showpiece from the windmill's past – and left to hang there like a side of dead meat.

Except that it wasn't dead. It groaned again and as I drew nearer twitched convulsively.

I could now see the blood streaking the yellow anorak, washed with rain. "Hang on, Len," I grunted with what must have seemed to him a ludicrously unfortunate choice of phrase.

I stuffed the Luger into my pocket and the torch into the soft earth, so that I could at least see something of what I was doing.

The blood seemed to be coming from his head and when I stepped in and gingerly lifted the yellow hood of the anorak I could see it seeping from a deep wound at the base of his skull. He groaned again. "Okay, okay . . ." I murmured soothingly, "I'm going to try to lift you off this thing . . ."

I backed in against the wheel and shoved my shoulder gently beneath him, his head lolling on to my chest. Straightening up slowly I clamped a hand into the small of his back and heaved slowly, taking his full weight on my shoulders and raising him from the wheel.

He weighed a ton.

Carefully I edged away from the wheel and eased myself down to my knees. I couldn't see where the hell I was putting him. As limp as a rag-doll he rolled on to the muddy verge. I thought he'd lost consciousness but as he touched the ground he gave a muffled sort of a moan far worse than a full-blooded scream.

I reached for the torch. The legs were strangely buckled, both knees, it seemed, severely damaged. His jeans were black with glutinous blood. I picked gingerly at the soaking denim wondering helplessly if there was anything I could do to relieve his pain. I played the beam of the torch on to each of his legs in turn.

My stomach lurched. I squatted back on my haunches and shut my eyes tight. "Oh Jesus God . . . Jesus . . ."

His kneecaps had been shot away.

I peered at them again trying hard to assess the damage rather than dwell on the savage brutality which had caused it. Without removing the jeans there was no way, and I certainly wasn't about to try – not here in the middle of the night surrounded by mud and muck . . . It was an operating theatre he needed, surgeons and nurses, care and a ton of courage.

"Len, listen . . ." I knelt up, shading the beam of the torch from his eyes.

The face staring up at me was not Len's.

The eyes were open, the pupils fixed. He was dead.

I took a handkerchief and wiped the tear-stained face, gently cleansing it of blood which, seeping from the wound at the back of his head, had crawled across it with thin spidery fingers.

I had never seen him before but I knew who he was. Young, dark haired, hazel eyes like his father's . . .

A sudden shout of warning came from behind me. Len's voice.

Turning quickly I caught one brief glimpse of a dark figure rearing above me only a few feet away, a gun coming up and levelling at my head.

Hurling the torch into his face I flung myself headlong towards him, scrabbling along the ground on hands and knees. There was a strange splat of sound and the whip of a bullet as it passed close to my head. My hands closed on his ankles. I raised my head and butted him hard in the crutch.

I heard the wind go out of him and clawed desperately for the gun. He was immensely strong, his gun-hand forcing the weapon slowly downward to my face, the long, black-eyed silencer no more than a few inches from my eyes.

It was time for prayers.

I was trying to think of one when it occurred to me that his finger was no longer on the trigger; the weapon was clutched awkwardly in his fist, my initial attack having presumably dislodged his hold of its butt.

I ducked my head under the gun and clambered up the full length of his straining body using his clothing as handholds. I caught hold of his hair and slammed my knee into his guts with all the force I could muster. He grunted like a wounded wart-hog but still managed to hold on to me with a manic strength, both arms clasped about me in a rib-crushing bear-hug.

We waltzed around like a circus act for what seemed the best part of ten minutes but was probably no more than a couple of seconds, until, tiring of the futility of it all, I released his hair and with the straightened edge of my hand hacked at his throat in a highly unsuccessful attempt at Shuto-Uchi: fortunate for him, disaster for me. The next thing I knew was that he had hooked my legs from under me and I was sprawled on my back with him on top.

I don't remember much more of it, until I caught sight of Len standing over us holding above his head what looked like a baseball bat which he brought down on my assailant's head with a sickening crack. If it had been his head that cracked I would have crawled out from beneath a dead man. But it was only the blunt instrument which went, spraying us with splinters, bringing Len to his knees with his exertions, and depriving us both of my late adversary, who, scrambling to his feet, sized up the unequal situation and hastily departed before either of us realised he had gone.

"Fucking West," snarled Len. I let it go.

"You all right, Tosh?"

"Thanks," I panted.

He played the beam over me. "You nearly bought it then, didn't you?" He sounded pretty neutral about it.

"I wouldn't have been the first," I told him. "Look behind you."

He shied like a frightened mare and swung around with the torch at the ready. He really was on the twitch. "There's a body at your feet," I told him drily.

With his back to me he stood for a second or two over what was left of Anthony Raven, the beam of the torch travelling the full length of the body, and back again to the knees. I saw his shoulders sag. "Poor sod," he muttered and switched off the light. "He's rumbled us, hasn't he?" came his voice. "The only good thing is that we've rumbled him as well."

"Who?" I struggled to my feet feeling a lot older than I really was. "Who're you talking about . . . West?"

There was a nod in his voice. "He's on to us all right." He added anxiously, "Do you think he's still around somewhere?"

"Could be." I hesitated. "What makes you think he's on to you?"

His voice went up a notch. "For Chrissake, look what's he done to poor old Tone. Kneecapping only means one thing. Listen, I don't know who the hell you are or who you're working for, but I'm willing to believe you're on our side, right? Okay? But let's bloody well get out of here while we've still got our kneecaps to walk on."

My foot touched a heavy object. I stooped to pick it up. "He dropped his gun." I relieved him of the torch. "Which is a step in the right direction. If he hasn't got a gun he can't shoot our legs away, can he?" I examined the weapon, another Luger – a later model than the P08 I guessed.

I was in the act of unscrewing the silencer when we both went rigid. The corpse was moaning.

"Oh my Gawd," muttered Len and leapt behind me with a fine demonstration of togetherness.

With a small whinny of relief I knelt beside the stricken figure. He was still alive. The eyes, though still unfocused, were moving slowly, painfully. I kept the light off his face.

"Len," I spoke over my shoulder. "The Ranger's house is over there where you can see that light. Knock him up and tell him to call an ambulance and the police . . ." I was shrugging myself out of my heavy trenchcoat. "Len . . . ?"

I was on my own again. I could hear my doughty companion making off into the distance quite fast. I delivered myself of his favourite expletive very loudly and felt no better for it.

Carefully I spread the mackintosh over the wounded man doing my best to keep the weight of it off the injured knees. I leaned in to him. "Can you hear me?"

After a second he gave a guttural grunt which I took to mean that he was with me. "I'm going to get help. I'll only be a couple of seconds."

The Ranger himself wasn't on duty but his deputy was highly organised. I told him there'd been an accident and someone was lying by a big wheel out there bleeding a lot and in need of medical attention and could he do something about it?

He eyed my muddy clothes with suspicion and said yes he could, and what was my name? I told him Tom Eliot and would he telephone for an ambulance or would he like me to walk up to the Parkside Clinic and try to get help there?

He reached for the telephone.

"I'd better go and stand by him," I said shuffling towards the door, "in case he wants to make a last request."

He shouted at me to wait until he got through and he'd come with me, but I'd already gone. Like Len, the last thing I needed was a chat with the police.

I reached the grass verge and beat it fast in the direction of the Honda, only to beat it fast back again when I remembered that I had left a couple of pounds of lethal ironmongery in the pocket of the mackintosh covering the wounded man.

I recovered the gun and then for about one half of a second considered the mackintosh itself. Somewhere about its person there was sure to be something which would lead the cops to me. I whipped it off the recumbent figure which gave off a resentful groan. I leaned in towards him. "They're bringing some blankets," I whispered hoarsely, my eye on the Ranger's house. "Help is on its way."

I left before he could start an argument.

Chapter Eleven

To suggest that Sam was in a towering rage would be to misrepresent the facts. Sam didn't tower, he hunched, he rolled himself up into a ball and crawled into it, inwardly digesting his spleen and only when he was ready, released it, bit by bit, in grinding grunts and groans, steaming through nose and ears and, most awesome of all, fixing the object of his discontent with an eye like a bloodshot boiled egg designed to deprive that hapless individual of any lingering vestige of self-respect.

During the confession of my evening's activities he had successfully worked himself up to this pitch of unreasonable behaviour, so that when I eventually ground to a halt with a sheepish sort of grin and a lame, "And here I am . . .", I had a feeling that what was about to break would not be all that pleasant. So I sat back in my chair and allowed it to wash over me. Having caught the general gist of his complaint – I was far too tired to listen to it all – I shut down a bit and let him go on until he'd finished, watching him humping himself around the room in a curious woolly sort of grey garment which might have been an overcoat but was probably a dressing-gown.

Finished at last, he stood over me, breathing heavily and looking like an elderly actor playing Uncle Vanya.

"Well," I said half jocularly, "there it is. No good crying over it now, is there? It's done. What we've got to do now is grab West before he does away with someone else – me for example. I care about my kneecaps even if you don't."

He roared back, "I didn't say I didn't care about your kneecaps."

The door opened and Mildred put in her head replete with pink plastic hair-curlers. "What on earth are you two going on about? You'll wake the neighbours."

"Bugger the neighbours!" growled Sam succinctly as he edged away.

"What are you so cross about?" she persisted.

"Nothing," said Sam. The look he passed to me was one of caution. "Revelations from the Boy David here, that's all. He's been stepping out of line if you want to know."

She gave me a sympathetic look and shook her head with a smile. "You should be married to him. Now, why don't I make you both a nice hot cup of tea, then you can settle down and talk about whatever it is quietly."

"I don't want any tea," barked Sam. "Go to bed, woman."

"I wouldn't mind some," I said making a wry face at Mildred. She gave me a smile full of understanding and withdrew.

Sam had drawn back the curtain and was glaring out of the window as if the neighbours were lining up in the street outside armed with cudgels and pitchforks. "Bloody neighbours," he muttered darkly.

After a moment I ventured, "Should we ring Linda, do you think? Tell her about Anthony. She should know, shouldn't she – just in case he – er . . ."

He took a long time answering then shook his head heavily. "No . . . no. I don't think so. Not tonight. Tomorrow. Time enough tomorrow. Anyway, got to find out where he is first."

I got up quietly and padded out into the hall where I had left my coat and the airline bag I'd found on the *Chessene*. I bundled the firearms out of the mackintosh pockets.

Mildred came to the kitchen door wondering what all the clanking was about. At the sight of the weapons she shook her head sadly. "Will he never give up?"

"It's not him this time, it's me," I told her.

She shrugged it off. "I'll bring your tea in a couple of shakes. For goodness sake, try to defuse him."

He was still at the window. I clanked the hardware on to his desk. "That P08, unless I am much mistaken," I said quietly, "is the thing that killed Geoff Earnshaw."

Slowly he turned from the window, calm again. He eyed the wicked looking weapons glinting on the desk, head sunk into his shoulders, his lower lip protruding, the way it did when deep thought overcame him.

"Somehow we're going to have to explain those away, aren't we?"

"I couldn't have left them there." I sounded defensive.

He placed a delicate finger on the gun West had left behind. "That one you could. That could have led them to West."

"Anthony Raven could do that."

"If he survives."

After a short brooding silence he cast an enquiring eye at the airline bag. "What's that? Earnshaw's effects?"

I unwrapped them and placed them, one by one, on the desk beside the guns.

The heavy silence continued as he regarded them with sober intensity, eventually lifting the bracelet with one finger to study the inscription. Frowning, he shook his head, replaced the bracelet with the rest and flicked the yellow duster over them.

"With every forward step, we put up one more black with the law. Hodder should be in possession of those." He leaned heavily on the desk, his knuckles white on the battered surface. "It gets more complicated by the minute and we become more involved than I'd intended. If I were sensible I'd ring Hodder right now and let him take it from here, but . . ." He broke off and raised distressed eyes to mine. "These were found in Anthony's hideout and Hodder would jump to the obvious conclusion – he'd have to – that Anthony killed Geoff Earnshaw. And I just do not believe that. I know that boy. He may not be up to much but he's no killer. So either these were planted on him or he found them and held on to them as evidence against . . ." He shook his head. "Who? The method of Anthony's disposal suggests the IRA – kneecapping is one of their less endearing hallmarks – but I just don't believe it's them. If it is, why don't they say so? They're not usually so backward in coming forward. A bomb goes off and they're on the phone before the dust settles."

He creaked into his chair behind the desk and frowned vindictively at the two pistols and silencer. "This SWALK thing is something else. They've left their calling cards everywhere. At the cemetery this morning – ye gods, was it only this morning? – the fire down in Wapping." He looked over steepled fingers at me. "I – er – incidentally, I went over there to have a look, did I tell you that? I didn't, did I?"

It was his turn to confess. He had appropriated Mildred's Allegro once again and driven himself down to Wapping to observe the burning building suspected of containing arms and ammunition. By the time he got there the blaze was under control and several firemen had braved the remaining flames and brought out the steel boxes only to find them empty, whilst several wooden packing-cases stacked alongside and suspected of containing firearms were now heaps of blackened ash with not a weapon in sight.

The place had been littered with leaflets bearing the now familiar inscription, SWALK.

"You say Anthony's note was written on the back of one of those. And there was a stack of them on the boat. I wouldn't mind betting there's one stuffed into Anthony's clothing somewhere . . ."

The note from Anthony was still in my pocket. I laid it on the desk in front of him.

He narrowed his eyes at me. "You shown this to anyone else?"

"Not a soul."

"You're quite sure?"

"Positive."

"Then how the hell did West know you'd both be at the windmill tonight? Anthony would hardly be likely to tell him."

"Well, I certainly didn't. I haven't seen anyone. I didn't even tell you."

I stopped suddenly, remembering. I *had* seen someone.

Sam was eyeing me like a bird of prey. "What? You've thought of something."

"I saw Cath," I told him in an almost sheepish whisper. That little escapade was the one thing I had opted not to tell Sam.

"Cath?" A dangerous note had crept into his voice.

I tried to ignore it casting my mind back instead to the sequence of events. Just after the boy had passed me the note,

I had registered Cath's eyes on me. I remember thinking she had seen the exchange. Later she had been waiting for me at the cemetery gates with that challenging look in her eye, inviting me back to the *Chessene* . . . bath . . . bed . . . She'd undressed me and while I was in the bath she'd hung up my wet clothes to dry . . .

"She must have gone through my pockets," I muttered. Slowly and carefully, I told him exactly what I thought had happened.

"And then you snucked up in bed together?" He sounded suddenly very weary. I didn't attempt to deny it.

Silence ticked through the room like a time bomb then he said slowly, "And you call yourself a detective."

After more telling silence he said, "We don't know where she is now of course, do we? Cath, I mean."

"She wasn't on the boat, I know that. As I said, there'd been a fight of some sort, not a lot, she'd thrown a book at someone . . ."

"It *was* she who rang? It *was* her voice? You're sure of that?"

At that moment Mildred insinuated herself around the half-open door and the unbearable tension mercifully slackened for a bit. She bore a heavy tea-tray and shoo'ed me away when I tried to help her with it. "Just clear a space on the desk for me, there's a good boy. It's always like a pig-sty in here but he won't let me touch it." She placed the tray alongside the guns. "There you are, I've made you both some sandwiches, so for goodness sake eat something." She looked at me severely. "When did *you* last eat?" Her face suddenly crumpled as she took in my appearance for the first time. "And just look at you! What have you been doing? Look at your clothes!" She grabbed the sleeve of my anorak and then went for my jeans. "You're wet through, and you're covered with mud. You've been fighting."

"Leave him alone, Mildred, will you?" moaned Sam.

"Give me that jacket at least," she insisted. "I'll dry it out for you."

"Mildred dear, he likes it that way. Mildred . . ." he added in a firmer tone as she was about to remonstrate "He's found Anthony . . ."

With widening eyes she stared at him for a long moment, then transferred them to me. I gave a despondent nod.

"Is he . . . ?"

Sam interrupted her. "He's alive. But in a bad way. He's probably in Roehampton."

Her voice tightened. "*Probably* . . . ? Don't you *know* where he is?"

In a low practical tone he told her just as much as she needed to know and no more. When he had finished she sank uncomfortably on to a pile of books in a chair.

"Does Lindy know?"

He shook his head. "Not yet, no."

"His father?"

He raised a hand. "First thing is to find out where they've taken him. No good telling anybody he's on the critical list if we don't know whose critical list he's on."

"I'll talk to his father, if you like," she said. "I get on with him so much better than you do. I don't mind doing it in the least . . ."

Sam stared at her with sudden emotion. "Go to bed, Mildred darling, will you? I'll be up in a little while – when I've got rid of Boysie Oakes here. We've got to – talk for a bit longer, then I'll be up."

She got to her feet wrapping her warm dressing-gown about her spare frame with a strange sort of dignity. She touched my arm. "Don't keep him up too long, he needs his sleep. So do you by the looks of you."

"Bed," said Sam firmly.

"It won't be any good," she said. "I shan't sleep."

When we were alone again I poured Sam some tea and put a sandwich in front of him. He was hunched behind his desk like some sort of oriental panjandrum with rigor mortis, inscrutable, grim-faced, eyes closed.

I carried tea and a sandwich for myself over to his father's refuge of an armchair and let myself slowly down into it. It folded itself around me like a warm bath.

A full minute of charged silence followed, broken only by the sound of slurping tea and the steady mastication of sandwich.

Without warning life stirred suddenly behind the desk and from a pile of rubble Sam unearthed a telephone. "I know the

Ranger," he told me as if revealing that he was on intimate terms with someone at Buck House.

Dialling a number he mumbled his way through introductions. "You had an accident case up there tonight, I believe. Wondered if you knew where they'd taken him? . . . I think it might be my son-in-law . . . Queen Mary's Hospital, Roehampton. Right, I'm obliged to you . . . What? . . . Who? . . . Tom Eliot . . . ? Never heard of him. Thanks a lot. Goodnight." He hung up and made a wry face. "The police want to interview a bloke called Tom Eliot." He disinterred a telephone directory from a drawer, riffled through its pages and made another call.

Anthony had been admitted to Queen Mary's Hospital in Roehampton and was in Intensive Care. No visitors.

Our eyes met for a second as he sat brooding and irresolute, one huge hand dwarfing the telephone, then with a heavy sigh he lifted the instrument once again.

"Linda?" I enquired.

He shook his head. "George Raven. Lindy first thing in the morning, I think. Much sooner tell her face to face. Mildred or I will pop round."

The sound of the dialling seemed to screw up the tension. The room had become so quiet I could hear the ringing tone loud and clear. Sam transferred the phone to his other hand and reaching for a pencil began doodling on the back of an envelope.

"They're either all in bed or dead," he muttered.

I closed my eyes. I heard the sudden squawk of a metallic voice and then dozed off into a mesmeric haze. It was probably psychological; I didn't want to hear the shouting. Sam's mumblings were comforting and soporific, like breakers on a seashore.

The telephone gave a ping. I opened my eyes. Sam was saying in a wondering tone, "Reprieve . . . Dad's in Germany. A call from Berlin this afternoon took him off to a conference there. I gave Marvell the details. He'll pass them on to Sir George when Sir George makes contact. If we want to talk to him directly he's at the Schweizerhof." A pause while Sam doodled some more. "I don't think we need bother him, do you?"

"How long's he going to be away?"

He made no answer. Instead, he was staring steadily at his doodling, leaning forward a little and frowning ferociously.

"What is it?"

He said softly, "Cath's not a Kate is she, by any chance?"

"What do you mean?"

"With a 'K'."

I recalled the name inscribed in *Kidnapped* on the *Chessene*. "She is actually, I think. Katherine with a 'K'. It was in the book I found . . ."

He was writing again, almost feverishly this time. I got to my feet. With a triumphant flourish he leaned back in his chair and twisted the envelope around so that I could see what he had written. "How about that?" He stared at me with sombre eyes. "You see, sometimes it pays to put things down on paper. S-W-A-L-K." He spelt it out slowly. "Their initials . . . Skip, West, Anthony, Len and Kath. They're all in it. A little gang of . . . What are they doing, Mark? What, in the name of God, are they up to? Murder, maiming, kidnapping, arson, desecration . . . They'll get the whole bloody book thrown at them. They could be put away for life. And one of 'em's my son-in-law . . ."

I perched despondently on the edge of his desk, weary and unhelpful, still staring blankly at his list of names. It had been a long, long day, this Friday the thirteenth, and it wasn't over yet. I didn't know the answers any more than he did. Except perhaps . . .

"If they're such a close-knit group, as this stupid acronym would have us believe, why is one of them – to wit, West – in the process of scaring the living daylights out of the rest of them? Because that's what he's doing. When Cath rang me tonight she was under some sort of stress, I'm quite sure of that." I warmed to my theory. "Now let's just suppose: he hoves up at Chelsea – and don't ask me why, for God's sake. So far as we know she has no reason to mistrust him. He's a paid up member of the group and according to Len holds the purse-strings. In all innocence she tells him of the rendezvous at the windmill. *If* he thinks Anthony is going to turn Queen's Evidence, not only about the kidnapping and the money but also about the aims and the purposes of the group, he's got to

153

put a stop to it, hasn't he? So he forces Cath at the point of the gun to fetch me over to Chelsea while he goes off and, unmolested, maims Anthony. How's that?"

"Why doesn't he kill him?"

"To all intents and purposes he does. If I hadn't found him on that wheel he'd surely have been dead of exposure by morning – if he isn't already."

Sam shook his head laboriously. "And now we've frightened everyone off; they've all disappeared into the woodwork. Len, for instance: he took to his heels because he didn't want to get involved with the law and I can't say I blame him. Does he know who you are, by the way?"

"Depends what other people have told him. *I* didn't give him a name and he never got a good look at me. I dripped a whole lot of poison into his ear though. Incidentally, what I told him about that bomb in the coffin being timed to go off during the ceremony may not be as daft as it sounds. Everyone was standing around that grave – but everyone! Sitting ducks. Cath, Len, Skip . . . you . . . Linda . . ."

Sam's eyelids flickered. "I find that difficult to go along with."

"But can you check on it somehow?"

He gave a doubtful shrug. "I'll have a go. All right then, back to base. Len's gone and we don't know where. That's one. Two, Skip Roberts. He might be easier to trace. He's a buddy of Cath's so Lindy might know where he hangs out. Anthony Raven, three, and he's not likely to be all that communicative during the next week or so. Four, West. Now he's the big hang-up. He'll have gone firmly to ground and very deep, I guess."

"I know his phone number."

"He's not going to be there waiting for us, is he?"

"Maybe not, but we could have a look." I jotted down the number on his envelope. "That's the year I was born," I told him, passing it before his eyes.

"Fancy," he said.

"You've got contacts who can put an address to that, I'm sure." I hesitated. "And then there's Cath . . . five."

He screwed up his eyes at me. "Yes, Cath . . ." He thought for a moment. "After the phone call to you what did she do?

Was it *then* she threw the book at West – if it *was* West? And when he'd gone on his errand of grievous bodily harm – presumably removing the gun from her head – why, if she realised where he was going, didn't she ring you back and warn you?"

"Perhaps she did, I don't know. I was out of that place like a dose of salts. She wouldn't have got a reply." I took a deep breath. "But if she'd gone anywhere – on her own account – she'd surely have left a message."

Sam studied his hands for a moment, steepling the fingers. "Mark . . . try looking at it in another way . . ."

"Cath in cahoots with West, you mean?"

"Why not?"

"Why?"

"Half a million quid?" I turned my back on him. "You're not smitten with her I hope, are you, Mark?"

I shook my head wearily. "No . . . no, not really; not in the way you mean. She's just – different, that's all. Probably what makes her attractive. It turns my stomach to think that she might be . . . with him. But until we get to the bottom of it we won't know *how* deeply she's involved, will we? In the meantime I prefer to give her the benefit of the doubt. Anyway, that's my pigeon, not yours."

I got up and idled over to my chair, sank into it and closed my eyes tight. "God, I'm knackered. This has been one of the worst days I can remember – and I've lived through some bad ones in my time. Why don't I just go back to the simple life? Acting's a piece of cake compared to all this rubbish."

He nodded. "Why don't we turn in then? God knows we've done enough for one night. You go and have a nice hot bath. Tomorrow's another day."

I groaned. "I hope to God it's not going to be anything like this one."

But I had a shrewd idea that it would be.

Chapter Twelve

I was told later that ever since our gloomy confrontation at the cemetery, Detective Inspector Hodder of the CID had been worrying about me. It's usually quite nice to have people worrying about you, not so nice when "people" turn out to be representatives of the law, and utterly unnerving when the chief worrier appears in the middle of the night, screwed firmly to your doorstep and wearing a big black hat.

Such was the situation when I bubbled into the home-stretch of my cul-de-sac three minutes after I had left Sam at two o'clock in the morning. The pitiful glimmer of the solitary forty-watt street-lamp picked out the sable-hatted figure on the top step of my abode, one resolute finger stuck to the doorbell like a limpet. A gangly and shadowy companion hovered, as befitted one of lower rank, one step down. The engine of the badly parked car was running, keeping the driver warm.

I swung the Honda around on a sixpence and quietly bubbled away again to the phone-box on the top of the hill.

Sam's gravelly voice answered after one ring.

"Sam," I said, "tomorrow isn't another day. It's the same one. Hodder's pounding on my front door."

The grunt he gave was a quiet and unintelligible expletive.

"Where are you?" I told him. "Did he see you?" I thought not. A moment of silence then he said, "Can't afford to lose you now. You'd better come back here. I'll leave the garage doors open. Park your machine behind the Allegro where it can't be seen and close the doors behind you, right? See you." He hung up.

He was at the front door waiting for me, bustled me into the house, shot bars and bolts, turned keys in locks and slid a sturdy chain into place. I felt like Edmond Dantès saying hello to the Château d'If.

In his lamentable front room once more, he made straight for the window where he peered between the curtains, grunted again, and drew them carefully and securely closed.

"It's Wimbledon out there," I told him feeling slightly giggly.

"It's Tom Hodder out there," he countered grimly. "I wouldn't put anything past him. If he's busting down your front door, mine'll be the next. You and me are indivisible – like Castor and Pollux."

"How the hell did he get on to me, that's what I want to know?" I asked with a touch of petulance.

"Tom Eliot at the Ranger's house let you down, I reckon." He heaved himself on to his desk which creaked alarmingly beneath his weight. "Your friend up there who phoned the ambulance probably told the cops that Tom reminded him of that ex-actor laddie who'd had the accident and went off the rails – what was his name? Mark Sutherland, wasn't it . . . ?"

"Rubbish," I said, my eyelids on the droop. "I fade into the landscape."

"Sure you do," he nodded. "Like Quasimodo's hump."

Then Mildred swept in, pink plastic curlers and a dressing-gown with a school badge on its pocket. "Your bath is ready and I've made up the bed in Lindy's room. Come along, there's a good boy. Say goodnight, Sam."

"Goodnight, Sam," growled Sam.

"Goodnight, Pollux," I said.

"Mark . . . ?"

I unglued my eyes. Mildred was standing over me. "Cup of tea?"

I blinked painfully. The room was shafted with sunlight but the bedside lamp was still burning. "I left the light on," I mumbled.

She put tea and morning paper on the table beside me and opened the curtains. "Sorry to call you so early. You can blame Sam for that."

"How is he this morning?"

"Out for his walk." She hovered for a second in the doorway. "I don't think he slept at all. He certainly didn't come to bed." And she was gone.

I sipped slowly at the hot strong tea. Every bone in my body ached. My eyes were sore and full of grit. But at least the sun was shining.

I reached for the newspaper and life stirred slowly as I focused on the headlines.

The abrupt emergence of SWALK had not only made the front page in a big way but had confused the correspondent almost as much as it confused me. The single point of interest was the suggestion – 'it is believed' – that the organisation calling itself SWALK had contacted 'various sections' of the press and categorically denied responsibility for the placing of explosives in Earnshaw's coffin, stating moreover that it was a newly formed vigilante group committed to wage a war of attrition against terrorists and the growth of terrorism in this country.

It admitted liability for the firing of the derelict property in Garnet Street, stating that the building was being used as an arms dump by an unspecified terrorist organisation. Whilst the police admitted the possibility of the house having once been used for such a purpose, there was no evidence that at the time of the fire it had contained anything other than abandoned crates and boxes which 'might at one time' have housed arms and ammunition.

Along with the bedclothes I cast the paper aside and creaked slowly into an upright position.

Sam returned from his constitutional looking twenty years younger than he'd been the last time I saw him.

"Lovely out," he said rubbing his palms together vigorously and warming his baggy tweed trousers in front of the sitting-room fire. "Sleep well?"

I nodded. "Which is more than can be said for you, I'm told."

"Don't need a lot of sleep at my age. Ask anybody. I've been on to Roehampton, by the way. He's managing. They're quite hopeful in a depressing sort of way. He may not walk again on those legs but it's too early to say. Something might be done. I also called in on Lindy."

"How did she take it?"

"With difficulty." He frowned. "I didn't have the guts to tell her the full extent of the damage; the doctors'll have to do that. She'll have been on to them by now, I expect." He shook his head. "God only knows what she sees in that lad. He never amounted to much in my eyes."

"That's because you're her father."

His eyes glinted. "*His* father didn't think so either."

A hoot from the kitchen called us to breakfast.

"You've got some good digs here," I told Sam, winking at Mildred as I crunched my way comfortably through a plateful of eggs and bacon, toast and marmalade, and downed a couple of pints of blazing tea. On a chair beside me Magnificat had taken up his position and watched me speculatively with acid green eyes and mouth a-dribble.

"I come here quite a bit," said Sam. "Known the landlady for years." He eyed me over the rim of his cup. "How would a ploughman's lunch at the Prospect of Whitby grab you?"

"That's Wapping, isn't it?" He nodded. "You've already been to Wapping."

"Wouldn't mind going again though. Especially as that phone number of West's belongs to Messrs Thorkel Mane Limited of Skalds Wharf, Wapping Wall." He gave a fat chuckle at my surprised eyebrows. "We never close," he went on smugly. "Garnet Street, the venue of yesterday's fire, flows into Wapping Wall at the very moment it becomes Wapping High Street. So you see, it might well be worth shimmying down there to have a quiet nose around."

"Quiet? We'll stick out like sore thumbs."

He ran a mild eye over my creased clothes. "*You* might but I doubt if *I* will. It's quite civilised down there now in the daytime. Most of the wharves have been taken over by design centres, photographic studios and the like. Anyway," he glanced at Mildred, "I wouldn't mind getting away from here for a bit today. If Hodder's on *your* back, he's certainly on mine too. I've been pipping him at the post for the past two days and he's not going to like that." He gave a small snort of merriment.

"Leaving *me* to cope when he turns up on our doorstep, I suppose," cut in Mildred.

"Leaving you to tell him all you know – which is precisely nothing."

"Except that you've gone to Skalds Wharf and if he really

needs to contact you, you'll be having lunch at the Prospect of Whitby. What time, do you know?"

It pulled him up for a second but only until he caught the glint in her eye. "You dare, woman . . ." he whispered.

The cordoned off, burnt-out house in Garnet Street, no more than a shell and still smouldering, was giving off oily black acrid fumes. A couple of firemen stamped about in their big boots checking for glowing embers. The whole place stank abominably and, though a write-off, had clearly been so even before the fire had devoured it.

What little was left of it bore all the signs of dilapidation and disuse. Sheets of blackened corrugated iron, plastered with charred posters advertising out-of-date pop concerts, had long since taken the place of windows and outside doors.

At the rear of the building Sam pointed to a green steel box upended in a corner. "Ammunition box. There were a couple of dozen – all of them empty."

Suddenly, with a quick glance around, he ducked beneath the cordon tape and crunched over to a boarded-up doorway which had escaped the flames, the door hanging at an awkward angle from a single hinge. He stooped and closely examined a rusted padlock still in place.

One of the fireman caught sight of him and commenced an approach. When I cleared my throat loudly Sam retreated without haste, rejoined me and together we wandered off, a couple of bored and disillusioned tourists.

Sam was rubbing his right thumb and index finger together like Shylock counting his ducats. "Oil," he said shortly. "That padlock's been pretty well in daily use, I'd say."

I glanced over my shoulder. "That fireman's standing there watching us."

He looked at me sideways. "You're slouching, that's why. You look hunted and suspicious."

We turned into Wapping Wall where vast, grim-looking wharf buildings and warehouses towered between us and the river, shutting out the sun from the narrow cobbled street.

Sam jerked his head. "There," he murmured. High on a wall in huge letters of peeling blue paint were the words, *Skalds Wharf*.

We lounged across the road to the building's entrance which in contrast with the rest of it had been freshly painted and refurbished in olive green and cream. A board bearing the names and occupations of the building's tenants was fixed to the wall beside the door.

Five floors, five names. No Thorkel Mane Ltd. Sam gave a disgruntled snort. "We'll just have to ring the bloody number, that's all, see who answers. That's the last thing I wanted to do."

"Hang about . . ." I placed a finger on the second name up, Floor B. "*Thespis,*" I read aloud. "*Dance and Movement.*"

Sam frowned. "Thespis?"

"Father of Greek tragedy," I told him in case he didn't know. "It's a school of drama, that's what it is. And didn't your Linda mention a drama school?"

Sam's slow smile gave way to another until his whole granite face was awash with them. "By golly, we've found it. Well done us!" He shoved open the door.

"Hang on a minute." I laid a restraining hand on his arm. "What are we going to do? Ask for an audition? We can't just barge in."

"Who's barging in? I've opened a door, that's all. You have to open a door if you want to go in anywhere. I thought we might have a scout round the back."

"That sounds obscene."

He gave me a pained look and pushed through the door with me hard on his heels.

Facing us at the far end of a wide, stone-paved corridor which ran the full width of the building were two vast, red-painted doors, one of which was slightly ajar and opened on to a vista of the river.

"That's a bonny sight," said Sam and ploughed off to investigate, his pounding feet producing a resounding echo from the lofty walls. He pushed open the door.

We were standing fifteen feet or so above the river. Immediately below us the low tide had laid bare a small beach of shingle and unsightly flotsam. "Can't you just smell it?" enthused Sam, drawing in gusty lungsful of mud and diesel oil. "I love this river. If I had my time over again I'd be in the River Police."

"I'd be a baritone and sing Wagner," I told him.

He didn't care what I'd be and, grasping an iron stanchion on the outside wall, half launched himself into space, leaning out far over the beach to study the wall below us with interest. "Wonder what's down there?"

Still clinging to his handhold he glanced back over his shoulder down the corridor and out on to the road. "Cellarage? Storerooms? . . . Be under water at high tide."

He was talking to himself so I didn't comment, just registered the fact that the board hadn't said anything about a cellarage of any sort. A glass panelled door on our left appeared to be the only way up to the offices. *Entrance*, it said. *All Floors*. And that didn't mention a cellar either.

"You can see the Prospect of Whitby down there," called Sam still leaning out at an angle and nodding down river. Screwing up his eyes he then peered upwards. "There's an iron ladder set in the wall. All very handy."

He came back to me and we stood for a couple of seconds looking down the wide sweep of brown river towards the great bend of Limehouse Reach. Apart from a couple of lads paddling solemnly in blue kayaks and a white tourist craft surging up from Greenwich, there was no traffic at all. A few moored and tarpaulined small boats bobbed sluggishly on the water a little way upstream.

"How do you feel about SWALK being anti-terrorist?" asked Sam out of the blue, ostensibly still intent on the scenery.

"I like it. I like it much better than the alternative."

"Believe it?"

I thought about it then said, "I rather think I do. Any reason why not?"

As if by tacit consent neither of us had previously mentioned the implications of the morning newspaper report; and now, having broached the subject, he seemed disinclined to continue but stood nodding his head, breathing deeply and gazing amiably down river at the approaching vessel. He pointed suddenly. "There's a cormorant, look . . . there, see? . . . between us and the boat."

I saw what looked like a black duck with a long neck riding on the oily glint of water; if he said it was a cormorant that was all right with me.

"Good sign, that," he went on. "Means the river's more salubrious than it was. Lots of birds coming back."

"Sam . . ." I said. He looked at me. "Do *you* believe it – the anti-terrorist thing?"

He shrugged and turning on his heel strolled towards *Entrance. All Floors.* "I see no reason not to. Doesn't get them out of the wood though, does it? Vigilantes are nobody's favourite people. They're the lynching mobs. The law may be an ass but at least it's methodical and dispassionate – the vigilante is neither."

He gave the glass panelled door a shove but it didn't budge.

"All right then . . ." A predatory finger hovered over the buttons. "How about . . . *Thistle Design Studio?* Floor E, right up top. By the time we're due to arrive they'll have forgotten they asked us up." He gave the button a prod. A voice squawked out of the wall. "Maintenance," Sam told the grille gruffly. The wall made a rude noise and I pushed open the door.

To the right a sturdy iron staircase reached upwards. Our feet rang on the metal treads. "Sounds like Wormwood Scrubs," commented Sam.

Floor B Thespis: Dance and Movement announced a painted board in gilt Gothic lettering; a small vestibule with a wall full of photographs of people in balletic poses. A large blow-up of John Gielgud doing his Richard of Bordeaux on a door marked *Studio* was offset by a portrait of a pop star with a phallic-shaped microphone halfway up his nose.

As Sam moved purposefully towards one door another opened behind us. "Can I help you gentlemen?"

The beautiful young man who stood before a slowly closing door marked *Toms* was, I thought, not only capable of helping us but also of answering almost everything either of us wanted to know.

Clad in a scarlet boat-neck sweater, full black tights and scarlet leg warmers, he jibbed a little when we turned to face him, his welcoming smile sobering as he recognised Sam and extended a slender brown hand. "Chief Inspector Birkett. What a surprise. We faced each other yesterday morning – across Geoff's grave. I'm Skip Roberts."

Sam nodded and took his hand. "Chief Inspector no longer,

Mr Roberts, just an out of work busy-body needing answers to a question or two." His affability matched that of the coloured youth who now transferred his gaze to me, proffering his hand as he did so. "Mr Sutherland . . . meet an ardent fan of yours."

"Savage is the name," I told him more gruffly than I intended. Since I fell off the ladder recognition has always embarrassed me.

"Mr Roberts . . ." said Sam.

"Skip, please."

"We need information."

"Unofficially, I guess?"

Sam gave his head a wobble. "At the moment, yes, but it's not going to stay that way. It's only a matter of time before officialdom catches up with us. As you're obviously aware I am personally involved in the affairs of your – er – acronymic organisation."

The smile disappeared from the handsome face. A split second's pause then he said, "You're as close as that, are you?"

An attractive blonde piece in a slinky yellow catsuit shoved open the studio door and making for another labelled *Cats* eyed me intently from beneath lowered lids as if I were the mouse she'd been looking for all her life.

"We can't talk here," Skip Roberts said. "I've got to go anyway, I'm in the middle of a class."

"Where? When?" Sam pressed him. "It's urgent."

"Midday at the Prospect, turn right just outside. It's usually pretty quiet at that time. Okay?"

He was turning away when Sam said, "Oh, by the way, you have a telephone here, I imagine?"

"Sure we have."

"Could you give me the number – just in case we get caught up with other things." He brought out a notebook like the policeman he'd been most of his life and jotted down the number.

As Skip Roberts pushed through the studio door I could hear that dreaded honky-tonk echo of a piano one associates with all dance rehearsal rooms.

We clattered down the iron staircase and into the pale

sunlight. "That lad's an innocent," remarked Sam. "Caught up in something he doesn't understand – just for the kicks probably."

He was eyeing a low, red-painted doorway barely four feet high let into the wall of the building we had just left. "I thought so . . ."

"What?"

"There *is* a cellarage. There had to be. That means there's got to be another entrance – riverside probably."

We moved on to the end of the warehouse. Between it and the next building was a narrow alleyway with a notice which called it *Thorkel Steps*.

"Curiouser and curiouser," muttered Sam.

He gave a covert glance around; no one seemed to be interested in us. A lot of shouting and clanking was going on across the road where workmen were unloading a truckful of iron scaffolding with considerable verve.

When I looked back Sam was halfway down the passage, his wide bulk filling it out like a cork in a bottle. Beyond him and between us and the river a barrier of loosely erected planks prevented access to Thorkel Steps which would presumably have led us down to the water's edge.

Sam stuck his head between a couple of the planks and contemplated the scene.

"Someone's been down there," he mumbled. "And not all that while ago." Withdrawing his head he glanced over his shoulder. "Watch my back, will you, while I have a go at this."

I strolled up to the open end of the passage and stood for a moment or two looking like someone watching someone else's back.

When I turned to check on Sam's progress he was no longer there. The crossed planks were there but Sam had gone.

I rattled my way up the passage and set my eye to a gap. Sam was halfway down a flight of worn and weathered stone steps. Squinting closely at the planks I put my hand on one which looked suspicious; it moved aside easily, pivoting on a nail set low in a crosspiece leaving sufficient space for even Sam to get through.

165

I joined him on the steps. He was examining a cigarette-end with interest. He passed it to me, pointing to the step on which I stood. "Dropped there. Interesting?"

I nodded. "Very. Dunhill's filter-tip. Like the ones in Cath's boat."

"What else?" He squinted over his shoulder at me like a rubber reproduction of a gargoyle. "Anything else?"

He was testing me. I made a face at him. "Dry," I said in a prissy voice. "It's dry. And since it pissed with rain throughout most of the night, could only have been thrown here this morning – since the last high tide, whenever that was."

"Oh, well done, that man!" he chortled with a low crow of pleasure. "We'll make a detective of you yet."

"Shog off," I told him rudely.

The dozen or so steps led down to the ramshackle beach which was treacherous with slimy green stones and pebbles, broken glass bottles and black soggy stumps of rotting timber. The river lapped and slurped at our feet barely a yard away, sluggish undulations of filmy brown liquid – no one could call them waves – adding their quota of rubbish. I watched an elderly ham sandwich and a contraceptive take their places side by side on a flat green stone.

"Glad you mentioned about the river being more salubrious," I observed mildly. "I'd never have guessed."

"Shog off yourself," returned Sam with a smug chuckle. He was enjoying himself immensely, like a schoolboy playing truant.

I shivered suddenly. Down here the wind was keen. I huddled into my anorak and wished I'd brought my trusty trenchcoat. My companion was crunching his way along the narrow beach towards a short flight of weatherbeaten stone steps which led up to a heavy iron door opening on to a small landing. At the head of the steps Sam pressed his ear to the door like a safe-cracker on the job. He held up a warning hand and then stopped breathing while he listened again.

As was expected of me I too held my breath. Down river a ship's hooter gave off a melancholy moan. Sam's broad shoulders twitched irritably, then he straightened up, frowned at me and made off again.

I caught him up. "What did you hear?" I whispered hoarsely.

"Nothing," he whispered back.

We crunched along the full length of Skalds beach, found nothing of interest, and crunched back again, loitering once more at that bloody iron door. Sam eyed it with increased frustration. "Can't you pick the flaming lock?" he demanded with sudden and unreasoning asperity. "I thought you were supposed to be able to do everything."

My jaw sagged. "Have you seen the size of that thing? You'd need a damn great . . ." I stopped in dismay. "Oh shit . . ." I muttered.

"Not here, dear boy, not here."

I gave him a miserable look. "I think I may have found the key to that door."

He fixed me with a flinty look. "But?"

"It's in the pocket of my mack – hanging on a hook in your front hall."

I explained how I came by it on the boat in Anthony's raincoat pocket.

He shrugged it off. "We'll just have to come back another day, won't we?" He consulted his watch. "Come on, it's nearly twelve – time we were going."

At the foot of the steps he shambled to a halt and pointed a histrionic finger at nothing at all down river. "Someone up there behind me is keeping an eye on us," he murmured without moving his lips. "Left of that obelisk thing. *Don't* look now . . ."

"I wasn't going to," I said huffily. "We're trespassing, that's why he's looking."

"People bawl at you if you're trespassing. That one ducked out of sight."

We made it back to Wapping Wall without mishap. "Maybe I was over-reacting," said Sam. His eye nevertheless was as watchful as my own and when someone cranked up a pile-driver somewhere behind us we all but leapt out of our underwear.

Chapter Thirteen

Business at the Prospect of Whitby was not exactly booming at that hour. A couple of early tipplers propped up the long bar, one at each end, while a smart young barman appeared behind it to attend to our needs – Guinness for Sam, lager for me and a promise to talk to a lady backstage about a couple of ploughman's.

"You," said Sam quietly in my ear, "owe me fifty pence."

"Why is that then?"

He nodded at the tabloid newspaper folded on the bar beside the nearest imbiber. Only the headline was visible: *Kiss of Death Outrages*.

I passed him a 50p piece without comment and carried my lager through to the rear of the building where long tables and benches were set up on a sort of dais so that customers could get a good view of the river through the windows. And very fine it was too if you liked that sort of thing. I did, so clearly did Sam. He grunted with pleasure and with lips firmly set to his Guinness swept the long reach of the river with the sort of keen understanding one might have expected of a hardened mariner.

His head ducked a little as he caught sight of a bird hanging almost motionless high in the pale sky; only the wings trembled. "Kestrel," he murmured. "Look at him, will you? I know just how he feels, sitting up there waiting to make his kill. Split second timing, that's what it's all about. There he goes . . ." He craned forward as the bird stooped suddenly, a fearsome projectile hurtling towards its prey; then in a flurry of wings it seemed to hesitate, tilted and planed away upwards again. "Missed!" Sam shook his head. "Amazing how often they get away. And he's the *real* professional. It's that one moment that matters – botch it and your dinner's gone."

I grinned. "You're being homespun, Sam."

"You want to make something of it?" he growled. "Homespun or not, timing's what it's about, I tell you. Look at old Hodder for instance: he's missed the bus all the way along the line. He hasn't got the nose for it, you see. And I'm beginning to think I haven't anymore, either. I used to have it. And hated it, do you know that? That final swoop with the talons out . . . God how I hated it. That was during the bad old days of course, when the gallows were there . . ."

He stared at his Guinness for a morose second, then took out his notebook. "What was that telephone number in Len's diary?" I told him. "The Thespis number is different. Which means," added Sam, "that West has a line all to himself somewhere in that building."

"In the cellar."

"That would be my guess."

"Two ploughman's," called a comely blonde from behind the food counter. I pointed at Sam's empty glass; he nodded and made to get up. I pressed him back. "Beauty before age," I told him.

We took our ploughman's outside to a patio boasting a gaunt and leafless weeping willow; its drooping stems reached down to the ground like so many lengths of string. "*Salix Babylonica*," said Sam regarding it with approval. "In summer you could sit beneath that and never be seen."

"He's late," I said quietly.

"You've noticed that."

As if he'd been waiting in the wings for a cue the late arrival chose that moment to burst through the door and into the sunshine, a dazzle of scarlet and black and white flashing teeth, full of excuses and apologies, none of which we listened to and most of which were clearly genuine.

He wouldn't be eating, he said when he'd got his entrance over, and the strongest drink he'd take would be lemon juice. Supplied with this he sat facing us with his back to the river and for several moments none of us knew how to begin. Until Sam quoted the phone number from Len's diary. "Whose number is that, do you know?"

"West's," said Skip promptly.

"And *where* is it?"

"Where?"

"Yes. Where is the actual instrument which bears that number?"

Skip blinked a couple of times then shook his head. "Would you believe it – I've no idea. I've never been to his place. Somewhere around here I guess . . . West's a bit of a screwball, you know. Keeps to himself most of the time. Not what you'd call the sociable type."

"What can you tell us about him?"

His eyes flickered from Sam to me, then back again to Sam. Caution gathered over his head like a cloud.

"Where's Cath, Skip?" I put in quickly before he shut down altogether.

"Cath?"

"Yes, you know Cath. The 'K' in SWALK, lives on a houseboat, builds her own motor-cars . . ."

"Okay, okay man . . . I never said I didn't know her, did I? I don't know where she is . . . not at this moment if that's what you mean. Have you tried the boat?"

I glanced at Sam. The fact that she'd gone missing last night didn't mean she hadn't returned this morning. We hadn't tried the boat . . .

Sam said, "Skip, bear with us, will you? If we're confusing you it's because we're a mite muddled ourselves. We think something may have happened to Cath . . . something fairly nasty." He held up a hand as Skip was about to interrupt. "We need your help, believe me. We've got some of the answers but we need a lot more. Have you seen the papers this morning?" Skip made no answer. "Of course you have. Some of the facts aren't correct, are they? Or maybe some of them have got hold of the wrong end of the stick. *Did* you blow up Geoff's grave? It was you who rang the press and denied it, wasn't it? It could only have been you – there isn't anyone else. From what I gather Len wouldn't have had the nous, and if Cath had contacted them they would hardly have failed to mention the fact that it was a woman's voice on the phone – they like that sort of thing. Have you noticed how they drool over woman terrorists?"

"Cath is not a terrorist," Skip suddenly burst out angrily.

"She's the next best thing though, isn't she? You all are.

You're terrorist-busters, trouble-shooters, vigilantes . . . a lynching mob. If the law isn't up to its job, take it into your own hands and show them how to do it . . . clean up the world." He raised his voice as he went on. "I'm not blaming you, Skip Roberts, understand that. I'm not *blaming* any of you. For the state this country's in at the moment we all have to shoulder the guilt. But with your less than well-laid schemes, Skip, things have gone sadly awry, haven't they? Something else happened last night – too late to make the final editions of the morning papers. Did you know that your friend, Anthony Raven, is in Queen Mary's Hospital with both his kneecaps shot away?"

The dark handsome face seemed to change colour; the eyes were blank, their brightness gone. "Why?" he whispered hoarsely.

Sam shrugged and said gently, "You set yourselves up to fight terrorism; you should learn to know your enemy."

"But kneecapping for Christ's sake . . ."

"The standard reprisal for treachery."

"Tony would never betray anyone."

"He was prepared to," I put in quietly.

Skip turned his eyes on me for the first time, shaking his head slowly. "No . . ."

"Yes. Unfortunately West got there first."

"West?"

"The cuckoo in your nest," Sam said.

"West . . ." Skip repeated the name mechanically as if to fit it into some incomprehensible mental jigsaw puzzle.

Behind me the door creaked open followed by a babble of voices as more people brought drinks out on to the patio. The pile-driver started up again nearby.

Sam told Skip what little we knew about West, our suspicions, surmises and fears. It wasn't much and when it was over Skip finished his lemon juice and stared into his empty glass.

"Len knew about West?" he asked in a low voice.

"I told him."

"Where is he now?"

"Len? No idea. He galloped off into the night."

"Holed up with his bird probably."

"Wanda?"

"You know her?"

"The hairdresser lady?" I tossed out a hopeful guess.

"No, she's got that craft shop in the market – Jubilee Market, you know?"

I nodded. "Of course she has."

"If anyone knows where he is, she will. They live in each other's pockets, those two. I didn't know about the hairdresser – she must be new."

Sam was making a note in his book. Another visit to Covent Garden. Now I knew where Cath and Skip had got to on the night of the drop when they had so effectively dropped out of sight: they'd simply walked into Wanda's shop.

"Tell us about the kidnapping," said Sam in an almost casual voice.

Skip stirred impatiently "It wasn't a kidnapping. If you know everything else you must know that. It was a set-up to get some funds out of Tony's old man."

"You didn't stint yourselves."

"He can afford it."

"And whose idea was it? Anthony's?"

Skip communed with himself for a second or two then shook his head vaguely. He couldn't remember who had actually mooted the idea; it had evolved from a discussion about the IRA and the way they'd tried to dispose of Mrs Thatcher and the rest in Brighton. While none of them approved of either Mrs Thatcher or her politics, they weren't prepared to see her blown to bits by a mob of terrorists. Someone had criticised security and someone else had said he could have done better himself with one arm tied behind his back – West, he thought – and had gone on to say that a citizen army sort of thing might make more sense than security people dressed up as policemen with big flat feet. "Nothing personal, Inspector," Skip had added glancing surreptitiously at Sam's feet. "I know, I know . . . it sounds crazy now, but at the time it seemed to make sense – you know how it is, one thing leads to another. The thing came to a head a couple of weeks later when Cath received a letter from an aunt of hers in Ireland telling her that her uncle – someone quite high up in the Royal Ulster Constabulary – had been ambushed and killed by the

IRA. She was in a terrible state and very, very angry. After that we just talked and talked about having a go at the bastards ourselves – even a small group like us might do some good."

"Us?" interrupted Sam. "Who's *us*? Just the five of you?"

"By the time we actually got around to giving it a name there were only five of us, yes."

"You mean, some backed out?"

"Geoff Earnshaw backed out."

"And was later found dead on the Common . . ." I put in abrasively. "I found his watch, ring and bracelet tied up in a neat little parcel on board the *Chessene*. He was murdered."

Skip stared at me with open mouth.

"The parcel incidentally was hidden in a bag belonging to Tony Raven."

His reaction was violent. "Tony? He would never do a thing like that."

I nodded. "We don't think so either. But who have we got left? Cath, Len, you . . . ?"

"And West."

Sam put in mildly, "The police would call it unsubstantiated guesswork, but it's also educated guesswork. And my elderly friend Mark, here, *was* set upon last night by a manic West intent on murder, who had, it seemed, already bashed Anthony over the head, shot away his kneecaps and left him to die of exposure. So we may as well work on that theory, even though the courts might discount it." He paused. "Tell me something, Skip, why did Geoff walk out?"

He shrugged. "He just wasn't sold on the idea, I guess. He said we hadn't got a cat's chance in hell of getting away with it."

The IRA, he had pointed out, wasn't just a muddle-headed collection of Irish maniacs got together to frighten the British. It was an organised army, fully equipped and highly trained in urban guerilla warfare and fighting a strategic war. And he, for one, was not going to start blowing up ammunition dumps belonging to an army far more devious and subtle than anything we had to offer. When West had asked him how he knew so much about it he had lost his temper and had yelled that his bloody father was Irish and had been a member of a splinter group of the IRA operating in Birmingham and if West or anyone else thought that he, Geoff, was going to tangle with people like that then they had another think coming.

"There's no doubt about it," went on Skip, "he did know quite a lot about them. He had lots of books on the subject – IRA, Carlos, terrorism in general. He showed me some of them and, man, they turned my blood cold. They really were scarey and nearly persuaded me to pull out too. Like the man says: this thing was too big for the likes of us to be fooling around with."

As if by mutual agreement the three of us took time off to watch a vessel, only the masts of which were visible above the parapet, as it chugged down river. A radio blared on board.

Sam said, "How does West come to be in with the rest of you? He strikes me as an odd man out."

Skip shook his head. "Not really. He and Len help out at the studio."

"Doing what?"

"Karate. He specialises in karate. Teaches it."

"Balls!" I said rudely. "He knows as much about karate as my Aunt Fanny. And I ought to know. If West was even 1st Dan, which would mean at least a year's practice, he'd have had me out at the windmill. And if he isn't 1st Dan he has no right to be teaching anybody anything. He's been having you on," I told Skip.

"What about Len?" asked Sam. "How does he fit in?"

"Len came with West."

He went on to tell us that he, Geoff and Anthony had first met up a year or so before when Anthony had been interested in promoting a pop group which had shown promise at an amateur talent competition. Skip added modestly, "I was on the drums and was probably about as good as West was at karate. I was pretty hot on rhythm and movement."

"Do you also roller-skate?" I asked casually.

The question floored him for a second then he said shortly, "Sure I skate."

"Were you responsible for the choreography at Jubilee Market on Tuesday last?"

He regarded me for some time in silence, his head on one side.

"Don't be ashamed of it," I said, "it was superb."

"You saw it?"

"Wouldn't have missed it for the world."

He frowned, smiled, then looked sheepish. "Okay, yes, I arranged it. Skating is a passion of mine – roller and ice. I do my best to pass it on to others. That's one of my – subjects. Incidentally, West knows his skating too. He's very good."

"There were five. You, West . . . Cath?" He nodded. "Len?"

He shook his head with a grin. "Len can't even stand upright. The other two were from the workshop."

"And all that screaming in the wings?"

"Some of the kids. Also from the workshop. They had no idea what was going on. They did it for the kicks. But it sure worked, didn't it? It was West who thought we ought to lay on something of the sort – just in case the fuzz had been called in."

"The fuzz, as you call 'em," put in Sam drily, "were called in only later when you knocked over and injured several innocent bystanders. Not very clever if I may say so – and hardly part of the choreography, excellent though it was."

"You were there too?" Sam nodded. "Seems like everyone was there."

"I was Sir George Raven," admitted Sam with a modest blush. Skip stared.

"What was Geoff Earnshaw able to contribute to a theatre workshop project?" Sam continued. "He was an electrician."

Skip grinned. "He could wire up a cat and make it talk. There are more things to be taught in a theatre workshop than just acting." He glanced at me. "You should know that, Mr Sutherland."

"Savage. I was even taught how to sweep a stage."

"Cath was having a ding-dong at the time with Geoff and decided to go along with us."

"And what did she know about anything?"

"She was at RADA and did quite a bit of acting before she got bored with it and took an engineering degree – believe it or not."

I gave him a quirky smile. "Sounds a funny sort of theatre workshop – an electrician, an engineer and a drummer. And a what? A playboy? *Was* Anthony a playboy?"

Skip hesitated. "If anyone was the odd man out it was Tony. He was just desperate to do anything. He wasn't a playboy. He hadn't got any money for one thing. His old man hardly gave him a thing. Tony was the result of an unhappy and miserable upbringing, hated his home and would have done anything to get back at his dad."

"And did," put in Sam sourly.

"The only good thing that ever happened to Tony was Linda – your daughter."

Sam said sharply, "She wasn't in on any of this, I hope?"

"Tony wouldn't have it. By the time we'd hired the studio we were also into the anti-terrorist lark and Tony just wouldn't have her anywhere near the place. I don't think he even told her where it was."

"I'm bloody glad to hear that," growled Sam.

"Like I said," went on Skip, "he was desperate to do anything. I don't think he ever realised the sort of trouble we might get ourselves into by tangling with the IRA and such like. But at least he got us the money and jumped at the chance of doing down his old man."

"So you got the money . . . and you got the weapons?"

"We got some, yes."

"Where did they come from?"

"West knew a man."

"Ah yes, of course, he would know a man, wouldn't he?"

"An American, he said. He wouldn't tell us who he was but said he was reliable and, in fact, dealt legitimately with Tony's father." He stirred uneasily and glanced over his shoulder conscious for the first time of other people on the patio. "I remember that particular night because it was the night Geoff got killed. For some reason, and I suppose it was because things were coming to a head and he realised we were going through with it, Geoff got into a screaming rage. Said we were stark staring mad and he had a bloody good mind to grass on us – to the cops, to Tony's dad, the lot. I don't think he really meant it, but he was pretty far gone, I thought, and then just pissed off in a rage. And that was it. All this happened at Tony's place in Wimbledon, and on his way home over the Common he was bumped off."

"By West," said Sam.

"West was with us."

"For how long after Geoff had left?"

There was a long silence then Skip nodded slowly. "He could have done it, yes. When Geoff left we all packed it in and went home. I guess we were shaken by what Geoff had said." He stopped suddenly.

"You've remembered something?"

Skip frowned. "I remember Len saying to West, 'You coming then?' and West saying, 'You go on, I want to think this thing through.'" He remained silent for some little time then added, "Oh Jesus, he went after Geoff and killed him, that right?"

Sam nodded. "That's how I see it. He didn't trust Geoff not to blab. And I believe that even then he had decided to double-cross the lot of you – once the money was in his hands. A cool half a million doesn't happen every day of the week, and whether he intended to make off with it for himself or use it as an entrance fee into a terrorist organisation on his own behalf we may never know. I think the latter is true. I don't know why but there's something about his behaviour which would seem to fit, and my nose is twitching with it. If he was only after the money he could have been in South America by this time, safe and sound, without fear of extradition."

The patio was becoming crowded. Sam said restlessly, "I think it's time to move, don't you? You all right for time, Skip?"

"Sure. We could go back to the studio. No one will be there for half an hour yet."

Getting up, he moved slowly towards the parapet and, stretching his whole body, sensuously, like a cat, leaned forward over the parapet to stare down at the river below. Sam struggled into his overcoat while I gathered up glasses and crockery. The pile-driver next door had taken up some sort of insensate rhythm of its own.

"Skip . . ." called Sam.

The young Negro turned, skin glowing like polished ebony in the pale sunshine . . . until suddenly, nightmarishly, everything changed. The face became distorted and wracked with a hideous spasm of pain, one of the brilliant eyes disappeared in a dark well of glutinous scarlet. Thrown back against the parapet by the impact of the bullet, he hung suspended and writhing for a moment, then somersaulted backwards over the edge. In a terrible silence broken only by the incessant thudding of the pile-driver everything seemed to wait for the sickening shock of sound as the plummetting body struck the beach below. Then all hell broke loose.

Sam was yelling at me, people were shouting and screaming and running for cover, I dropped glasses and crockery and ran to the parapet to stare dumbly at the lifeless figure sprawled obscenely among the rotting flotsam below, Sam bawling at me to get away from the parapet . . .

I cannot ever remember being so angry as I was at that moment; it seemed to grow in me like some monstrous superhuman force, beating in my ears and behind my eyes like that bloody pile-driver. I swung round and stared up at the steep bank which rose above the patio and at a broken wall beyond it. The shot had come from somewhere up there.

A flight of steps led upwards. I leapt for them, shoving Sam aside and conscious that people were streaming, chattering, from the bar anxious to know what was going on. The pile-driver was thudding in my ears. I leapt over a notice which said *No Entrance* and floundered upwards. I jumped an iron railing . . . He was up there somewhere.

I yelled at the top of my voice, "West! . . . West!"

I stood sobbing with exertion, breathless and homicidal, staring around like a trapped animal. Nothing. I clambered on to a wall and looked downwards. Below was the street, packed with parked cars and lorries and loud groups of workmen shambling back from lunch break . . .

No sign of him. I turned away, studying the ground, kicking at the grass, possibly in search of the rejected shell of the bullet which had ploughed into Skip's face. I didn't find it.

I stumbled down again to the now crowded patio. A few

pale faces stared up at me curiously as I approached, the rest were glued to the parapet peering down at the monstrosity below; they roared and chattered and made wild gesticulations, explaining to others how it had happened. I even heard someone laughing . . .

Chapter Fourteen

It was Sam who led me away from that place, a rough urgent hand on my arm, half dragging, half pushing me through the press of sensation seekers.

"We can't leave him there," I protested fighting off his hand.

"We can and we must." He shoved me into a corner. "Listen, Mark, there's nothing we can do; we can't help him; he's dead, for God's sake. If we hang around they'll hold us for questioning and we can't afford the time. Now come on, we've got other things to think about."

He pushed me ahead of him.

He'd forgotten where he'd left the car and so had I but we ran it down somewhere off Cable Street and clattered off in a cloud of blue smoke passing an ambulance and several police vehicles going in the opposite direction.

"This is where we came in," I observed sinking low in my seat to keep out of sight.

He gave a little snort of pleasure. "It's a new experience to be running from the law."

"'Running'," I pointed out as we took a corner at all of two miles an hour, "is not the word I would have chosen."

He patted the dashboard. "It's not her fault, poor old duck. Mildred's wrecked her engine; she never gets her out of second gear. She trots her down to Safeways twice a week and on a good day might even take her over to Richmond for an airing in the park. She used to be an Allegro – she's a Molto Adagio now."

"Sam," I said suddenly. "Wouldn't it be best if you left the rest of this to me? Or come clean with the cops – now, before you get in any deeper?"

"*I am in blood stepp'd in so far . . .*" intoned Sam.

"Oh shut up, will you?" I moaned. "You'll land yourself in

the most awful shit when they catch up with you – and they will, you know that, don't you? They have to." He wasn't even listening. "Sam . . ."

He was looking into the future.

"*Birkett's Last Case* is what I'll call this when I get around to putting it all down on paper. And stop beefing, will you? You're like an old woman. I'm having a whale of a time. Anyway," and a tight grimness entered his voice, "this is a personal issue, you know that. If you want to get off I'll stop the car and you can get out right now."

I half opened the car door. "I could get out right now without you having to stop. I could walk faster."

And that was the end of it. Sam giggled like a schoolgirl in a gymslip.

Mildred, however, wasn't giggling when we finally got back to *chez* Birkett. She was lying in wait for us at the front door, her hands floured, her hair dishevelled. "Not only have the police been here," she announced, "but George Raven's been roaring down the phone for you."

"What police?" asked Sam mildly.

"Your Inspector Hodder."

Sam exchanged a glance with me. "He's not *my* Inspector Hodder. Heaven forfend!"

"They both want you to ring them the moment you come in. And they didn't sound amused either."

She turned on her heel and huffed off into the kitchen pausing at the door to call over her shoulder, "Oh, and there was George Prewitt too, *he* rang. At least he was polite, unlike the other two."

"*Now* she tells me . . ."

Sam hurried into his front room. I stopped off at the hall-stand to retrieve the outsize key from the pocket of my muddy raincoat, then, deciding to attempt a peace probe on Mildred, sauntered into the kitchen.

She was thumping away at a slab of pastry. "Don't be angry with him," I ventured in a small tentative voice. "There's been another killing; he's just working it off."

She paused in the pummelling of her pastry and leaning on it heavily with both hands stared down at it with hopeless eyes. "Why doesn't he stop, Mark? Why doesn't he just give it all up and rest – let other people do it, younger people who are paid to do it – accept his retirement like any other sensible man . . ."

"He will after this, I'm sure. It's hit him where he lives, that's the trouble. He won't give up now, not till he sees the end of it."

She brushed back her unruly hair with a forearm. "And when will that be?"

I hesitated. "Tomorrow," I said.

A half amused expression touched her lips. "Tomorrow?"

I nodded. "You can bet on it." It sounded all right but, like Polonius, I had been accounted a good actor.

She raised her eyes to mine and I was startled to see tears in them. "Keep an eye on him, will you, Mark? Please." She added in an unnaturally harsh voice, "I don't want to lose him now, after all these years. He's too old to be out on his own."

I smiled and touched her arm. "Tomorrow, Mildred. I promise."

I found Sam hunched at the window of his front room with his back to me. "You were right, Mark," he said. "There's a big question mark over that bomb in the cemetery. George Prewitt has been ferreting away with the technical people. The consensus of opinion suggests that it was set to explode at eleven fifteen and didn't go off until five hours later. Nobody knows why except that these home-made things are never foolproof. The bastard who planted it must have unfastened that rear window in the undertaker's chapel when he viewed the body before closing time, and let himself in again *after* eleven fifteen that night, set the clock and planted the thing in the coffin. The experts think that even with six feet of earth above it, the blast would still have been powerful enough to kill."

He turned slowly and looked at me with sombre eyes. "He's a maniac, Mark. There were at least a dozen of us around that grave. He could have killed the lot of us . . ."

We sat in doleful silence for a moment then I said, "If only we knew something about him. All we've got is a bloody telephone number."

"Couldn't we use that?"

"How?"

"Get Len to give him a ring."

I cleared my throat. "'Hello, West old man,'" I said. "'Len here. Sorry I bashed you over the head last night. It was a mistake. Actually I was aiming at the other bloke. Could we meet for a jar sometime? . . .'" I shook my head. "It won't do, will it? Besides, we've lost Len along with everyone else."

"We haven't tried Wanda yet."

"Or Cath," I said quietly. "We haven't tried Cath either."

It was like dropping a pebble into a stagnant pond; the sluggish circles of silence spread outwards into the room and beyond it to that empty creaking cabin with the splintered picture-glass and the damaged book on the floor, the muddy footprints, trampled cigarette-ends . . .

The strident pealing of the telephone bell shredded every nerve in my body. Sam's hair was standing on end too, but that may have been a trick of the light.

He hung over the jangling instrument, glaring at it but making no effort to answer it. Mildred beamed in hot-foot from the kitchen and stood in the doorway drying her hands on a towel.

"Aren't you going to answer it?"

"I was just hoping it might go away," said Sam.

She came into the room. "It's probably that awful inspector. I'll tell him you haven't got back yet."

Sam lifted the receiver as she was reaching for it. "Birkett," he said.

Mildred and I exchanged wary glances as a lengthy series of angry squawks erupted from the instrument. Sam, holding it several inches from his ear, made a face at us and mouthed "George Raven", then said patiently into the mouthpiece, "I did try. You were in Germany, I believe," nodded attentively for a second or two then added, "This minute if you like. Both of us?" I gave him a belligerent shake of the head, which he returned with a nod and a beaming smile. "He'll be delighted."

Hanging up he looked at Mildred. "We may be gone some time."

She said stoutly, "Don't let him get the better of you."

"Mildred darling," he grunted, edging himself cautiously

around a corner of the desk, "you live in Cloud Cuckoo Land. He's going to have us for his tea."

Apart from a nod and a gesture indicating that we should be seated, George Raven made no move as we were shown into his presence by the taciturn Marvell. I stole a glance at Sam; he had perched himself on the very edge of an armchair in close communion with his old tweed hat poised securely on his knees like a well-behaved cat.

George Raven, in the absence of any further move from either of us, spoke first. "Mr Savage, Linda has told me of the part you played in the rescue of my son. I am in your debt. At least he is still alive – a mixed blessing as I see it. He's no longer in the intensive care unit . . ." He trailed off into silence.

Sam hadn't moved, nor did it seem he ever would again. I therefore embarked on a somewhat woolly distillation of events as they had happened and as nearly as I could remember them. When I had finished I sat back and wondered how most of them could have happened on a single day.

"This man West," Raven said, "where can he be found?"

Sam stirred into life. "We have a telephone number and an address in Wapping and that's it. Both were encouraging but after this morning, I'm not so sure. The place is within a stone's throw of the spot where Skip Roberts was killed and will now be swarming with police. If I were West I wouldn't go near the place."

"On the other hand . . ." I hazarded.

"What?"

"It might be the very place he'd be safest. It's the sort of quirky thing that happens. The last place you'd look for a bolted horse would be his own box."

"It's not a horse we're looking for." He sounded tetchy.

George Raven said, "If a telephone number and an address is all we've got, then it stands to reason that's where we start." He stared at us as if we were a couple of idiots. "Doesn't it?"

When I told him that Sam had already suggested that Len should be persuaded to ring the number if only to ascertain that West was in residence, he nodded and said, "Why not? Good idea."

I nodded back. "All we've got to do is find Len."

"Right. And when we find him we get him to tell West that we are about to launch an exploratory expedition into his territory. That'll surely persuade him to make a move of some sort?"

I said patiently, "*If* we manage to run Len to earth and *if* we persuade him to make the call, it'll be with a gun at his head, which would hardly help him give a convincing performance. West would rumble him and be off like a dose of salts."

"How about money instead of a gun?" asked Raven with mild cynicism. "I'd be willing to go as high as five hundred."

"Pounds?" My jaw sagged. "*I'd* do it for that."

"That might not be a bad idea," put in Sam.

I hurried on. "The other small thing is that if West knows in advance that we're going in on a raid he'll be ready and waiting for us, with a damn great bazooka in his hand. What's he got to lose?"

"His life," growled Sam.

"If he's got a screw loose or he's kamikaze, he might not care about that." I looked at him. "You ought to know more about homicide than the rest of us. Pathological killers get a lust for it, don't they? With half a million quids' worth of someone else's money in his pocket he has to get rid of the someone elses, right? So he decides to blow 'em all up at the cemetery – if other people happen to get in the way, tough! After all it's only like blowing a crowded plane out of the sky to get at one bloke. If it had worked, bully for him, but unfortunately the bomb didn't, so he's back where he started. Now he's running around like a chicken without a head, making it up as he goes along. He's on his own." I glanced at Sam. "Born terrorist he may be – mentally – but there's nothing professional about him. He's an amateur like the rest of them."

I got up and began ploughing up the carpet in my impatience. "What does your boy Anthony know about terrorism?" I demanded of George Raven. "Sweet Fanny Adams! And Len O'Toole? Len's a heavy; brainless muscle – a henchman. The exception was Skip Roberts . . ."

I felt suddenly deflated and pulled up at the window to look out over the cheerless Common. Between the trees I watched a small boy trying to get a green and yellow kite airborne.

"In my opinion," I went on slowly, "Skip was a professional in everything but terrorism."

The child on the Common was running, holding the guide-string high, his head turned over his shoulder, watching the kite pitching and floundering in his wake.

"What a crying shame he should ever have met a sod like West." I paused. "I also think he was sold on Cath – probably in love with her, who knows? I sensed something of the sort when I first saw them together. I'd like to bet that she's the only reason he was caught up in all this."

The kite was fast in a tree. The child stood beneath it, tugging without hope at the string.

I turned back into the room. "And talking of Cath . . ." I said almost in a whisper.

There was a long silence.

"Is there a telephone on that boat?" asked George Raven suddenly. I nodded. He reached for his telephone and I gave him the number.

I could hear the ringing tone over and over again as I prowled uneasily about the room knowing there would be no reply. Then, all at once, came a loud metallic click and a harsh voice shouting impatiently into the receiver. I seemed to grow roots.

I saw Sam's shoulders twitch slightly as he straightened up in his chair, his hat falling unheeded to the floor. I moved in a couple of paces watching Raven's face as he spoke Cath's name and listened intently as the disembodied voice gabbled on. His eyes strayed across at Sam, avoiding mine. "Er . . . just a moment." He suddenly interrupted the flow. "I think I'd better hand you over to Chief Inspector Birkett."

He offered the phone to Sam who was already halfway across the room to take it. With his back to me he mumbled for a second or two. I heard him say "*ex* Chief Inspector", then the voice took over again in chattering cacophony.

I moved up alongside him; he transferred the phone to his other ear. I moved on to the window. The small boy was still there, talking now to a middle-aged man and pointing upwards to his lost kite. The man removed his hat, tucked his walking-stick beneath one arm and awkwardly began to climb the tree.

Behind me the telephone pinged. I turned slowly. Sam was looking at me.

"They've found her," he said gruffly. "A neighbour saw her caught up in the mud under one of the houseboats. Rang the police. They thought at first that she'd fallen overboard and hit her head . . ."

My chest was hurting like hell. "But she hadn't?"

He frowned and moved away. "Her neck was broken."

Blindly I turned again to the window. I knew it. I had known it since last night, sensed it.

The blindness cleared after a bit. I watched the man in the tree hook the kite from its perch with the crook of his stick. It came away easily and fluttered to the ground at the feet of the waiting child. The boy picked it up, gingerly hugged it in his arms, then turned and ran off without a word or a glance at the Samaritan halfway up the tree.

Chapter Fifteen

Driving through certain parts of London in a Rolls Royce on a Saturday afternoon put me in mind of what it must have been like during the early days of the French Revolution when Parisian gentry began to think twice before calling up their *équipages* for fashionable jaunts through the park.

Marooned at the occasional set of traffic lights, we were the centre of attraction for various underprivileged persons who came over to make faces at us through the window. Others shaded their eyes with their hands and peered in hoping for a glimpse of a film star or one of the royals – or if their luck was really in, a millionaire pop group.

They must have been pretty disappointed with Sam and me lolling about on the back seat. George Raven was all right, looked fairly impressive, I thought, up there in front behind the wheel.

It was George Raven who had put this particular operation into motion. The admirable Marvell had looked up the telephone directory for anyone who might be trading under the name of Wanda and come up with *Wanda's Boutique* at an address in Covent Garden. He had, his employer informed him, struck oil.

"We'll all go together in the Rolls," Raven had declared as if arranging a trip to the Balearic Islands. "You two on your own could frighten him off . . . if he's there at all, of course."

The whole idea seemed cockeyed to me: five hundred pounds for someone who might not be there, to make a telephone call to someone else who also might not be there.

But I was in no fit state to form any sort of opinion one way or the other. The news of Cath's miserable and violent end had turned me into a zombie programmed for revenge, concerned only with ways and means by which I could destroy

West. I needed him to die slowly and, if possible, in screaming agony.

As we whispered over Waterloo Bridge I was jolted back to the present by the unnerving realisation that my thoughts were those of a terrorist, and that Sam, George Raven and I were hooked into the sort of operation deplored by us when devised by a group of muddle-headed but well-intentioned discontents who had called themselves SWALK.

With a steady stare I regarded the bundle of morose silence beside me that was Sam Birkett until, becoming aware of my scrutiny, he turned his head and met my eye with a ferocious glare of enquiry.

"What?"

"You sure about all this, Sam?"

"About all what?"

"Taking the law into our hands."

He looked at me levelly. "Cold feet?" he asked. There was no contempt in the question, only challenge.

"Pretty cold, yes." I sounded more belligerent than I felt. "But there *is* an anti-terrorist squad in existence, isn't there? Better equipped and more able to cope." I pressed on as he tried to interrupt. "Aren't we doing the very thing we're trying our best to prevent – privatisation of the law, so to speak?" I turned away watching the crowds milling around outside the Aldwych Theatre as George Raven swung the big car into Drury Lane. "Flushing out a man like West – armed and desperate as he is, to say nothing of his being unhinged – might be a lot simpler if we had several more bods to help – preferably in pointed helmets."

"Two against one is enough," grunted Sam surlily.

"Three," came Raven's voice from the driving seat. "And more if needed – but without pointed helmets. I have only to snap my fingers."

"No." Sam shifted uneasily in his seat. "No private armies, George, for God's sake. We don't want a gang-war on our hands. West may not be as alone as we think."

"All the more reason . . ." I began.

He cut me down tartly. "Let's just concentrate on the job in hand, shall we?"

I gave him a surprised look. His face was grim, his lower

lip protruding with aggression. Winston Churchill was back.

That was the end of the discussion.

Miraculously George Raven had found a space and was parking the Rolls with the sort of carefree abandon that I would have slid the Honda into someone's front garden. The space was only miraculous because it was staked out by a couple of red and white police bollards which he dealt with by simply moving them a few yards up the road.

"This is Russell Street," he said returning to us, dusting his hands and reaching into the car for his smart grey homburg and silver-topped cane. He looked like an actor-manager with a success on his hands.

Wanda clearly thought so too when he bustled into her tiny boutique, removed his hat and breathed *bonhomie* all over her. After blinking her disbelief of him she settled down a little, prinked delicately at her lank, shoulder-length blonde hair and swayed her hips a couple of times – always a good sign.

She was the girl of the photograph in Len's wallet, pert and pretty, slightly overblown but with an unexpected shrewdness in her wide blue eyes.

Those eyes were for George Raven alone, though they did flick a casual glance over his shoulder in my direction. Sam was not with us; he had taken his chronic policeman's suspicion off to the rear of the building to check the possible existence of a back door.

The little shop was full of shadows; small spotlights on chromium stands and rails cast narrow white beams, directing prospective customers' attention to heaps of glitter lurking beneath glass on black velvet trays. Several revolving pyramids of inexpensive costume jewellery, cascades of silk scarves suspended head high, metallic belts and chains spread over the backs of two chairs whose seats displayed various forms of female headgear – all these hazards served to rivet me to the square yard of empty floor space just inside the door.

Apart from Raven and myself the shop was thankfully devoid of custom, nor did Wanda appear to have an assistant. She stood behind the bijou glass counter and eyed Raven with speculative appreciation as he fingered a pair of ear-rings and held them to the light to catch their sparkle. Beyond her, in the far corner, a flight of open wooden steps led to the floor above.

She nodded and was smiling at some innocuous remark Raven had made about the jewellery, when I was struck violently in the small of the back. The door opened behind me and the place became over-populated as Sam's gargantuan presence was added to it. His arrival, together with the slight shake of his head directed at me, brought a sudden flash of alarm to Wanda's alert eye.

George Raven said suddenly and quite loudly, "Does Mr O'Toole happen to be on the premises?"

The stealthy creak above our heads told us that *someone* was, and I was past Raven and Wanda and halfway up the stairs before Wanda could shout a warning.

A face drawn with sudden panic stared down at me from the stair-head.

"Hello, Leonard," I greeted him. "How are things with you then?"

He backed away as I moved slowly upwards, his face ashen, his eyes flickering about him as though searching for a weapon of some kind.

"We come in peace, Leonard," I assured him comfortingly as I took in the tiny room which though uncluttered by downstairs excesses was no more negotiable. A large settee bearing a pillow and some folded blankets, a table with a television and the remains of a meal upon it, a couple of upright chairs, an armchair and several open crates stacked about the walls and containing merchandise for the boutique – plus Len of course, and now me – made the doorless and narrow-windowed room claustrophobic to a degree.

As I moved resolutely towards him he collapsed backwards into the armchair. A moment later we were joined by George Raven and Wanda, with Sam bringing up the rear with the news that he had shut up the shop. Shrinking back in his chair Len goggled up at us with wide-eyed alarm, Sam making a particularly fearsome impression on him.

But Sam was lightness and joy. "Hello, Mr O'Toole," he smiled proffering a hand which Len was too frightened to accept. "I'm Linda Raven's father – saw you at Geoff Earnshaw's funeral yesterday, didn't I?"

It was George Raven who took control. Seated at the table and carefully setting aside a half-consumed plateful of congealed chips, he spoke quietly of our good intentions, mentioned only a few of the details leading up to our present visit, and with a plea for the necessity of speedy action, handed the meeting over to me with as nearly a satisfied smirk as one of his stature could be expected to muster.

I looked Len in the eye. "Cath's dead," I said bluntly. As he opened his mouth in disbelief I added, "Skip too."

"Skip?" whispered Wanda behind me.

"This morning," I nodded. "Both killed by your friend West. And, of course, you know what happened to Anthony." I paused. "S-W-A-L-K," I spelt out quietly. "You and West are the only two left, and if we don't act fast, it'll be only West. If *we've* been able to track you down, it's only a matter of time before he does too. So you've got to trust us and help us. Haven't you?"

Len blinked up at us like an idiot barely taking in what I had been saying. "Cath too?" he whispered.

"When you and I met up last night on that boat she was already dead – in the river with her neck broken."

Wanda gasped and Len started up angrily in his chair. Where he thought he was going, God knows. I shoved him back again.

Wanda said, "Why should he want to kill Len?"

"Because Len's in his way, that's the simplest explanation. And West is on a killing spree, and a very successful one at that." I turned again to Len. "The five of you cooked up a scheme to defraud Sir George here of half a million pounds. You told me last night that West was the one who was handling the money. He handled it so well that not one of you ever had a glimpse of it, and two of you are dead and one crippled for life. Which leaves you, Len, out on a very shaky limb."

Sam intervened. "Did you fire the building in Wapping last night, Len?" Len gave an unwilling shrug. "Why?"

"It was an ammo dump, wasn't it?"

"Was it? There wasn't any ammunition in it when you blew it up."

"They moved it, didn't they?"
"Who did?"
"How do I know? The IRA lot, I suppose. It was their stuff."
"Who said?"
"West said! He was still in touch with some of 'em. He knew what was going on."
"With the IRA? Does that mean he was *with* them at one time?"
"So he says, yes." Len was becoming more belligerent by the second. "That's what made us think we could pull it off in the first place. Five of us could have done 'em a hell of a lot of damage with the sort of inside gen he'd got. He knew it all . . . where they were, safe houses, ammunition dumps, all that sort of stuff. It was a piece of cake, I tell you, we could have slaughtered 'em."
"Were you ever one of them?"
"One of who? The friggin' IRA?"
"Who else are we talking about?"
"I never was – never. I wouldn't touch 'em with a barge pole."
"You're Irish though, aren't you?"
"I was born in Liverpool."
"And you're a pal of his." Sam was snarling. "Didn't you come in on this together?"
"Come in on what?"
"That's what Skip said. You and West came together, he said."
Len shouted suddenly, "So bloody what? That doesn't make me a Provo, does it?"
"Cool it, Len," put in Wanda soothingly. "Tell 'em what you know, for God's sake."
He turned on her violently. "You keep out of it."
She overrode him. "If you won't, I will."
Again Len half rose in his seat; again I shoved him back. She turned to Sam. "West let it slip one night when he'd had a few . . ."
"Shut up, Wanda!"
"You owe him nothing, Len," she flung back at him. "He's got you just where he wants you, don't you understand that?

All he's got to do is to wait till the heat's off, then he'll just come in and kill you like all the rest. Don't make any difference to him now, does it, how many he kills? Well, does it?"

Len subsided as suddenly as he had been roused.

She turned back to Sam. "West – apparently – had grassed on someone big, back in Ireland. So he had to get out fast. He came over here, changed his name and has been lying low more or less ever since – over a year now. He's frightened out of his wits really, but he'd never admit it, of course. God, *I'd* be scared too if I was in his shoes and that lot was looking for me. Well, Len got mixed up with him in Liverpool just after he'd got off the boat. He was looking for someone to latch on to, I reckon, someone simple like Len here, someone who would help him, and smooth the way and all that. This was all before Len and me met up, so I only know what Len's told me about him, but I've always thought he was a bastard. I've always hated him. I can't hardly be civil to him, you know that, Len, don't you? I've said it over and over again, haven't I? I've always been afraid that one day . . ." Tears began to well in her eyes. "I never thought it'd get this bad . . ."

Sam put a hand on her shoulder. "It needn't get worse." He eyed Len for a moment in silence. "She's talking a lot of sense, you know that, don't you?"

He looked sullenly at the backs of his hands and made no reply.

"Len," I tried quietly, "last night, when you bashed him over the head on the Common, you saved my life. I've no doubt about that at all. If you hadn't been there he would have killed me. So I'm not going to repay that sort of debt by getting you into more trouble, now am I? What we're asking you to do won't get you within ten miles of West; if it works, as we hope it will, he'll be out of your hair and everybody else's for good. And if you're worrying about grassing on him, don't – forget it; loyalty to someone like him is not just misplaced, it's bloody dangerous." I exchanged a glance with Sam; he obviously thought I was doing fine so I went on. "You told me you don't know where he hangs out, that right? You've no idea where he is?"

There ensued the longest silence yet. It went on for so long that I began to wonder if I'd asked the question. Sam and I had another look at each other while George Raven sat immobile, his chin resting on hands folded over the silver top of his cane – Sergei Diaghilev watching a dancer with two left feet.

I was about to repeat the question when Wanda came once more to the rescue, smouldering anger quenching her tears.

"Len, if you want to get out from under West, now's the time to do it, don't you see that? Why don't you tell them?"

The only answer was a tight, almost involuntary clenching of his fists.

She sighed loudly and turned again to Sam. "All right, I'll tell you what *I* know, but don't be too hard on Len, right? It's just not his day, is it? West has buried himself in some cellar or other down in Wapping – in the same building as the studio where they work out. Well, the night before they blew up that dump – Thursday I think it was – West had Len over there with him working all night, moving that stuff from the dump in Garnet Street to his own place in Skalds Wharf. Right so far, Len?"

"Is that right, Len?" snarled Sam when there was no answer. Len nodded miserably. "Why?" Len shifted uneasily in his chair. "Why, Len? If you were going to blow the place up on Friday, why move the stuff out on Thursday?"

"He said . . ."

"What? What did he say?"

"That we might as well save the stuff for ourselves. Why blow up good guns, he says, when we can use 'em for ourselves? Just leave some of the empty crates and boxes, he says, to fool Skip, he says, when we put down the charges . . ."

"Why try to fool Skip?" I asked.

"Skip wouldn't 've done it, would he, if he knew he was just blowing up an empty house?"

"So you spent all night humping the stuff into West's cellar . . ." I looked at Raven, ". . . which he was then going to pass off as the first consignment of arms bought in the name of SWALK with *your* money, Sir George, but without spending a penny of it. Clever . . ."

"Not really," put in Sam drily. "It would have been cleverer if he'd left some of the cases intact. The police might then have accepted that a genuine IRA arms dump had been destroyed, and the IRA themselves might have accepted the loss. As it is, they now know that someone looted the place beforehand. What the idiot has done, in fact, is to draw their attention to his part of the world, and, indirectly, to himself. If I were West, I'd be on the move right now – like the clappers."

"It's a tangled web," commented Raven after a pause.

"It's that all right," nodded Sam. "Unfortunately for him, he's the fly that's caught in it."

He stared thoughtfully at Len for a second. "Well, Len, you've been a great help and don't think we're not grateful. You just lie low for a couple of days, see? Wanda, keep an eye on him and don't let him out on his own."

Wanda said, "He's got a room over in Fulham. After last night he came over to my place, but I put him up in here. I thought he'd be safer here – West might not think of the shop."

I nodded. "Quite right too. Oh, and incidentally, Len, while you're in the giving vein, what reason did he give you for – detaining me on the boat?" Once more he hesitated. "Oh, come on, for Christ's sake!"

"He said you were one of them," he blurted out galvanised by the sudden threat in my voice.

"One of whom?"

"One of the Provos from the dump. He said you were on the snoop looking for Tony. So would I go and take care of you. He said he had to do something in Wimbledon, like I told you, or he'd have seen to you himself."

"I'll bet . . . Right," I looked at the others, "now it's crunch time, Len. What we want you to do is so simple you'll want to laugh in our faces. We want you to give your old buddy West a friendly ring, that's all."

He didn't laugh in my face, he just blinked at me as if I'd gone mad. Wanda moved in but Sam restrained her gently.

"Just pick up the phone," I smiled, "and dial the number you've got stuck in the back of your diary and say, 'Hello, West old man' and Bob's your uncle!"

He was getting to his feet. I gave him a prod in the chest and he sat down again. "I can't do that," he spluttered.

"Why not?"

"He'd roast me alive. I nearly killed him last night."

"You didn't do anything of the sort. Listen!" I held up a finger as he was about to shout at me again. "It was dark, right? He's your friend, right? And you saw him being attacked by this maniac, so you went to rescue him with your tree trunk. Are you still with me? Now, in the dark, you hit the wrong one, didn't you? Instead of hitting the maniac you hit him. 'I'm sorry, West old man, that's how it happened, and I've been worried about you, wondering if you're all right, blah, blah, blah . . .'" I smiled at him. "There, what do you think of that?"

"I won't do it."

"I think you will."

"I won't," he assured me with a twist of bravura at the corner of his mouth. "Not for a hundred quid I won't."

Ten seconds ticked by. "How about *two* hundred?" George Raven, quiet and persuasive.

Len took another breath, paused, thought again and expelled it slowly. He stared at Raven with eyes like marbles. "Pardon?"

George Raven knew about timing. An avuncular smile came first, warm and trusting, full of teeth; he then slowly reached into his pocket, drew out a wallet and in devastating silence produced four newly minted fifty-pound notes which he placed with meticulous care one by one and side by side on the table before him. They looked lovely and I coveted them because they looked so new. But not nearly so much as Len coveted them. He stared at them with a new light in his eye which he then transferred to Raven, whose smile now resembled that of a barracuda, then on up to Wanda whose face was without expression.

"For making a telephone call?" he whispered at last.

"That's how important it is," said Sam.

"But why?"

"Yours not to reason why," said Sam.

"We want to know if he's where we think he is," I said more helpfully. "If he is, then, Len old chap, we'll go in and get him and after that all your troubles will be little ones."

He craned his head to get a better view of the crisp, pristine notes. They did look good I must say.

The silence in that room was intense. Outside, someone was

playing some Beethoven flute variations on a clarinet; people do that sort of thing at Covent Garden for no particular reason other than to pick up the odd penny.

"Why can't you telephone yourself?" asked Len. "If he answers, just hang up. You'd know he was there, then."

"That's exactly the sort of thing that would make him take to his heels – someone breathing down the phone at him. It's got to be someone he knows; a friend, and you're about the only one he's got left."

"He's not *my* friend."

He was still dithering when George Raven played his trump card. Skilfully he laid another note alongside the other four. "Two hundred and fifty," he muttered softly.

Len cleared his throat stealthily. "The phone's downstairs in the shop," he whispered hoarsely.

I allowed him to get up without further harassment.

Chapter Sixteen

Sam and I sat opposite each other in a steamy corner of an all-night cafe called Pat's Quay, an unsalubrious establishment affectionately known among the locals, a Thames River Police buddy of Sam's had assured him, as Cat's Pee. Be that as it may, the steaming black liquid in chipped mugs on the table between us bore no resemblance at all to cat's pee but was thick and slab and would have supported a spoon in an upright position – had one been supplied.

At one-thirty in the morning the clientele was thin. Apart from the immoveable Chinese insomniac behind the counter staring with inscrutable sloe-black eyes at the enamel teapot, and who might or might not have been Pat, only one other nightbird shared our vigil: a drunken female person wearing a Union Jack and a complicated grey wig, on whose wet lips a rocky version of the 'Marseillaise' occasionally bubbled. In the blotchy mirror above Sam's head I watched her drawing idle patterns on the wet table-top before her with trembling, mittened fingers.

My eyes dropped to Sam, leaning back against the wall, his face tired and pale and looking its age. The weariness hadn't reached the eyes however; beneath the brim of his hat they glittered like tiny chips of broken glass.

"Why are we doing this, Sam?" I asked after a long silence.

"Don't start that again." He peered at his watch. "Another half hour and we can go."

"Why wait?"

"Because I like two o'clock," he growled. "His resistance will be at its lowest. I'd like it even later but you would be impossible. Be patient now, will you, like a good lad?"

"He might not be there."

"He's there. I feel it in my water."

He'd certainly been there when Len had finally phoned

him. We'd heard the grating voice as he had lifted the receiver. Len had held the instrument away from his ear so that Sam and I, hanging close, could hear what was going on.

Len had done quite well, his performance difficult to fault; a slightly falsetto tone perhaps, a quaver to it, but easily explained by nervousness. After the first few seconds of gabbled explanations and apologies about hitting West over the head by mistake, West had sounded magnanimous, said he understood and why didn't the two of them meet up tonight for a quiet jar. Sam had shaken his head violently and mouthed "tomorrow". Len said he had a date that night but could manage any time tomorrow.

"Where you speaking from?" asked West. Even at second hand the casual question dripped with ulterior intention.

Sam put a finger to his lips. Len said he was in a call-box which was fair enough: Wanda's phone was coin-operated.

"How about me coming round to your place?" West suggested. "Eleven tomorrow morning, how's that?" Sam nodded peremptorily. "Okay, right," Len gulped. "Great. See you then."

"We can get pissed together," said West.

When he hung up Len was quite white.

"Not to worry," soothed Sam. "I doubt you'll ever see West again."

In silence I fervently hoped that he was right. Another meeting with West would undoubtedly be Len's last.

I caught a glint in George Raven's eye as he counted the five beautiful fifties into Len's waiting and slightly trembling palm. I grinned back; he'd saved two hundred and fifty on his proposed original deal.

When Sam burrowed in his overcoat pocket for his woolly gloves he also produced with them a folded sheet of paper. It was the one he'd picked up at the scene of the fire in Wapping earlier that day – SWALK printed all over it. He held it under Len's nose. "Where'd you get these done?"

"Cath did them. She knows someone who has an old printing machine. He let her use it."

"*Knew*," said Sam pedantically.

"Pardon?"

"Cath *knew* someone, Len. She's dead. Should you be

tempted to use that phone again after we've gone, remember that, won't you? As Wanda said, he's got nothing to lose now by killing you. You're the only remaining thorn in his side."

"Don't worry," promised Wanda holding on to Len's arm. "I'll see to it."

"With any luck," frowned Sam, "we might well keep Len right out of it." He crumpled the paper in his large hand and turned to me. "We never found out who the 'L' stood for, did we, Mark?"

"I never did," I said stoutly.

As we prepared to leave I asked Len what the intention of the pamphlets had been – advertisement or what?

Len gave a shrug. "So's people would know it was us. When we found out our names made that word we thought it was a good idea to leave those things behind whenever we did a job like, you know? And Skip said he'd let the papers know we were sort of – well, like freedom fighters – know what I mean? When the public saw them hand-outs they'd know we were on their side and meant business. We thought it'd sort of catch on like . . ." he had concluded feebly.

Now, looking at Sam across the cafe's messy table, I felt a sudden warmth for him, affection even. Tough, implacable, pugnacious, sometimes utterly unreasonable, he was, nevertheless, possessed of an almost febrile sensitivity which expressed itself in an appreciation of ornithology, classical music, books and good theatre; he was obviously a splendid, though sometimes wayward husband and a doting father; he cared about people and had an irrepressible schoolboy sense of humour which endeared him to me almost more than anything else.

He had fought forthrightly for *his* cause throughout his adult life and here he was, approaching his seventies – if he wasn't there already – pale, bone weary and dog-tired, sitting in a shit-house of an all-night cafe, ready and willing to move in on an armed and possibly homicidal maniac.

He was watching me. "What?" he demanded in his usual pugnacious and succinct manner.

I gave him a twisted smirk. "You wouldn't thank me for it even if I told you."

He held my eyes for a second then said, "Come on then, let's get out of here, it's time we were on the move."

If Saturday afternoon on Lavender Hill was the prelude to the French Revolution, the early hours of Sunday in Wapping was the Reign of Terror.

Our five minutes' walk from Pat's Quay was a nightmare.

Shadows stirred and shifted in dark doorways, unseen feet scuffed, disembodied secret whisperings and wet giggles crawled from the echoing black mouths of narrow alleyways like paint peeling off rotting wood; the sudden glow of a cigarette almost at my elbow revealing a nose and a mouth and the glitter of eyes made my stomach sit up and beg; I even heard the creak of his clothing as he breathed. From the same source a second later came a low wolf-whistle of invitation.

"Wish to God we'd never come," I muttered disconsolately to Sam who was rolling alongside me like a drunken sailor.

"Slouch, boy, slouch!" he grunted crossly. "You're poncing about like a sub-lieutenant leading a charge. You'll get yourself raped if you go on like that."

"I should be so lucky," I grumbled eyeing with apprehension a huddled group of night-prowlers slouching towards us beneath a pale pool of unnatural street-lighting. To ease Sam's mind I adopted a stiff-legged macho swagger, sunk my head into my shoulders and thought pornography until we were past them.

"We should have brought those bloody guns," I told him.

"No guns." He sounded angry. "I've broken the law more times than I can remember on this little jaunt, but guns I will *not* carry."

"Fine for you. What about poor defenceless little me?" When he didn't answer I added, "Old George Raven would have humped along a flaming great arsenal."

"That's exactly why I wouldn't let him come."

They'd had quite a stand-up fight about it. Raven would have given his eyeballs to be in with us on this, but Sam had been rudely adamant. He was right of course. Wapping Wall was no place for the second richest man in the country to be picked up dying in a pool of blood.

When Raven had eventually caved in, with extremely bad

grace, I had felt sheepish and overdid everything, talked too much and laughed a lot, the way you did when you see a colleague pissed on from a great height and would like him to know it wasn't you who did it.

We were there.

Casually we drew into a patch of deep shadow and took a peer around. The group of layabouts were just turning into the High Street, otherwise not a soul was about. Sam stared up into the sky as if in a moment of silent prayer. A soft rain was falling – not much but enough to make it unpleasant. "What is it?" I whispered. He waved me to silence. I stood rooted for a moment then, leaning in to him, I whispered confidentially into his ear, "I'll tell you one thing . . ."

"What's that?"

"I'm beginning to smell."

He looked at me steadily. "You only just realised that?"

"I haven't been allowed to change my clothes for two days, have I?" I told him defensively.

But he had gone, disappeared into the gloomy maw of the passage which led to the cross-planking and the steps down to the river's edge.

I picked my way carefully in his wake fumbling a couple of loose stones underfoot on the way. Then I cannoned into Sam who had come to a standstill. "You're like a herd of rampaging elephants," he complained.

A tiny pin-prick of light from his torch aided him as he gingerly manipulated the barrier of loose planks, holding the crossed one aside and allowing me to clamber through before letting it pivot back into position.

The river was black before us, slurping stealthily at the foot of the steps; a few lights from the opposite bank reflected a fitful glitter on the sluggishly running water. Away from the sheltering bulk of the buildings an icy wind coming up from Limehouse way made me huddle suddenly into my anorak.

I had left my heavy trenchcoat with the bike, back at Pat's Quay, tucked away in a shed at the rear of the cafe having come to a monetary understanding with the insomniac Chinaman who had promised to look after it until we got back. "Wise," he had nodded pocketing my fiver. "Here, leave bike in street, come back, no wheels." Confucius himself couldn't have put it better.

The broad shadowy shoulders of Sam hove up ahead and brought me to a halt. He was waiting on the lowermost step, the water lapping at his feet. The river was high, swirling around the narrow wooden walkway which on our previous visit had been a good four feet above the now submerged beach.

My stomach gave an unpleasant heave of apprehension as I followed him on to the slippery planks and half crabbed my way behind him towards the iron door set into the wall of the warehouse. I checked on the outsize key in my pocket and resisted the temptation to take it out; with my sort of luck I would have dropped it into the drink – then where would we have been? Keyless in Wapping, that's where.

When I joined Sam on the tiny stone landing-stage he was standing quite still; against the dark sky I could see that his head was bent, listening. Behind us the water swirled and gurgled, lapping at the top step.

His hand drew me in towards the door and I pressed my ear against it. I could hear a muffled growling sound, quite regular, as if someone was hauling up a heavy weight over wooden tackle. Glancing questioningly at the dark mass that was Sam's face I realised with some surprise that his teeth were bared in a wide smile. There was nothing to grin about, I thought sourly, then, as the origin of the sound dawned on me, I found myself smiling too and nodding happily. It was snoring. He was asleep. Wallowing, I hoped, in a drunken stupor.

Kneeling, I placed an eye to the large keyhole, relief surging through me as a nagging doubt at the back of my mind was set to rest. I had half expected another key on the inside, which would have rendered our present strategy null and void.

In the room beyond, a dim, yellow light was burning, a candle perhaps. The shadows were heavy. I could make out a stack of something which looked like crates but little else. Nothing moved.

I relinquished the keyhole to Sam who had a lengthy look until, regaining his feet, he gave me a nod.

As I drew the key from my pocket I saw him reaching for something in the waistband of his trousers. He gave me a momentary flash of his torch so that I could see it and I was only just able to repress a loud snort of pure pleasure. It was a policeman's truncheon.

He'd had that thing stuck halfway down his trouser leg all evening and hadn't even bothered to mention it. I did my best not to think of the discomfort he must have suffered perched on the back of the Honda.

I set the key to the lock and slowly, with a prayer, put pressure on it. Nothing happened. I stared up at Sam's dark silhouette in sudden dismay. I tried again. Nothing. Slowly I straightened up, shaking my head.

He shook his head too and gently shoving me aside had a go at the key himself. The damned thing refused to budge.

I couldn't see Sam's despair but I felt it.

Suddenly he bent to the lock again and this time I could have sworn I heard the smooth movement of sliding wards. He looked up into my sweating face, his index finger three inches from my nose slowly making a gentle clockwise motion. As with his previous despair I could now sense his smug smile. I remained unimpressed. How many right-hand locks did *he* know, I wondered, which unlocked themselves with a clockwise turn of the key?

Slowly he pushed open the door. Not a squeak.

I could see the truncheon poised threateningly in his hand. I didn't even have a toothpick. The acquisition of a weapon of some sort was my first priority.

Stepping carefully over the high sill I silently pulled the door to behind me.

After the keen salty tang of the river, the heavy atmosphere of the cellar struck me in the face like a physical blow and momentarily closed down my breathing apparatus. Not only was the place blue with tobacco smoke but it stank of oil and spirits and stale sweat. It was like a visit to the losing side's locker-room after a six-nil defeat: you needed to breathe but lacked the courage to chance it.

For one of his age and size Sam moved with remarkable agility, stepping silently and deftly over various articles of rubbish which littered the floor and were revealed to me only by an occasional helpful flicker of his torch behind him.

As we drew near the source of light an upended crate

leaning against the wall on my right caught my eye . . . a gleam of dull blue metal . . . crated guns. Half squatting, I eased one gently from its mounting and squinted at it closely. A German MP40 submachine-gun, heavy and handy as a club if for nothing else. The lack of a magazine was just as well; in present circumstances I would not have cared to trust myself with a loaded weapon.

Sam's torch flashed impatiently in my direction. Hefting the gun in my hand I joined him as he stood looking down at the unlovely sight sprawled on a lumpy mattress at his feet.

In the yellow light of a hurricane lamp which stood on an upturned crate I studied the face I had expected to see, the gleam of gold in the gaping drooling mouth, the face I had seen at the pub window on the day the whole thing had begun, the one belonging to the skater who had kicked me in the teeth.

Sketchily clad in a grubby blue undervest and a pair of half-unzipped jeans, his head pillowed on a pair of mud-streaked gumboots, he was an unwholesome looking object. Alongside the boots and within easy reach of the twitching fingers of his right hand lay a hefty revolver, a Smith & Wesson .38, beside it a half-empty bottle of Bushmill's Irish.

I held my breath as Sam manoeuvred his bulk silently around the head of the snoring figure, hooked the gun adroitly into his huge hand and passed it to me. I salted it away in the roomy pocket of my anorak.

Following up a through draught, I discovered that the iron door through which we had come was not the only entrance into the cellar – how else, I thought, could he himself have got into the place if the river entrance was locked as we had found it and no extra key available?

A heavy trap-door was set at the head of half a dozen stone steps, an open padlock hanging from it. Unhooking the padlock and raising the trap noiselessly I peered through a narrow crack at the wide stone corridor from which Sam and I had watched his cormorant. The huge doors where we had stood looking out over the river were now closed, as, I assumed, was the door at the opposite end of the corridor which led into the street, for all was in utter darkness.

I lowered the trap and turning back into the cellar snapped

the padlock closed. One less exit was one less chance of escape for the sleeping beauty.

Sam was crouching over the crates. I joined him. He flicked the torch over their contents and we moved silently from one to another with a lowering of spirits brought on by the knowledge that we were looking at only one armament dump of perhaps dozens.

Whilst it was impossible to estimate the number of weapons and rounds of ammunition, there were certainly enough to launch a small war: mortars, hand-grenades, submachine-guns, carbines, a crate of Kalashnikov assault rifles, SRS automatics, some American Armalite rifles and ammunition of all calibres – boxes of it.

I picked up a cigarette-end. How the hell he had the nerve to smoke cigarettes and light hurricane lamps surrounded by all this lot, beat me. I peered at the stub. A Dunhill's filter-tip. I held it for Sam to see. I felt the skin of my face tighten as I thought of Cath, her beautiful Nefertiti neck snapped by that rank, snoring barbarian. Sam picked up my thoughts, and my rage was momentarily stilled by the heavy pressure of a cautionary hand on my arm.

To block out my memories I found myself wondering about the diamonds when a sudden ear-splitting hoot from a vessel on the river sent my heart into my mouth and in the hollow, reverberating silence which followed I realised with dismay that West's snoring had ceased.

I covered the ground between us in about two seconds flat, to be greeted with a tableau straight out of a waxwork museum.

West, eyes wide and bloodshot, was leaning up on an elbow glowering at Sam straddling above him, the truncheon poised, outstretched, ready and threatening.

As I arrived at a run the tension broke, West taking me in with startled eyes, reaching for the gun that wasn't there and taking a blow on his wrist from the truncheon that all but incapacitated him. He gave a yell and started to his knees, his damaged wrist tucked into his armpit.

"Not another move," warned Sam in a malevolent growl.

As he knelt, frozen into immobility, West's already unzipped jeans crumpled slowly about his knees revealing narrow, muscular thighs and some really unsightly underwear. As West made a grab for his jeans, Sam raised his club threateningly. "Leave them . . . just as they are."

With some difficulty West found his voice, his now frightened eyes flicking from Sam to me and back again to Sam. "Who the hell are you?" His speech was slurred and he was none too certain of his balance, with or without his trousers.

"Oh come on, Mr West," smiled Sam relaxing a little. "We don't have to go through all that, do we? You know perfectly well who we are and what we want. Your life is what we'd *like* but I doubt if they'll let us have it. So, failing that, we'll settle for your liberty, all right? With any luck you can spend the rest of your days safe and sound and cared for by Her Majesty's Prison Service."

West's eyes narrowed as they slid around the cellar searching for more of us. I watched the powerful hands clenching spasmodically as he realised we were alone. A large bruise was forming on his damaged wrist.

"Two of you?" He grinned, regaining as much of his composure as his addled brain would allow. "Just the two of you? Is that the lot? You're a brave pair of boyos." His grin broadened as his eyes lingered over the MP40 in my hand. "And a great deal of harm you'll be doing with that thing pointed at me stomach. Did you forget to load it, little man?"

I threw it full in his face. It caught him across the nose and opened up his cheek an inch or two. Toppling backward with a muffled cry he twisted himself around in mid-air and hampered as he was by his half-masted jeans tried to scrabble to his feet. From nowhere at all a gun had appeared in his hand. As it came up to threaten me Sam's truncheon descended on his wrist with a crunching blow. The gun flew from his grasp and he was kneeling again, this time with his body bent inwards, his head touching the mattress as he rocked himself to and fro, blubbering like a child, clutching at the wrist which I felt quite sure must this time be broken.

Sam and I stood quite still, silently watching.

I felt nothing but hatred. If the gun in my pocket had been in my hand I know I would have killed him, happily, in cold blood and with no remorse.

Sam's anxious eyes were on me. "You all right?" he mouthed silently. I nodded, turned away looking for the gun West had dropped, and at that moment my ankles were seized. West's arms wrapped themselves about my calves like tentacles, dragging me down. Once again I felt the vice-like grip of those powerful arms; my ankles were locked together and, as his head butted me behind the knees, my balance went and I lunged towards Sam like a felled tree, fouling the blow he was aiming at West with his club.

I heard Sam shout. He caught me violently with his left arm and spun me to the floor as a gun-shot almost exploded my eardrums. I heard the bullet strike the wall behind and ricochet on to another. The air was full of choking blue smoke and everything began to slow down, like a film projecter losing speed.

West came slowly into focus. He was in a terrible mess. I remember blinking at his unprepossessing figure swaying from side to side and wondering whether that might be my final view of the world. I tried to concentrate on the gun in his hand; if it was about to send me into eternity it would be nice to know who had made it. I used to be quite an expert on guns – in the good old days when I was an actor and they fired only blanks.

He caught me looking at it and shuffled back a couple of paces out of range of any attack I might be contemplating.

His trousers were now about his ankles; another step and he'd trip over them. He seemed to realise it too. The gun was in his undamaged hand and looked steady enough; if he was ambidextrous I'd be dead before I could move a muscle. Reaching down with his right hand, his eyes never leaving my face for a second, he began hauling awkwardly on the jeans, the muzzle of the gun never wavering. He was a born killer.

Again that sniggering laugh. The trousers were now up over his hips; he was having some trouble with the wrist which, amazingly, was unbroken. Sam, I supposed, would have been taught in a tough school; he would know just where to strike with that thing to cause maximum pain with a minimum of obvious physical damage.

West was struggling with his trouser zip, his body wriggling like a bloody nautch-girl – all except for the hand which held the gun; that was as steady as a rock. His eyes, those watery bloodshot eyes, never left us for a moment.

"You two first . . ." he was whispering, "then Len – good old Len – tomorrow."

"Then what?" came Sam's voice from behind.

"Then I'm home and free."

"And where's that? Ireland?"

The eyes narrowed. "What's that to you?"

"Just interested, that's all," shrugged Sam. "One way and another you've been quite clever – which is more than I can say for the rest of us. I'm glad I'm not still a copper. Getting into a jam like this would have got me slung out on my ear."

"You're out on your ear anyway," he snarled. The jeans were back in place, the zip finally fastened. "And pig will always be pig, no matter what."

"That's what I'm saying. *We* haven't moved with the times, *you* have. When I was on the Force you were all muscle and nothing on top. Now look at you: you think for yourselves, you've learnt to use your brains, and that's the only thing that matters if you want to survive."

I sank back on to my haunches with a silent sigh. Now we were playing for time; waiting for the cavalry to arrive. What cavalry?

The gun was a Ceska .38. I recognised it now. Clumsy and inaccurate, but at this range lethal.

"That's why you Provisionals are so successful," Sam was going on. "You go off and get trained properly. Where did *you* train? Libya, Lebanon . . . ?"

West spat suddenly and viciously; I felt the spray on my face. "To hell with you! Them too. I'm on my own now. I'm not lickspittling to anybody. I'm getting out, see?"

"With half a million in your pocket."

"That's right." He gave a braying laugh. "I'm a rich man, aren't I?"

"So why didn't you get out before, while you could? You've wrecked it all now, haven't you, killing all those kids? You, a pro, killing kids. Why?"

"Because they *were* kids, that's why. Playing games. Amateurs. I've never seen anything so pathetic – setting 'emselves up against professionals. They're worse than your lot – they gab and grass like a lot of old women. That's why Geoff had to go. I *liked* him, you know. He knew all the theory, had all the books, but when it got down to the practicals – oh no, not for him. Then he saw this picture of me in *An Phoblacht* and that was it . . ." He shook his head suddenly as if to clear it of the drink. "Recognised me, didn't he?" His eyes seemed to be losing focus. "Couldn't let him go . . . but he was too quick for me even so – he must have passed it on 'cos Tony knew too – I think . . ." He trailed off, a puzzled expression in his eyes.

I had a loaded gun in my pocket. Behind us was a trap-door which, in my zeal, I had locked, and between us and the only other exit stood West. If he went on talking like this maybe he'd talk himself to sleep. His recent exertions had pumped some adrenalin into him but now, perhaps, the alcohol was on the move again.

Sam said, "I don't think Tony knew."

"He did. He came down here on the snoop, stole some of my things. I knew it was him – left his glasses behind, didn't he? His black glasses. Wore 'em because he thought someone might recognise him, 'cos he was *supposed* to have been kidnapped. Can you imagine anything so amateur? He would have taken 'em off down here 'cos it was dark, and when he heard me coming, panicked and forgot 'em . . . went out that way." He jerked his head at the door behind him. "I didn't know about it till I found the glasses . . . little bastard." He was breathing heavily. "You can't live with people like that . . ."

He mopped at his damaged face with his forearm; blood streaked the bare skin.

"Can I get up now?" I asked mildly.

He looked at me startled. "You stay where you are."

"Can I have a cigarette then?" He frowned as if not understanding the question. I added, "Executioners usually allow a last cigarette."

He seemed to like that. "That's right, they do, don't they? Trouble is . . . I've smoked 'em all."

"Never mind, I've got some." I put my hand into my pocket, even felt the butt of the gun – and then thought my last moment had come. I saw the knuckle of his trigger finger whiten, I heard him growling like a dog. At the same moment the iron door behind him swung silently open. I could see the lights reflected on the river.

A heavy figure stood silhouetted in the doorway.

"Mr McGlusky . . . ?" asked a calm voice.

West swung violently on his heel, the bullet meant for me ricocheted wildly about the cellar. Almost simultaneously came another, a flash of flame from the still figure in the doorway.

West gave a horrendous scream, the gun flew from his hand, his body arched as it hit the floor, squirming and wriggling like a wounded snake; the screams continued, tearing at my eardrums. One of his flaying hands clutched at the hurricane lamp toppling it from its perch on the crate and crashing it to the floor . . . a burst of flaming oil, spreading fast, soaking into the mattress . . . I stared at it stupidly.

I heard a gasp from Sam, then he was past me, struggling out of his overcoat and flinging it with himself headlong on the blazing mattress. I joined him with my anorak, frantically beating at the flames licking up from beneath him until the danger was past.

Thick black smoke welled out from beneath us as if we had quelled the flames of the other place. Sam, making a cumbersome effort to clamber to his knees, beat half-heartedly at his smoking overcoat.

West's screams had turned into agonised whimperings. I too got to my knees. Blood seemed to be everywhere; West's blood. He was stashed up behind a crate. I crawled towards him shoving aside the crate with a shoulder. He gibbered with fear as my face loomed over him.

His right kneecap was smashed.

A cold voice said behind me, "The first instalment, Mr McGlusky."

I looked up into the basilisk eye of George Raven. In one hand he held a huge American Colt .45, with the other he offered to help me to my feet.

"Sam all right?" he enquired.

Sam appeared over the crates slowly rising to his feet. His hat was gone; his hair stood on end and his face was streaked with oil and lamp-black. He looked like a survivor from the stokehold of a sinking ship.

He collapsed panting on to a crate, staring solemnly at the trembling West cowering at Raven's feet. "What did you call him?" he enquired without interest.

"McGlusky – Steve McGlusky. At least, that's what he called himself in Ireland. Whether it's his real name or not I personally couldn't care less. But he's wanted over there pretty badly, isn't that right, McGlusky? The best we can do for you is to send you back to them and let them deal with you as they see fit. This is a tea-party compared with what they'll have in store for you." He smiled suddenly. "Hurt your knee, have you?"

West's eyes were screwed shut with pain. "You bastard, you bastard . . ." he moaned.

"You still have another kneecap," Raven reminded him silkily. "Try not to forget that, will you?" And after a long moment of silence he added in a low voice, "You should not have touched my son."

Slowly West opened his eyes.

Raven smiled. "Ah yes, I forgot to introduce myself, didn't I? My name is George Raven – Anthony's father."

With a low groan West closed down again.

Raven snapped the safety on to his gun and stowed it away in his overcoat pocket. "So, what *are* we going to do with him?"

"How did you know who he was?" I asked coming out of a daze. "How did you know anything at all about him?"

"McGlusky?" He gave an easy shrug. "Oh, I know quite a few of them. We sometimes do business together." He glanced down at West. "I've never actually met this one, but I know something of him. He had quite a record over there and threw it all away, blotted his copy book, so to speak; grassed on a colleague who, I understand, displeased him. When Len was talking about him earlier on, I had an idea it might be McGlusky. The timing was about right."

I eyed him curiously. "How do you come to be so well-informed?"

He shrugged again. "It's my job. I'm a businessman."

"You do business with them?"

"With anybody if the price is right."

Sam said in a low voice, "Guns? Armaments? This sort of stuff?"

"Not directly, no. There are various devious methods of trading, of course, but we don't make a song and dance about it. A gun is a gun, and if Uncle Sam or John Bull refuses to sell, you may rest assured that Comrade Ivan will . . . . and many, many others. These days none of us can afford to live in Cloud Cuckoo Land."

Sam and I stared blankly at each other for a mute moment then I said, "We'd better contact someone, hadn't we?" I nodded at the pain-wracked West. "Get rid of him down there. And then I'd like to go home and sleep for three whole days if that's all right with you two."

Sam considered. "I could ring the Wapping cop-shop I suppose, it's only just up the road. They can hold him there for the night and good luck to 'em."

I pointed out the telephone on the wall and he trudged off wearily to make the call.

George Raven and I were left for a lonely moment of mutual embarrassment, then he took me gently by the arm and led me out of West's hearing.

"Mark, listen . . . I wouldn't want you to think badly of me. I don't deliberately supply arms to terrorists, but the buying and selling of such things is a tricky business. Impeccable references may sometimes fall short of the truth."

"That I can well believe," I said sourly. "And I don't want to talk about it, if you don't mind. What you do and who you trade with is your affair and on *your* conscience, not mine. The whole stinking planet is a time bomb and it's a matter of indifference to me who presses the button. I'm only sorry that there are so many – sods in the world, that's all . . ."

Anything further I might have wanted to say was thrust abruptly from my mind by a sudden shattering commotion behind us as a packing case crashed to the floor and a consignment of submachine-guns were strewn all over the place. West, supporting himself precariously against another crate, was standing facing us, swaying dangerously on his one good leg.

I sensed Raven go for his gun but before he reached it West ducked his head quickly and with his teeth removed the pin from a hand-grenade. With his finger pressed to the clip he held it towards us like Paris offering his apple of discontent.

"Get off the phone!" he shouted. A second's pause and then the ping of the replaced telephone.

I can't remember ever having heard silence so intense as that which passed during the next few seconds. I could almost hear the hair stirring on the back of my neck.

Like a crippled bird he hopped towards us, a primed grenade in each hand. Sweat mingled with the blood on his face, his blue undervest was black with it, but the triumph of certainty blazed like a madness in the wild, bloodshot eyes.

Raven's gun was in his hand. West raised an amused cackle of laughter. "Shoot me, Anthony's father, and we all go up." We backed away slowly as he continued to hop towards us. From the corner of my eye I could see Sam moving ostensibly towards us, also towards the open door.

"Your benighted son was the cause of all this," railed West. "He loathed you, do you know that? Without him and without your money this would never be happening. He was a thief too, did you know *that*? He broke in here and stole my things – Geoff Earnshaw's things – but he confessed it all before he died. Oh yes, I squeezed that out of him before he died."

Tears were streaming down his cheeks.

George Raven muttered in my ear, "Make for the door." Aloud he said, "Anthony isn't dead. I talked to him only this morning." He added in a whisper to me, "When I say go . . ."

West had stopped and was staring stupidly at Raven. Sam, a few paces to my left, was immediately in front of the open door.

"He's dead. Tony's dead," whispered West shaking his head in disbelief. "I left him dead."

"Alive," said Raven. "Don't you understand plain English, you stupid Irish . . . go!" he yelled suddenly.

I went for the door like a greyhound, gathering up the startled Sam as I went. Outside for a split second we hesitated on the small stone landing-stage. Behind us I heard a shot and a shrill scream.

"Jump!" I yelled at Sam. "Jump!" I shoved him headlong into the river and, half turning, caught the blast from the erupting grenades full in the face. I was flung backwards into the air; my ears were still ringing with the echo of the explosions as I struck the water hard. The ice-cold river swallowed

215

me whole, winding my clothing about me like a shroud, tugging at my leaden shoes and dragging me down. Fleetingly I touched the bottom, pulled on desperate arms and fought my way back to the surface. My only concern was for Sam. With bursting lungs I broke into the air, shouting his name and plunging around in a tight circle searching for him. Oil and salt blinded me.

When I caught sight of him he was half a dozen yards away and I couldn't tell whether he was treading water or drowning. "Swim!" I shouted. "The whole place is going up." Oily water poured into my mouth. I spat it out and almost vomited.

He was swimming, thank God.

The disintegration of Skalds Wharf began in a comparatively small way with the two grenades exploding in West's hands. A split second before those initial explosions I had caught a glimpse of Raven silhouetted in the doorway and beyond him the ungainly figure of West crumpling to the floor. The confused memories of those few moments plastered themselves across my retina and have remained there ever since. I saw Raven flung backwards against the doorjamb and go down as the explosions began to take over, each more devastating than the one before. George Raven could never have made it to safety.

We were ploughing laboriously down river towards the Prospect. The water was high and the tide, I guessed, on the turn, which made the currents tricky. I kept Sam carefully in my sights; he was a couple of yards ahead now and swimming quite powerfully. Behind us explosion followed explosion lighting up the sky and turning the river into a stream of gleaming metal.

"Keep close in," I yelled to Sam who seemed to be floundering a little. I churned up alongside him. He was spluttering but bared his teeth gamely at me. I moved over on to the river side and began edging him towards the bank. The current fought back at us.

A huge detonation shook the night. Over my shoulder I could see the flames licking upwards; the building appeared to be folding in on itself.

I shoved Sam bodily nearer to the bank. Now I could make

out an iron ladder stanchioned into a high blank wall. I caught Sam about the waist and piloted him towards it, took one of his hands and clamped it to a metal rung.

I ranged up alongside him and we hung there, heaving and shivering together, for an eternity, listening to the distant sound of shouts and running feet and the roar of fire.

Eventually, and as if by mutual consent, we began to climb, hand over hand, and rung by rung, slowly and exhaustingly . . .

Chapter Seventeen

I remember crawling on to my bed on all-fours at four o'clock that morning, burying my face in the pillow and collapsing like a deflated balloon. My last thought was whether I would live to keep the date I'd rashly made with Sam for eleven o'clock. That's all I remember. I probably slept on all-fours. I don't know.

The way back from the river had been about the worst journey I had ever made in my life – worsened by the fact I felt unimagined responsibility for a man of seventy who had been immersed in the River Thames for the best part of half an hour, and then, huddled on the back of a speeding motorcycle, had travelled from Wapping to Wimbledon in sopping wet clothes in a temperature only just above freezing. And not once had he raised his voice in complaint, other than to inform me at one moment, while steaming gently in the airless kitchen of Pat's Quay, that he thought he might drop a line to the Port of London Health Authority about the state of their river.

My admiration and respect for Sam Birkett increased that night by a hundredfold.

The insomniac Chinese proprietor of Pat's Quay – Ah Foo he said his name was but I doubted that – had been suitably appalled by our melancholic appearance when we staggered into his premises to collect the Honda. He had sat us in his steamy kitchen and plied us with hot black tea for which he declined payment. He loitered instead in the doorway.

"Big fire at wharf," he said.

I nodded. "So I believe. We heard the fire-engines."

Still he waited. "You fall in river?"

"Our boat sank," said Sam and sneezed violently.

"Ah so . . ." said Ah Foo, his eyes wise and black and flat. Then he departed.

When we crept into Sam's place, stiff and frozen and barely

living, Mildred, fearsome in hair-curlers and a gaberdine raincoat, descended upon us and harangued us like one of the Trojan women, railing at poor Sam as if there was no tomorrow.

Since no word of defence escaped his lips she then retreated in good order and went off to prepare a hot bath for him, to return a split second later to inform me that I too would be having a hot bath.

Sam took her hand gently and told her that he and I were far too elderly to bath together.

Five minutes later I was back in my own flat running a hot bath of my own and wondering uneasily about the amount of muck we had taken into our stomachs during our flounderings in the river. We'd probably contract typhoid. To hell with it – typhoid couldn't be worse than a performance of *The Trojan Women* at four o'clock in the morning.

When the alarm roused me at ten I was rather less certain. I felt decidedly queasy so I went and sat on the loo for a couple of lugubrious minutes and when nothing was forthcoming, settled for typhoid and took a couple of Alka-Seltzers instead.

When I let myself out of the flat, the despondent face of my downstairs neighbour appeared around the edge of his door. "Two policemen have been asking for you, Mr – er . . ." he informed me with a tentative look over my shoulder into the street beyond. "Twice," he added with a warning note to his voice.

"Ah good." I handed him his bottle of milk from the step and gave him an encouraging grin. "They're friends of a friend of mine. I've been expecting them."

Without knowing why, I was feeling decidedly better and the shadow of typhoid was passing. The sun was shining, God was doubtless in his Heaven and I was certainly in my favourite leathers.

I swung the bike into Sam's drive, churned up his gravel a bit, parked the Honda and pushed my way into the ever open door.

Schiller's 'Ode to Joy', aided and abetted by some of the most encouraging sounds ever devised by the mind of man, welled out into the hall and greeted me. No one was about so I followed my ears to Sam's office and, shoving open the door, stood in respectful silence while the music lapped around me like a balm. How could it be, I wondered, that a miracle of such immensity could have been composed by a man who was stone-deaf?

Sam was hunched in his chair, his head sunk into his shoulders, his eyes closed. I pushed the door to, slunk into the room and folded myself noiselessly into his father's armchair.

When the symphony eventually blazed to its end we both sat listening to its echoes until the tape clicked itself off.

Sam neither moved nor opened his eyes. He simply murmured, "I wish *I'd* said that." After a second he added, "How are you, this bright and shining morning?" Then he opened his eyes.

"Thought I was getting typhoid earlier on."

He nodded sagely. "We should have had a jab. Too late now though. Didn't dare tell Mildred where I'd been. Said we fell in a pond together. Remember that, if she asks, will you? If she knew it was the river she'd have us both in hospital."

"*You* all right?" I asked.

"Never better." And he looked it too. He said after a pause and looking at his watch, "I've asked Hodder over for eleven thirty. Together we'll face him and tell all."

"He's not going to like it."

"He's going to have to lump it. What's done cannot be undone. And he'll have a lot of answers to questions he'd never even thought of asking. It ought to make him happy."

"It won't."

"No, you're quite right, it won't. Still . . . it's going to be difficult for all of us – especially as we're going to have to wait until Anthony's *compos mentis* for some of the answers. He's coming along fine, by the way. Lindy rang this morning; she saw him last night. He's still under a lot of observation as far as I can make out, but things look as well as they can . . ."

"Did you – tell her about George?"

He shook his head. "I haven't told her anything about last night. Not yet. We've got to be certain about things. He might have made it, who knows?"

"No way. I saw him go down. And not into the river where he might have survived."

A long depressed silence ensued then he said, "So Anthony might even now be the second richest man in the country."

I stared at him bleakly. "Why don't I feel anything? All that carnage and I feel nothing."

"You will, Mark, you will. Tomorrow or the next day. It'll come. Then it'll be terrible." He leaned back in his chair and there was a small *clop* of sound as he switched off the cassette player. "It's like the last act of bloody *Hamlet*, isn't it? Bodies everywhere, nothing to show for it, nothing gained. Earnshaw, Cath, Skip Roberts . . . George, all gone."

"And West," I said.

"And West. The killer royal. I don't suppose we'll ever learn much more about him. Tom Hodder will follow him up of course, but if he was an internal problem within the IRA's ranks, for example, he won't come up with much. He'll go unmourned, and serve him right. How about some coffee? I'd ring for the landlady," he added with a sly grin, "but she's out at the moment."

I made a face. "How is she this morning? She still speaking to you? She hasn't left home, has she?"

"Hold on to your hat – she's gone to church."

I stared at him. "Good God, I had no idea she was that way inclined."

"She's not – not really – only when she wants to give thanks for something."

We stared at each other with sober eyes. I said, "P'raps *we* should be there too."

He nodded at the cassette player. "I've made my peace." He looked again at his watch. "Let's go and cook some coffee."

In the kitchen I perched on a stool while he busied himself with mugs and hot water.

He said, "Now, is there anything we ought to go over together before Tom Hodder arrives? Anything we don't know about?"

"There's quite a bit *I* don't know about," I told him. "I suppose we can piece it together somehow but most of the – protagonists are gone. *And* the witnesses, if it comes to that. I doubt if it'll satisfy Hodder."

"Tough," said Sam succinctly.

We went through it step by step – from the phoney kidnapping job to the death of West.

We assumed that Anthony had intended to lie low in the *Chessene* until such time as he decided to re-surface with idle tales about his treatment by SWALK, the members of which he would paint as shadowy and possibly sympathetic figures. He would then continue to combat terrorism with the help of the half million conned out of George Raven.

"All that bit, however," said Sam frowning at the steaming kettle, "turns out to be null and void since West, right from the beginning presumably, had decided to take the diamonds and run, and was just stringing them along until his *own* plans – whatever they were – had crystallised."

I shook my head in confusion. "How in hell could he have pulled the wool over their eyes? Apart from Len, who's a bit thick, they were all pretty intelligent people. Cath was *very* sharp, so was Skip. But only Anthony managed to get some sort of line on him."

"Only because Earnshaw put him up to it."

"So why didn't he tip off the others?"

He shrugged. "He probably would have done if he'd thought they'd have been able to cope with West on their own. But suddenly to realise you've got a homicidal maniac curled up beside you – that's something else, isn't it? They'd have been more out of their depth than they were already. To expose him to the cops would have exposed their own kidnapping set-up. So he decided on an outside job. You. 'Meet me at the windmill . . .' and all that. Cream?" He drew alongside with a mug of coffee in each hand. I took one and shook my head. After a tentative sip I deliberately mislaid mine. It was foul. Good detective he may have been, he just couldn't make coffee. No one I knew could make good coffee. Except me.

"Guesswork," I muttered.

Sam raised expressive shoulders. "Dear boy, that's the name of the game. That's how most cases get solved – or shelved."

"Well, Sherlock Holmes wouldn't have put up with it."

"Things were neater in his day." He gave me a sly look. "You never gave the world *your* Sherlock Holmes, did you, in your thespian days?"

"I only got as far as Sexton Blake."

He shrugged. "You'd have been terrible as Sherlock."

I ignored him. "West didn't realise Geoff's stuff was missing until he found Anthony's glasses. That's what he said, didn't he? Now that must have been Friday evening – after his failed bomb at the cemetery. He storms over to the *Chessene* and finds only Cath – Anthony's already left to meet me at the windmill. She knows where he's gone because she saw the note in my pocket, and, all unsuspecting, passes it on to West. To prevent me keeping that date he makes her ring me – at the point of a gun, I reckon. Only then does she realise what's happening. She tries to make a fight of it but he kills her, pushes her body into the drink, telephones Len to come and take care of *me* when *I* arrive – he probably told him to kill me but Len's not in that league. Are you with me still?"

He made no reply, just pulled up in his tracks and stared at me as if lost in admiration.

I went on. "Anthony, waiting at the windmill, gets the chop. West throws him over that wheel and leaves him for dead. How's that?" More silence. "Speak to me, Sam."

He wobbled his head. "Not bad, not at all bad. It wouldn't convince a jury of course."

"I'm not trying to convince a jury, am I? I don't have to. Murder's been committed and the killer's dead. *Everyone's* dead. No one's on trial, so there's no case. Just trying to convince *you*, that's all."

"And you're doing a splendid job." He moved off again. "We're just wasting our breath, you know. We're not likely to get any further until we talk to friend Anthony. And Hodder will be here in all of ten minutes thirsting for our blood. What are we going to tell him?"

"What we know," I said with what I thought was a bland smile. "Which is a damn sight more than *he* knows. Rightly or wrongly, for better or for worse, we've done *our* job. So let *him* do some work for a change."

He stuck out his lower lip in severe concentration. "Do you know something, Mark, dear boy?"

"What?"

"We might well go to prison for obstructing the police."

"He wouldn't dare." I pondered for a moment. "Would he?"

"You haven't drunk your coffee."

"No."

"You don't want it?"

"You've put me off it."

"Mildred says I can't make coffee."

"What nonsense."

"Quite. It's no good believing everything *she* says. That way madness lies." He looked at his watch and drew a long hissing breath. "Ten minutes to crunch time."

He wandered moodily round behind his desk and sank into his chair with a loud creak. "So what shall we do for ten minutes?"

I eyed his cassette player and gave him a smirk. "Play it again, Sam," I said.